TO WED IN *Scandal*

Also by Liana LeFey

Countess So Shameless

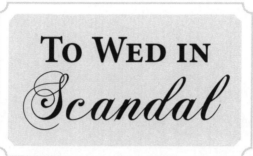

TO WED IN
Scandal

A Scandal in London Novel

Liana LeFey

Montlake
Romance

Text copyright © 2013 Liana LeFey

Published by Montlake Romance
P.O. Box 400818
Las Vegas, NV 89140

ISBN-13: 9781612185385
ISBN-10: 161218538X

Mama—as you typically are with everything, you were right about Sabrina. Thank you for helping me shape her into the heroine she was meant to be. And Daddy, you'll never know what it means to me that you tell everyone that your daughter writes romance novels.

This one is for you.

Acknowledgments

Deepest gratitude to:

Diana West, for the many years you've blessed me with your fabulous friendship. Thank you for the hysterical (and sometimes wildly inappropriate) laughter we've shared on so many occasions, for your constant encouragement, and above all, for your steadfast love.

"ZippyChica" Sonia Lara, for slogging through my gnarly rough drafts and giving me the feedback I need to polish them into something worth publishing, and for *Pride and Prejudice*—with the subtitles.

My agent, Barbara, for continuing to guide this fledgling into flight.

My Montlake/Amazon team, for being completely AWESOME.

Prologue

LONDON, 1713

*T*HE OAF HAD FINALLY LEFT—BUT NOT WITHOUT A parting gift. The thought of Montgomery finding the snake she'd secreted in his coat pocket brought a fierce grin to Sabrina's lips. She rather hoped he discovered it on his way home, for it was particularly satisfying to picture him trapped in the close confines of the carriage with the slithering reptile loose about his feet.

With delight, she imagined Montgomery leaping out onto the street, his conveyance continuing on its journey without him. He might even land in a large, noisome puddle. Face-first.

She smothered a laugh as she crept into Mama's room and hid behind the door. Being the youngest and smallest, her job was to listen in on her parents' conversation and report back to her sisters. It was especially important now, as the topic of discussion would surely be Montgomery's visit today. Papa wanted him for Eugenia, even though she had expressed strong wishes to the contrary.

She could not agree with Eugenia more. The man was simply horrid.

Sabrina reflected upon his many offenses with growing irritation. After her first few attempts to sabotage his suit, he'd taken to calling her the Red Pestilence. He had done it again today as he was leaving—and worse, he'd yanked one of her loose curls as he'd said it. Even now her cheeks burned. The thought of him as a brother-in-law was positively galling. It could not be countenanced. Thus, her slippery little present.

Last week, she had put ink in his tea. The result had been spectacular—and Papa had been livid. At least this time, no one but Montgomery would bear witness to her japery.

She shrank back as Mama sailed into the room, Papa close on her heels and already arguing in favor of Montgomery.

"Elizabeth, you know he's the best possible match. They are of an age, they already know each other and are on friendly terms, and he's—"

"She's in love with Afton," answered Mama.

Papa let out an exasperated sigh. "She's young. She can learn to love Montgomery."

"You know it doesn't work that way, Harry."

Her quiet reply was followed by silence. Sabrina peeked through the crack, just as Papa moved to stand behind her mother and place his hands on her shoulders.

"I know, my dear." Again, he sighed, only this time it sounded resigned. "Very well. I shall allow her to choose between them. Montgomery would provide a better life for her, but if it is her wish, I will give Afton my blessing."

Mama turned in his arms, and Sabrina caught a flash of her delighted smile. "I *knew* you'd see reason."

"Reason has nothing to do with it," answered Papa with a chuckle. "I simply know better than to cross you when you've set your mind on having things a certain way. Now, I have a surprise for you."

Sabrina watched as he produced a gilt box and held it out to her mother, who took it and opened the lid. "It's lovely, Harry. Thank you." Her voice sounded strange.

"Here, let me see it on you," he said softly.

"No, not just now," her mother quickly answered. "I must change for dinner, and it wouldn't go well with the gown I've chosen."

His face fell.

Stretching up, she placed a kiss upon his cheek. "I'll wear it for you later," she promised. "Run along now, and let me dress."

His disappointment vanished, replaced by a roguish grin. "I could play lady's maid," he suggested.

"You know better than that, Harry."

With a sigh, he released her. "Very well, my dear. I shall see you downstairs shortly."

Sabrina shrank back as he passed. When the sound of his footsteps had faded, she again peered through the crack.

Her mother stared at the necklace in her hand, her expression grim. "I wonder what the new one looks like," she muttered as she opened the bottom drawer of her jewelry box and tossed the necklace into it.

What does she mean?

Her mother finished her toilet and left the room. After waiting several minutes to be sure it was safe, Sabrina came out of hiding and ran over to the chest. Opening it, she took out the rejected gift: an emerald necklace. Even at her age, she knew quality when she saw it.

A noise at the door made her jam the necklace back into the drawer and shut it.

Jane, Mama's lady's maid, entered and squealed when she saw Sabrina there in the shadows. "Oh! You gave me a fright! Playing in her ladyship's things again, are we?"

Sabrina nodded.

Jane smiled. "I shan't tell. Only you'd best be getting back before Mrs. Tellane misses you."

Her governess had been taking a brandy-assisted nap when she'd tiptoed out to deliver her gift to Montgomery, but Sabrina knew better than to mention it. She left, grateful for not having to explain herself. As she made her way to where her sisters waited, she wondered about what she'd seen.

Why did Mama not want Papa's present?

Chapter One

LONDON, NOVEMBER 1723

"THE RIGHT HONORABLE DOWAGER COUNTESS OF Aylesford and the Lady Sabrina Grayson," announced the liveried footman.

Only a few heads turned to see the new arrivals, but that didn't matter. Nothing mattered now, save that London was finally at her feet. Sabrina stared down at the glittering world below, savoring the richness of color, breathing in air that seemed saturated with life itself.

Three years had been spent cloistered away from all such joy. But the gaiety promised at the bottom of these stairs filled her with gladness—to wear something besides black or grey, to laugh aloud, to dance with handsome young men.

*Papa...*Hard on the heels of elation, guilt and grief stifled her breath. Her step faltered. How could she feel any happiness without him here? He'd always taken such delight in his littlest girl. She remembered how he had laughed when she'd begged to go to her first ball on her fifteenth birthday. He'd said no, but had promised to find her a prince to marry the following year.

That year had arrived without him. Her heart wrenched. *Who will find me a prince now?*

Holding back the tears that threatened, Sabrina forced a bright smile for a gentleman who glanced at her in passing. The world would not permit her to wallow in her grief, at least not visibly. A sad, blotchy face would do her no good at all on the hunt.

I would never have trusted Papa's judgment, anyway, she thought, blinking away her tears. Birds of a feather flock together, after all. No doubt he would have selected a handsome charmer just like himself. No. It was better that she choose for herself.

And unless she wished to end as a governess for one of her siblings' children, she must cast her nets soon. A husband must be caught this Season.

Carefully, she appraised each of the gentlemen on display as they descended the long staircase.

Too round.

Too fidgety.

Impressively dressed, but ancient.

That one laughs exactly like—and unfortunately resembles— Lady Pinkerton's pet monkey. I hope for his sake he's extremely wealthy.

Throngs of girls milled about, all of them young and well dowered. *Most of them barely out of the nursery*, she thought. At nineteen, she could hardly claim the charm of their naïveté.

Perhaps an older man might be more suitable? Not too old, but mature. A refined, elegant man with impeccable taste and fine manners—and a more discerning palate when it came to women.

As though heaven itself had decided to have a laugh, Lord Falloure sauntered past, followed by a rush of warm air as every female in his wake sighed. Well, almost every female. She snorted quietly. Though older and undeniably elegant, the man was a confirmed bachelor with a known penchant for married women. She had no desire to see her husband's lovers at every social event.

No. She needed a discreet, sensible sort of man. A man who understood that there were more important things than carnal pleasures. A man who, therefore, looked right past the silly, giggling debutantes as though they did not exist.

A man exactly like...*that* one.

Examining her prey carefully from a distance, she guessed him to be in his mid to late twenties. Good.

The quality of his clothes marked him as a gentleman of adequate means. Also good.

He was well built, with gilt-blond hair and fine features. Their children would be handsome. Excellent.

And he seemed completely unmindful of the wistful stares and titters issuing from a nearby cluster of young females. The other gentlemen in his group occasionally glanced their way, but not him. Perfect.

"Mama, who is that?"

Her mother followed her gaze and sniffed, making a moue of disapproval. "Lord Francis Fairford, eldest son of Baron Middleton. He's managed to escape matrimony thus far, though he's been all but paying court to one Mrs. Geraldine Childers, but I don't expect a union to come of it," she confided. "The woman is a foreigner and without ties. His father will surely have forbidden it."

So, not engaged or married. "May I be introduced?"

Her mother's eyes narrowed. "It's still very early, my dear, and he *is* only heir to a baronetcy. There are many more eligible gentlemen here."

"Yes, Mama, but someone must be the first," Sabrina countered, keeping her tone meek.

After a moment, her mother relented. "All right, if you insist. Better that you test your wings on someone of little consequence before the real hunt begins. 'A jeweler first practices his skill on lesser stones before attempting the diamond,' Grandmama used to say."

Sabrina smiled as they made their way over to the menfolk.

At their approach, a silver-haired gentleman stepped forward. "How lovely you look this evening, Lady Aylesford."

"My Lord Sheffield," her mother murmured, pinking ever so slightly. "Allow me to present my youngest daughter, Sabrina."

Sabrina grinned as the corner of Sheffield's eye crinkled in a quick conspirators' wink. They were already well acquainted. A friend to her father for many years, he had become a great comfort since Papa's passing.

"Charmed and delighted, Lady Sabrina," he said as he bowed. "No doubt you, as your mother did once upon a time, shall soon have all the young men worshiping at your feet."

As he presented her to the younger men in his circle, she grew acutely aware that, while the majority appeared quite keen to make her acquaintance, the one she sought to impress in particular seemed vastly uninterested. Indeed, when it was his turn, Fairford's cool blue gaze flicked over her with what could only be termed poorly concealed disdain. His almost inaudible greeting of "Enchanted" fell flat and stale, and his bow was but the tiniest bend of the waist.

As she recovered from Fairford's blatant dismissal, a tall, curvaceous, blond woman materialized at his elbow—and she watched his demeanor transform. The chilly hauteur vanished, replaced by alert, attentive consideration of the new arrival.

This must be the infamous Mrs. Childers.

She rapidly tallied her rival's many deficiencies. Her smile was too warm, her manner too familiar. Her generous bosom was a trifle too exposed and her hips entirely too prominent below what had to be the most tightly corseted waist in Christendom. Somehow, Mrs. Childers had mastered the miraculous technique of remaining conscious without breathing, for surely the seams of her gown would burst asunder if she did.

Everything about the woman was "too."

A mistress, to be sure. She mulled it over. A union with the Frenchwoman was out of the question, her mother had said, which made Fairford perfectly eligible. She wasn't concerned about the wench. If anything, it was better to know about her now. It would make things so much easier, for there would be no danger of losing her head over him.

Mama had suffered devastating consequences for becoming too attached to her philandering husband, Sabrina's father. She was determined not to repeat her mistake. Anything beyond a mild fondness for one's husband was unacceptable.

She looked at Fairford. Provided they got on reasonably well, he would do. She put him at the top of her list. Then, cognizant that a young lady should never spend too much time eyeing any gentleman, she moved on. It wouldn't do to seem overly eager. According to her sister Eugenia, a gentleman preferred to pursue rather than be the object of pursuit.

All she had to do was gain his notice and then let him chase her to the altar.

The conversation at hand, a hushed discussion regarding the recent discovery of another unidentified woman's body on the banks of the Thames, should have held his attention. Not tonight.

Henry's mind wandered to the goings-on behind him, where a group of debutantes were discussing gowns and frippery. He doubted whether many of the girls were even aware of the strange murders.

"The French just seem to instinctively know what enhances a woman's appearance to her best advantage," one announced, earning sounds of heartfelt agreement from her peers. "If it weren't for their divine influence, we'd probably still be draped in linen and wearing crude leather sandals."

A wave of titters followed.

Closing his eyes, he sighed. *God. Why am I even here?*

He was just about to excuse himself when another voice spoke, one laden with sarcasm: "The only advantage to be had by wearing enormous baskets strapped to one's waist is their ability to mask an overly abundant posterior, should one be so unfortunate as to have one."

Silence fell like a stone, and he suppressed a chuckle. Whoever she was, that girl had bollocks of solid rock. Every Englishwoman he knew was a devout worshiper of all things French, despite the tension between their countries.

"Still, I must admit they do *usually* have impeccable taste," the bold female continued, clearly attempting to settle the feathers she'd just ruffled. "Perhaps the Spanish will at last learn how to dress, now that their young king has brought home a Bourbon princess."

Her comment was followed by agreeable murmurs. Unable to help himself, he glanced over his shoulder. A redhead. He might have known. He wished he could see her entire face, but all he caught was the curve of her cheek.

"Do you mean to say that you think the princess will cause the Spanish to wear panniers, too?" one of the girls asked, her expression vacant and confused.

The redhead laughed a little. "I doubt it. I understand she is most unhappy, being not fond of her husband. The Spanish court is equally displeased with her."

"Then I don't see why *we* need be concerned with her," another girl chimed in snidely. "Unless, of course, she brings Spanish prudery back to France with her. I should hate being forced to wear a veil over my hair in order to be fashionable next Season."

This garnered a few laughs. He waited to see how the redhead would react. He was not disappointed.

"What the Spanish choose to wear is of little concern to us here in England, 'tis true. But a Bourbon princess marrying Spanish royalty of Bourbon blood is. Their union only further solidifies France's hold on the continent. Don't you see? This is the Bourbons' way of circumventing the treaty."

When there was no response, the redhead sighed audibly. "The Treaty of Utrecht?"

Now he was intrigued. To hear a female discussing *any* politics, foreign or domestic, was most uncommon. To hear one speaking knowledgeably and with wit was even more of a rarity. But why was she trying to have this discussion with a gaggle of ignorant debutantes? Without bothering to excuse himself, he turned his back on his fellows and cleared his throat.

The redhead turned, a triumphant smile quirking her lips. Her delighted expression, however, quickly changed to one of irritation.

Clearly, the lady had been expecting someone else.

He opened his mouth to say something, but then hesitated. There was something strangely familiar about the hazel eyes that glared up at him. An impatient brow lifted above one, and he realized he was staring. He sketched a bow. "You must pardon me, my lady, but I couldn't help overhearing your conversation. Colonel Herbert, Viscount Montgomery, at your service."

Her gaze instantly grew wary. "Viscount *Montgomery*?"

As she spoke, a thrill of recognition ran through him. *No. Surely not.* He peered at her closely.

"Sabrina?" An enormous smile split his face. "By Jove, it *is*—the Red Pestilence!"

Her fine alabaster skin colored. It was then that he realized the other girls were staring at them in open shock. Grabbing Sabrina's arm, he led her away from the prying eyes and too-eager ears.

"How *dare* you insult me so, you horrid man!" she exploded the instant he released her.

It was hard to reconcile the image of this breathtaking—and very angry—woman with the mischievous child he'd known ten years ago. The delinquent imp had certainly grown up. "*I'm* horrid? If memory serves, you were the one putting snakes in pockets, not I. I never said a word until after you declared war."

"That was years ago! I am no longer a child, and for you to call me by such a name now, especially in public, is simply inexcusable."

Curiosity pricked him. "Exactly why *were* you so bent on being such a nuisance, if I may ask?"

The question caught her off guard, as he'd intended. She stared at him for a long moment before her chin lifted in the defiant manner he remembered so well. "I did it for Eugenia, if you must know."

"She put you up to all of those pranks?"

She looked uncomfortable. "Well, no. Not *all* of them." He stared at her until she blushed. "None of them, actually," she finally admitted.

"You needn't have bothered, you know. I had no intention of marrying her."

"You didn't?"

He shook his head. "I was dragged to your house by my mother on a weekly basis because she had hoped that your sister and I would take a fancy to each other. Aylesford wanted the match very badly as well, but the truth is that Eugenia and I were not suited for anything beyond friendship."

"But I thought—what I mean to say is that you *appeared* quite serious in your courtship," she said, looking at him with frank suspicion.

"Just because I didn't shout objections upon crossing the threshold didn't mean I was a party to their plans. I chose silence as my form of protest while at your house. Eugenia understood and reciprocated in kind."

"Oh."

She looked so crestfallen that he couldn't resist. "Unfortunately, I never did get to compliment you on your skill at devilry. An egregious oversight on my part, for you were a most gifted saboteur. Had I truly sought your sister's hand, the idea of having the Pest as a member of my family would have given me serious pause."

The look on her face said she wasn't sure whether to take this as a compliment or an insult. "I remember how furious Aylesford was with you for interfering, the few times you were caught," he continued. "I do hope your punishments were not overly harsh."

A queer expression crossed her features, and another memory assaulted him. His father had written him last year and in his letter had mentioned that Aylesford, who'd been gravely ill, had finally succumbed. The girl must have only just come out of mourning.

"Please, forgive me," he apologized at once. "I only arrived back home a few days ago, you see, and I'm afraid I simply forgot that…" He bowed his head, biting back a curse. "Truly, I beg your pardon. I did not mean to be an insensitive lout."

He watched her struggle for composure for a moment before she answered with a shaky but brave smile. "It has been over a year, my lord. The time for mourning has passed."

"It has been five years, and still I mourn my mother's absence," he replied.

She squirmed and looked away.

Damn me for an idiot! he thought, trying to think of a way to mend his disastrous misstep. As if echoing the awkwardness between them, the twang of stringed instruments being tuned drifted throughout the ballroom. Seizing the opportunity, Henry offered his arm. "May I request the honor?"

He might have offered to toss her off a cliff for the look she gave him. With visible reluctance, she accepted.

Chapter Two

*I*N SPITE OF HER RANCOR AT HIS HAVING HUMILIATED HER in front of her peers, the moment their naked fingers touched, rivulets of fire began to snake down Sabrina's spine, traveling all the way to her suddenly curling toes. Time slowed to a crawl as if, like her, it needed to pause for breath.

In that instant, everything came into sharp focus and she *saw* the man in front of her. Ten years had wrought great changes in him. Gone was the awkward, lanky youth, replaced by a man who projected strength, solidity, and confidence. His blue-violet eyes darkened to midnight as he stared back at her, eliciting a strange tugging sensation deep in her belly.

Hoping her face didn't look as flushed as she suspected it did, she jerked her gaze away. *What is the matter with me? Just because he's*—she grudgingly acknowledged the truth—*pretty doesn't mean he's not still a great oaf. Stay focused!* She wrested her attention away to see if Fairford was watching as they made their way to the dance floor. She couldn't see him amid the crush. If he *was* watching, would he care that she was dancing with Montgomery?

Her spirits rose. This little hiccup could work to her advantage, if she played it right. Let Fairford see her beauty and grace displayed on another man's arm. Let him see his fellow sex falling at her feet, and he'd soon be next in line.

Montgomery smiled down at her as they began moving with the music, a minuet. Breath barely made it into her chest for the clamor in her heart at the sight.

In a blink, Fairford was utterly forgotten. *Everything* was forgotten as they glided through the complex weave of turns and dips, touching and separating, touching again. And every time they made contact, the unsettling river of tingles intensified, pooling in the secret place between her legs.

The music wrapped around her like a living thing, seeming to carry her forward without any conscious effort on her part. When it finally stopped, she felt bereft, as if her body had somehow forgotten how to move without it.

Bowing over her hand, Montgomery brushed its back with his lips. "An honor and a pleasure, my lady."

Realizing she was standing there like a half-wit, she snatched her scorched fingers away. "Likewise, my lord."

"May I offer you something to drink?"

Damn! She'd hoped to excuse herself before he could say anything else, but…her mouth *was* parched. Her gaze drifted to the french doors leading out to the terrace. They were closed against the frigid flakes swirling beyond. It looked utterly miserable, and yet suddenly she longed to be out there in it, if only to escape the heat and turmoil boiling away inside her.

"Thank you. It is a bit warm in here," she finally said.

She watched as he snatched a glass from a passing tray and dashed its contents into a potted orange tree. He then went to the door she'd gazed at so longingly only moments before and opened it, letting in a blast of icy air and the snapping scent of clean snow.

Slipping and sliding his way to the balustrade, Montgomery scooped up a glassful of white from its top and came back. He held the goblet out to another passing servant, bidding him fill it from the bottle he bore.

She accepted the chilled wine and took a refreshing sip. It was delicious. "I doubt any gentleman here has ever gone to such lengths to fetch a drink for a lady," she said, smiling in spite of herself. "Thank you."

"You are most welcome."

She felt herself heating again from the inside out as his gaze lingered on her lips. She licked them reflexively and saw his eyes darken again. Her hand shook as she lowered the now empty glass. The way he looked at her was most disconcerting. She felt absolutely naked. Worse, she couldn't help wondering what *he* might look like without his clothes.

A bubble of hysterical laughter lodged in her throat. She ought to be thinking about cool, detached Lord Fairford. Golden, angelic Fairford. Not mentally undressing this black-haired devil! Lord Montgomery looked anything *but* angelic—unless one considered the fallen sort.

As if he could read her thoughts, Montgomery's mouth slanted. Her stomach again tightened. It was an almost uncomfortable response.

Almost. The same traitorous little voice inside her whispered that perhaps Montgomery might make a better husband than Fairford. The more she looked at him, the more pleasing the idea became. Thick, dark curls instead of fine, fair hair. Eyes of midnight rather than ice—dark eyes full of promises.

She watched, mesmerized, as something flared to life in those eyes, something infinitely, temptingly dangerous. The ache in her belly suddenly blossomed, sending another rush of heat to the place below. Panicking, she looked away and snapped open her fan, struggling to exude cool dignity as opposed to trembling idiocy.

How could she possibly think of her old *bête noire* with… desire?

She shifted to put a bit more distance between them. It was the height of irony that the boy who'd called her a pest now seemed to have the ability to set her ablaze.

"I must confess, I was rather surprised to hear a woman speak of politics so knowledgeably," he said, moving a little closer.

"I make it a point to keep well informed," she replied, annoyed by his patronizing tone—*and* by how close he was. "Papa always read the papers. Now, I read them. Every morning. Mama thinks it a waste of time for me to fill my head with such things, but I enjoy learning about the larger world."

"The pursuit of knowledge is never a waste of time," he agreed. "Ignorance by choice is a grave sin, but action taken in deliberate ignorance is an even greater offense."

A grudging smile formed on her lips. "That sounds like something Papa might have said." Sadness threatened to again overwhelm her. In spite of his many faults, he had been a wonderful father.

"Sabrina!"

As one, they turned to see a matronly figure parting the throng.

"Mama!" exclaimed Sabrina. "How very glad I am to see you. Lady Elsworth wanted me to relay Lady Bidewell's request for your assistance with—"

"Yes, yes. I already know all about it. Lady Boswell informed me," Lady Aylesford interrupted, gazing up at Montgomery with a most calculating look in her eye. "But tell me, who is your companion?"

Montgomery bowed, still smiling. "My lady, I must say it is a great pleasure to see you again."

"Henry?" Her hand fluttered to her breast. "Upon my word, how you have grown! Where is the rapscallion who used to pilfer my scones?"

"Still very much here, dear lady. And beware, for I still adore sweets."

Sabrina felt herself grow warm. He'd been looking right at her when he said it.

"Well, you cannot tell by looking at you," said her mother. "I can see I shall have to take you in hand. You are thin as a reed!"

Incredulous, Sabrina just stared at her mother. He was the epitome of health.

"My boy, you really must come and—"

Sabrina cleared her throat and shook her head a little.

Mama continued as though she had not noticed. "You *must* come to tea this Thursday. I simply will not accept a refusal!"

"My lady, I am most pleased to accept your kind invitation."

"Excellent!" replied Mama at once. "Sabrina, remind me tomorrow to invite Eugenia to tea Thursday. I'm sure she would love to see Henry again. Now, I beg you to excuse me. I hate to leave again so quickly, but I've sworn to assist Lady Bidewell with something and the need is urgent."

"But M—"

"You have far less need of my shepherding skills, my dear," her mother insisted, cutting off her protest. She flashed an arch smile at him. "I'm sure Henry will be happy to escort you the remainder of this evening, won't you dear?"

"I shall care for her as if she were my very own, my lady."

"Oh, pish tosh!" hooted her mother. "Do call me Auntie as you used to—there's no need for formality between *us*, dear boy. I knew you when you were in nappies."

She would be pinching his cheeks next!

"Of course, Auntie," he said, with far too much enthusiasm.

"Good boy. Now, I'm off to try and make a bride of the Bidewell girl." Her mother gathered herself as though in preparation for impending battle. "Wish me luck, for I shall have need of it."

Dread filled Sabrina. She knew exactly what her mother was up to, and it was absolutely infuriating.

Relax. She took a few deep, restorative breaths. If Fairford got the impression Montgomery was courting her…

"How is Eugenia?" asked Montgomery, pulling her back into the moment.

"Eugenia? Quite well. She recently presented her husband with their fourth child, a boy. The first three were girls."

"I *have* been away a long time," he muttered. "I suppose she is overjoyed?"

"She is arranging his marriage already, and he is but three months old," she replied, caught off guard. It struck her as odd that a man would be even remotely interested in such things.

"I'm pleased to hear she has finally taken to domesticity. I remember she was such a hoyden—rather like her youngest sister."

The glow in his eyes caused her stomach to flip again. Blinking, Sabrina shook herself. "I'm not nearly as adventurous as Eugenia," she said, aiming for "dull and proper" as she covertly scanned the crush. Fairford's flaxen head was nowhere in sight.

"I rather think you underestimate your own courage, Pest," said Montgomery, dropping his voice to an intimate murmur.

Despite his use of the hated nickname, a cascade of warm shivers ran across her skin. Desperate to escape the source of the unsettling sensation, she looked about for a means—*any* means—of escape.

About twenty feet away a tall, awkward-looking young man leaned against a wall. He was trying to appear bored, but the effect was ruined by the wistful looks he kept casting toward the dance floor. They'd been introduced earlier, but she couldn't quite…

Chadwick. Yes! He would do. She stared at him intently. *This way, you blind lump*, she thought.

It was an eternity before he finally took note, but when he did, her victim blushed all the way to his ginger roots. He glanced over his shoulder at the wall behind him, seeming startled to find it there.

Beneath her skirts, she tapped her foot. He turned back, surprise all over his face, and she had to refrain from rolling her eyes. *Yes, you! I'm not admiring the wainscoting!*

The lad gave her a shy, unsure smile, and she cast her gaze downward as if embarrassed by her own boldness. After a brief moment, however, she lifted her lashes to stare at him once more and watched in triumph as the red-faced young man obediently came to heel.

It was hard not to feel just a bit smug. Her sisters had taught her well.

"My lady, I'm so pleased to see you again," stammered Chadwick as he bowed before her clumsily. "May I beg the honor of your next dance?"

"Of course," she murmured, avoiding Montgomery's gaze. "Please excuse me, my lord."

Chadwick's smile nearly split his face in half as she placed her hand on his arm and allowed him to lead her away.

Five minutes. Five minutes and she could lose herself in the crush.

Sabrina stared, unseeing, at a point somewhere between her partner's eyebrows while they danced. Her mind was full of Montgomery, her body still alive with the memory of his touch. She had to stay as far away from that man as possible.

"My lady, might I dare hope for another dance with you later this evening?"

"Hmm?"

"I—I asked if I might hope for another dance with you," blurted Chadwick.

His urgent manner at last penetrated the fog in her mind. She came out of her reverie to see that Chadwick's boyish face was filled with fervent adoration.

Her heart sank. *Oh no.*

"I'm afraid that would be most improper, my lord," she said carefully. "My reputation would surely suffer irreparable damage were I to show you such favor."

It was just the right answer. She stifled a giggle as Chadwick's narrow chest puffed out. Really, she oughtn't laugh, but he looked perfectly ridiculous. Like a skinny rooster. She half expected him to start strutting and crowing.

She whipped open her fan and hid behind it until she could regain control over her twitching lips.

"I would never wish to cause you any distress, of course," he vowed, apparently mistaking her action for shyness. "I respectfully withdraw my selfish request."

A sigh of relief lodged in her chest.

"Yet, I must tell you that you have utterly captivated me, my lady," he continued with alarming vehemence. "Your beauty and grace know no rival. You outshine your peers as the sun outshines the very stars."

She choked down a wave of pure panic. Now the fat was well and truly in the fire. Just as she was contemplating the effectiveness of a good swoon as a means of escape, an idea struck her. *Thursday*...Montgomery was coming to tea on Thursday.

She looked at Chadwick. Perhaps not the most dashing rescuer, but what did that matter as long as he stood between her and Montgomery? It was too good an opportunity to pass up.

"I'm afraid that I may not dance with you again this evening, my lord, but"—she watched his Adam's apple jump as he swallowed, waiting—"I am receiving callers at tea this Thursday. If you would like—"

"It would bring me no *end* of delight, my lady!"

Ignoring his enthusiastic interruption, she smiled. He was obviously overcome, poor fellow. It was sweet, in an annoying sort of way. "I would be pleased to receive you as my guest, my lord. And now, I'm afraid I've lingered far too long. People are beginning to stare."

Chadwick's face lit with joy. "I completely understand the need for propriety, my lady. Shall I escort you to a chair?"

"I should like nothing better—but I'm afraid I *must* find my mother," she amended hastily. Fairford had just reappeared and was now speaking with the Duke of Bedford. She *had* to find a way to get his attention. "She is with Lady Bidewell."

At the mention of that name, Chadwick's face fell.

Too late, Sabrina remembered a conversation she'd overheard between her mother and Lady Bidewell regarding a possible union between her daughter...and this man. *Oh, sweet Lord.* Mama had left her with Montgomery to assist with the campaign.

She watched as his mouth hardened with determination. "I'll gladly take you to her," he said, slipping his arm beneath her hand without waiting for her reply. "I should very much like the opportunity to meet Lady Aylesford."

Hoist by her own petard, she had no choice but to go with him. Looking back, she fastened desperate eyes on the dwindling form of Lord Fairford.

Unfortunately, Lord Montgomery happened to be looking in her direction at that very moment. Their eyes met, and his lips quirked as he acknowledged her with a slight nod.

Sabrina's face flamed as she whipped back around.

Damn.

She felt utterly drained by the time she climbed into her carriage. Each of her sisters had been in raptures for days after *her* first ball—not so, for her. Never in all her days had she been so happy to leave a social event. Fairford had ignored all attempts to gain his attention, while Chadwick had managed to make a damned nuisance of himself, popping up at every turn and informing half the bloody ballroom of her having invited him to tea.

To make matters worse, Mama now sat across from her, seething with displeasure.

"What in heaven's name were you thinking, Sabrina? His father was a *merchant*," she groused, saying the word as though it tasted bad. "He's barely a genuine viscount, if you ask me."

Sabrina was sure she hadn't asked.

"His mother's family would never have agreed to such a union had they not been desperately in debt. I have it on good authority his mother deliberately compromised herself to guarantee the match, and that upon signing the register, the groom paid her family a ridiculous sum to have the estate freed. Chadwick's title was purchased outright."

"I don't plan to marry him, Mama."

"I should think not! I'd expect you to have better sense, certainly. But why waste your time on such as him at all? I thought you had your eye on Fairford? And let us not forget Henry."

Oh, let us do! thought Sabrina uncharitably. The very mention of him made her ears grow uncomfortably warm.

"He was quite taken with you." Her mother leaned forward, a gleam in her eye. "And I strongly suspect the sentiment to be mutual."

The temperature rose another degree. "I'm sure he is a very nice gentleman, Mama, but I think it a bit early to be making any wedding plans just yet." She'd managed to evade Montgomery, but there'd been a heavy price associated with her escape. If *only* Fairford had come to her rescue instead of Chadwick.

She sighed. It wasn't the lad's fault. Poor fellow only thought she was interested in him because, like an idiot, she'd deliberately led him to believe so. There had to be a gentle way of dissuading him. Perhaps her sisters could advise her? Georgiana and Augusta had both been highly sought after in their first Seasons…

"Young lady, I am talking to you."

She flinched. "Mama, I know I shouldn't have invited him, but I felt so sorry for him!"

"Charitable inclinations are *never* a good reason to encourage a man, Sabrina. It gives them ideas, encourages them to take liberties in the hope of possible gain. You are an earl's daughter. He is a merchant's son."

"I underst—"

"And worse, now Lady Bidewell is wroth with *me*! She had been working toward a match between her daughter and Chadwick for nearly a year when you blundered across his path. You've made a fine mess of things. The Season has only just begun, and already you've made an enemy."

Sabrina scowled. She already knew Chadwick might not easily be dissuaded, not with the likes of Miss Myopic Bidewell waiting in the wings to snap him up. And then there was Montgomery to deal with as well.

She looked forward to Thursday with all the anticipation of a walk to the headsman's block.

Henry held the cards in his hand and laid out a knave, not really caring about the game. It held no interest for him tonight. His mind was preoccupied with red hair and hazel eyes. Eventually, he tossed in his lot. "I'm done for the night, Percy. Just not in the mood for it, I guess."

"Feeling restless, are we?" the other man asked. "You ought to take a mistress. Just the cure for that sort of ailment."

"I've no interest in dalliances, old boy."

"Oh, I know a few ladies that could change your mind, believe me," teased his friend.

"I tried keeping a mistress once, but the experience left me unenthusiastic."

"Obviously, you didn't have the right one," said Percy. "Rotten bit of luck, that's all. You can't let one bad apple spoil the whole barrel."

A rueful smile lifted the corner of Henry's mouth. "I can only imagine Adorée's reaction to hearing a man compare her to fruit—rotten fruit, at that."

Percy sat up. "Adorée? *The* Adorée? When was this?"

"Before I went to India." He hadn't told a soul. She'd made him promise to keep their relationship a secret. Both beautiful and sensual, she'd been every man's desire—and she'd chosen him. She'd even gone so far as to call it "love," but the truth had quickly become apparent as her skilled hands had dug deeper and deeper into his purse. He'd given her as much as he could, which was no pittance, but it had not been enough to buy her loyalty. The moment a wealthier man had shown interest, she'd cooled toward him.

"Bloody hell, man," said Percy, frowning. "You could have told *me*, at least. I would have kept your secret and congratulated you on the coup. I've been trying to coax that woman into my bed for years, but I can't afford her." He leaned forward, his face eager. "Tell me, was she as good as they say?"

"Her expertise would have left even you breathless." Already he was regretting having divulged his secret.

"And yet you decided to forsake her perfumed perfection in favor of—how did you put it? Ah, yes—*pungent* India."

"I did not have much choice in the matter. Father insisted I take the post after I refused to accept the bride he'd selected for me." It was mostly true. Adorée's defection had wounded his pride in such a way as to make it the most palatable option. Despite the fact that he'd known her for a courtesan from the beginning, he hadn't been able to bear seeing her with another man.

"Well, if the carnal tempts you not, then tell me what will," continued Percy. "Name your vice, and I shall gladly support you in its indulgence."

Henry smiled and shook his head. "I am already in danger of hell's flames on several counts. And I think you've blackened your own soul quite enough without offering to aid others in their journey to moral turpitude."

"How *we* ever ended up being friends is a mystery," groused Percy. He let out a long sigh. "Very well. Off with you, then. Go home to your lonely bed."

"I'm not lonely."

It was a bold lie, and one that fooled neither of them.

Percy peered at him, all traces of humor gone from his eyes. "Normally I should shudder to say such a thing, but you might consider marrying before you wither away entirely."

"I'm not lonely, and I'm certainly not withering away," Henry said with a laugh.

"Then what is it that has you moping about of late? Is the lovely Adorée still to blame? Or is it something else that has effected your transformation?"

"What do you mean? I'm the same as I've always been—and I'm not moping."

"You've changed, Henry. You're becoming your father."

"Don't be ridiculous," Henry said, dismissing his friend's claim with a snort. But he knew he'd changed. He was vastly different from the brash young man he remembered being years ago. Time and experience had altered him irreversibly.

He *felt* older than the man before him, though they were the same age. *I might have been more like him, had I stayed here...* But he'd run away, plain and simple, not wanting to face responsibility.

And now it had found him and dragged him back to England. There was no escaping it. Father's health could no longer take the strain of managing the estates, and as the eldest it was his duty to take over their care. He sighed, feeling the weight settle across his shoulders.

Sabrina. Again, the memory of her intruded upon his thoughts. On the washed-out canvas of his life here in London, she was an unexpected splash of bright color. "The Red Pestilence," he chuckled.

"I beg your pardon?" said Percy.

Henry coughed. "My apologies, I was woolgathering. I think I shall call it a night."

"Suit yourself, I suppose," said Percy, looking disappointed. "You've not been yourself of late, you know. Admit it."

"Don't worry about me. I'll be fine." Henry signaled the footman to send for his carriage. "I shall see you at the Pendletons."

"Nighty-night, then," said Percy, tossing his cards to the table with a shrug.

Henry stepped out into the night air and breathed deeply. Immediately, he wished he hadn't. London hadn't had a good rain in days and it smelled like it.

As he climbed into his carriage, a woman walked past wearing a towering red wig. Once again, memory flooded back from happier times. Times when a fiery-haired little girl had caused him great amounts of grief—and had secretly made him laugh.

But Sabrina Grayson was a child no more.

Chapter Three

"HENRY! DO COME IN."

For a moment, Sabrina's mouth hung open. Mama didn't jump up to greet *any*one. Ever. Yet she'd done just that upon seeing Montgomery standing with the butler at the parlor door. Her gaze slid over to her sister, curious to see her reaction, but Eugenia was too busy to pay her any mind.

"Hello, Auntie, Eugenia...or Lady Afton, rather," said Montgomery, kissing the cheek presented to him by the elder and bowing over Eugenia's hand. "Congratulations on the arrival of your son," he murmured.

"Thank you, my lord," replied Eugenia.

Shifting his attention to Sabrina, he bowed formally. "A pleasure to see you again, my lady."

Snapping her mouth shut with an audible pop, Sabrina extended her hand and fixed her eyes on the wall beyond his left shoulder. Though she did her level best, it was difficult to ignore the way his touch caused her throat to become suddenly dry. Swallowing reflexively, she withdrew her fingers as quickly as manners allowed.

His violet eyes gleamed with mirth as he let her go.

"I'm so happy you could join us," said her mother. "Come, sit and have tea. I had cook make some of your old favorites just for the occasion."

In a rush, Sabrina sat next to Eugenia, purposely leaving no room on the sofa.

Montgomery shot her a knowing smile. "It has been so long since I was last here," he said, looking right at her as he took the cup offered by her mother. "I'm happy to find that not much has changed"—he glanced down—"although I welcome the lack of ink in my tea."

Sabrina's scalp tingled with heat, and she knew her cheeks must be the color of ripe cherries. "That was a long time ago, my lord. Things are quite different now."

"Indeed they are," he answered.

The way he said it caused her blush to deepen. She looked to her sister and saw that Eugenia was staring at her with a peculiar expression. She focused on taking a sip of her tea and hoped that he was finished. She hoped in vain.

"You are as unrepentant now as you were then," he said, smiling. "Some things never change."

She let out a weary sigh. "Are you planning to hold a grudge forever, my lord?"

"Not at all. I was most impressed by your bravery, actually. Not many little girls have the bol…"—he stopped and coughed, glancing at the other ladies in the room—"the courage to handle a live snake."

"Snake?" exclaimed her mother and Eugenia at the same time.

"What snake?" her mother persisted. "Henry, whatever are you talking about?"

Sabrina shook her head, silently pleading with him not to tell. Again, no such luck.

"She never told you?" His wicked eyes gleamed. "During my last visit here, Sabrina managed to somehow deposit a living snake into my coat pocket."

The unbelieving gazes of both women swung toward her, and she squirmed. "It was a childish prank, nothing more. And it was years ago."

"Sabrina! You must apologize at once!" demanded her mother. "I cannot believe you would do such a thing. What if it had bitten him?"

But Montgomery's laughter put an end to her tirade. "It was nothing more than a garter snake, Auntie, really." He turned his attention to her once more. "It might interest you to know that I made it all the way home before it decided to make known its presence."

Sabrina clamped down on her tongue. *So much for him leaping out and landing in a puddle...*Disappointment filled her.

"My valet discovered it as he was taking my coat," he continued. "He felt something in the pocket, reached into it, and found the stowaway. The poor man had a fit of hysterics and very nearly fainted."

In spite of herself, she felt the corners of her mouth lifting.

"There!" he said, pointing at her with mock severity. "You see what I mean? No remorse at all."

The laugh escaped her in the form of a soft snort. Unfortunately, it was the only sound in the room at that moment. She covered her mouth, mortified, as everyone else began to chuckle.

Just then, the butler announced that Lord Chadwick had arrived.

Thank God.

Her mother's smile faltered only the slightest bit at the sight of the eager face peering through the door. "Ah, yes. Our other esteemed guest," she informed Montgomery apologetically. She beckoned to the new arrival. "Do join us."

Chadwick entered, but stopped short upon seeing Montgomery.

Sabrina marked that in spite of the benign smile he wore, Montgomery's eyes carried a clear warning. Her temper flared. Who did he think he was? He had no claim on her whatsoever.

After only a moment's hesitation, Chadwick moved to stand before her. "My lady, you are the very spring incarnate," he gushed, lingering over the hand she held out. "Would that I were summer, that I might follow you for all eternity. You humble me with your extravagant beauty."

Beside her, Eugenia shook with suppressed laughter. Sabrina nudged her with a toe from under her voluminous skirts. "Thank you, my lord," she managed, smiling.

Once pleasantries had been exchanged and Chadwick had settled himself, Montgomery proceeded to completely ignore her. As if determined to make up for his lack of attention, Chadwick took every opportunity to be obsequious to the point of inciting nausea. Her patience with the whole situation was deteriorating with each breath. If she did not do something soon, she would scream.

"My Lord Chadwick, would you care to accompany me and my sister on a stroll in the gardens?" she at last cut in, interrupting his current soliloquy. "The day is warm, and I crave fresh air and sunshine."

The young man's doe-brown eyes widened in happy disbelief. He rose, in his haste nearly upsetting a footstool. "My lady, I'd be delighted!"

"What a wonderful idea!" her mother interjected. "Why don't we all take a stroll? It *is* lovely outside, and my new tulips have finally begun to flower. I've been dying to show them off."

Eugenia put down her cup and saucer. "Actually, I should really go up to the nursery and"—Sabrina grabbed her sister's other hand where it lay beside her and squeezed it, silently begging her to remain—"and check on little William," Eugenia continued, pulling her hand away.

Traitor!

"Of course, my dear," their mother cooed. "After all, it *is* his first time away from home."

Clenching her teeth in frustration, Sabrina allowed Chadwick to escort her from the room while Montgomery accompanied her mother.

Even if it wasn't exactly an escape, the walk was a pleasant change of scenery after the stuffy confines of the parlor. Or at least it would have been, had it not been for her companion. Chadwick clamped her hand in the crook of his elbow so tightly that her fingers were beginning to feel numb. She wriggled them, hoping to loosen his hold just a bit, but instead of releasing her, his other hand only moved to cover hers.

It was hot and sweaty and disgusting.

Not warm and dry like M—

She barely refrained from yelping in surprise as the thought was interrupted by the scrape of something—paper, she thought—being inserted beneath her palm. A note. She glanced up at her escort, only to have to look away again in dismay. The lad was staring at her like a moonstruck calf. Wrenching her hand away, she shoved the note into her pocket.

A deep laugh sounded from behind, and Sabrina looked back over her shoulder, worried that Montgomery had witnessed the clumsy exchange. But no, he was only responding to something her mother had said.

Her belly tightened at the sight of him. The planes of his face were softened in merriment, and his teeth flashed white as he smiled. The sunlight revealed that his hair wasn't actually black, but a very rich brown. Her fingers itched to learn its texture. Would it be soft and fine, or thick and wiry? It looked soft.

His gaze met hers.

She looked away. *Damn him!* Peeved at having been caught, she snatched a flower from a bush alongside the path and, without thinking, proceeded to shred the poor blossom.

"He seems to delight in vexing you," said Chadwick. "I can tell you are displeased by his presence. Why is he here?"

She looked at him, surprised by his keen observation and irritated with herself for betraying the depth of her upset. "Mama invited him. His mother and mine were childhood friends. *We*, however, were not."

"Then he is not courting you?"

"Good heavens, no," she answered with a little laugh. "He's far too old for me. The man paid court to Eugenia, once upon a time. You are correct in that he seems to enjoy bedeviling me. He did so when I was a child, and unfortunately, he appears never to have grown beyond such immature entertainments."

"My mother is fond of saying that though men age, they never truly become adults," said Chadwick, smiling again. "I intend to prove her wrong, of course," he quickly amended, his cheeks catching fire.

She repressed a smile of her own. He was trying so hard to impress her, but he just kept bungling it, the poor fellow.

Behind them, Montgomery and her mother laughed again, shattering the momentary peace she'd attained. She scowled. No doubt they were still discussing the snake incident. He'd waited ten years to tattle on her. Ten years! Not that it really mattered, now she was grown, but it still rankled. He ought to have been the one who'd discovered that snake, not his valet. "The Red Pestilence" indeed! If she lacked remorse for her childhood pranks, it was because his torment had been well deserved.

"Do not let him steal your enjoyment of the day, my lady," said Chadwick softly.

She looked into his sympathetic brown eyes. He was right. Montgomery was deliberately tweaking her nose, and she was letting him get away with it. No more. "Let us look at the water, shall we?" she said with a sweet smile.

Henry watched the couple ahead. Sabrina's prickly reaction every time he laughed was telling. She obviously still considered him the enemy.

Chadwick was, from the look of things, smitten in the way only a young man in the first blush of utter infatuation can be. The slip of paper he'd pressed on her was no doubt an impassioned plea for her favor.

Had he ever been that young and impetuous? Logic said yes, but experience said no. He'd never been so taken with a woman that he'd behaved like the man in front of him.

He watched as Sabrina, clearly dismayed by her escort's temerity, pocketed the note and moved farther down the path toward the water.

He turned to Lady Aylesford with a smile. "Being here brings back some wonderful memories."

"I should hope so," she replied. "You always seemed to like it here. At least until your visits were sabotaged."

"But those memories are some of my fondest."

She turned unbelieving eyes on him. "Surely you jest."

"No indeed. I looked forward to each visit." He laughed. "Truth be told, I could hardly wait to see what she would try next. She never failed to surprise me." He didn't tell her, but outwitting little Sabrina had been quite an elaborate and time-consuming game—one he'd thoroughly enjoyed, despite only rarely ever winning the battle. He ought to have been mortified to be bested by a child ten years his junior, but in truth, he'd only been impressed by her ingenuity and fearless attitude.

"In fact"—he hesitated—"I would like to ask your opinion on a matter of some delicacy."

She looked at him sidelong. "You wish to court her?"

Startled, he looked to see a knowing smile on her face.

"I was wondering when you would broach the subject. I could tell you were interested in her when I saw you together at the ball," she said with a soft chuckle.

"And you have no objection to my courting her? Even though I was once Eugenia's—"

She dismissed his concern with a wave. "That was years ago, and Eugenia was already in love with Afton. I told Harry it was a bad idea, but he insisted on giving it a go. You have my blessing to court Sabrina, if such is your wish."

"Thank you, my lady."

"Don't thank me yet," she said. "You'll have some convincing to do with that one, first." She nodded toward her daughter, who was down by the pond. "She still thinks of you in terms of ink and snakes."

A flash of red caught his eye. The breeze had snatched her hat away, and now it settled on the rippling surface of the water, leaving her fiery head exposed.

He let out a laugh as he saw her stamp her foot in frustration. Yes, indeed. Some things never changed.

Chapter Four

$\mathscr{A}$S SOON AS THE GENTLEMEN DEPARTED, SABRINA retreated to her chamber. Damn that Montgomery! Why did he have to ruin everything? The moment they'd come in view of the pond, he'd told another embarrassing story—the one about her falling out of the boat at the picnic. And this time Chadwick had heard. To his credit, he had not laughed along with the rest of them. He had, instead, been most adamantly *not* amused, which had been even worse.

Pulling out the little note he had pressed on her, she grimaced. She ought to toss it into the fire.

Still…it *was* her very first love letter. Giving in to curiosity, she broke the seal and unfolded the paper just as the hinges of her door creaked.

Eugenia peeked in. "May I?"

"Oh, of…of course," Sabrina stammered, trying to hide the paper. But it was too late.

"I see I've interrupted a bit of clandestine reading," said Eugenia, grinning. "Well, which one is it from?"

"Which one do you think?" Sabrina answered tartly.

Eugenia sat on the edge of the bed beside her. "Are you going to read it, or not?"

"How is little William?"

"Sound asleep—and don't change the subject. I've seen the note. It's pointless to try and keep it to yourself. Read it."

Sighing in defeat, Sabrina withdrew the letter. Her eyes rolled heavenward as Eugenia squashed in close beside her to read aloud:

My Dearest Lady Sabrina,

I have thought of little but your lovely face since the moment we met. You are the very sun in my sky, and I should love nothing better than to bask in the light of your grace and beauty for all eternity. Pray, do not make me wait overlong for the next sunrise.

Your Devoted Servant,
Tristan V. Chadwick

"Oh, that *is* lovely!" laughed Eugenia, plucking the page from her hands and setting it aside. "At least he refrained from trying to pass off Shakespeare's sonnets as original prose the way my first suitor did."

"Yes, at least there is that," Sabrina muttered.

"What, you're not thrilled about young master Chadwick's affection for you?" asked Eugenia, feigning shock. "Pity, I thought him rather sweet. He would break his neck to try and please you, you know. Not a bad thing in a husband, if you ask me."

"I did *not* ask. It's too bad you're not on the market—then *you* could marry him, since you like him so much."

Her sister stared at her knowingly.

"Oh, Eugenia, it's not that he isn't nice, but he just isn't—"

"Henry?" supplied Eugenia, her smile widening. "Your attitude toward him today was quite telling, sister dear."

"What do you mean? I did my best to try and ignore the brute."

"Precisely. Have I not always said that the best way to attract a man is to ignore him?"

Sabrina's mouth dropped open. How could she have forgotten the first rule? *Blast it all!*

"What I would like to know is why you should *wish* to be rid of him," prodded Eugenia. "He is perfect for you, and quite obviously interested."

"Interested? He brought up ancient history and threw it in my face. Then, after you abandoned me"—she glared pointedly—"he told even *more* embarrassing stories about me, and in front of an outsider!"

"Any man who calls on a woman ten years after she put a snake in his pocket is *definitely* interested."

"He's too old." She couldn't tell her the truth, that any man who could make her feel the way he did would have entirely too much power over her. Such a man would take her heart and soul as well as her body, and that was unacceptable.

Her sister's brown eyes twinkled. "My husband is thirteen years my senior, and I can assure you that I am quite happily married."

"He's insensitive, quarrelsome, and confrontational," Sabrina argued, refusing to concede.

"What man isn't? The main point is: Are you attracted to each other? I think you are."

"I think you're wrong."

"I think you blushed every time you looked at him—right to the very tips of your ears," sang Eugenia.

"And I think *you* are a busybody!"

"So you *are* attracted to him, then. I thought as much."

"I didn't say—"

"You don't have to, darling. I could see it as plain as the nose on King George's face."

Frustration filled Sabrina as she stared at her sister. Eugenia's face was set, her eyes far too knowing. *Fine. The truth, then.* "So what if I am? It doesn't mean I shall marry him."

"Why don't you tell me the real reason you won't consider him? And don't bother bringing up the fact that he once courted me, because he didn't. Not really. We weren't suited and we both knew it. Neither of us wanted to marry the other."

Sabrina could feel her teeth clenching. She'd kept it to herself all these years, and it just didn't seem right to let it out now. But there seemed little choice if she wanted Eugenia to understand and help her get rid of Montgomery. How ironic that they should switch places now, ten years after she'd played the saboteur. "I don't wish to marry a man to whom I am attracted."

Eugenia stared at her in bewilderment. "Why ever not?"

"Mama loved Papa, and look how she suffered because of it," she replied softly.

"Sabrina, you don't know that. Mama and Papa were—"

"I *do* know, Eugenia," Sabrina interrupted. "You were all so engrossed in your own affairs that perhaps you didn't notice that not all was well between them. But I did. All those times you had me play spy for you, I saw. I heard. It all started that day with the snake. After that, I began paying attention. Especially to the servants' talk. They speak quite freely about us when they don't know we're listening."

"What did they say?"

"They said that Papa had not shared Mama's bed in years. They spoke of how he took a new mistress every year and spent a fortune on her upkeep. They whispered about how his bastards pepper the villages around our country estate. It broke Mama's heart. And I know it all to be true, Eugenia. I heard them arguing, and then listened to her crying. I heard everything."

Eugenia said nothing.

Sabrina knew there was nothing to be said. Truth was truth. "At first, I was wroth with him over what I perceived as a terrible betrayal. But then I saw how much he genuinely cared for her and that he *tried* to make her happy in spite of her inability to…" She couldn't say that. Not to anyone, not even Eugenia. "Papa was not a heartless reprobate."

"No. He was not," her sister agreed. "He was a wonderful father and a doting husband. And I don't know what you heard or saw, but he and Mama were almost embarrassing in their openness of affection when *I* was a child." She shook her head. "Something terrible must have happened."

"What happened is that Papa was no different from any other man." It did not come out as she intended, and she faltered under the harsh look Eugenia directed at her. "Eugenia, we women must face the fact that at some point, *all* married men take a lover or mistress. Passion simply does not last a lifetime, at least not mutually. It cannot. Men have certain…needs." She felt herself blush, and hurried on. "Mama's problem lay in that she could not accept the reality. She expected too much of Papa. I will not make that mistake with my husband."

"I think you're wrong. About everything. Have you ever asked Mama about it?"

"It doesn't really matter, does it?" Sabrina cut in stubbornly, unwilling to answer the question. "The decision is mine to make, and I choose to marry sensibly. I have no desire to fall prey to the misery of loving a man who cannot be faithful to me."

"Then who will you marry?"

"I've selected the eldest son of Baron Middleton."

"Fairford? He's a bit aloof—and what about that Childers woman?"

"Exactly my point. He is a known quantity. Therefore, I shall have no illusions about him."

"But surely you wish to at least be on friendly terms with your husband?"

"And I shall," Sabrina replied with confidence. "A sensible man like him will understand my desire for a sensible arrangement."

"Henry is quite sen—"

"Montgomery is anything *but* sensible," Sabrina exclaimed, her patience at an end. "He is a pompous, irritating, immature, name-calling—"

"Pax!" cried Eugenia, waving her hands in laughing surrender. "The choice is ultimately yours, Sabrina. But if you want my advice, I'd say Henry is the better man. He's certainly a better man than most, and I ought to know. You would do well to snap him up."

"Again, I don't recall asking, but thank you for your opinion," Sabrina huffed. "Now, if you will excuse me, I wish to rest before changing for dinner."

"Of course, my dear," said Eugenia, rising. "I completely understand. Being besieged by one's admirers can be so exhausting." She ducked just in time to avoid the pillow aimed at her head. "Especially when they shower you with such ardent prose," she added, just before slipping out.

Even in her foul mood, Sabrina couldn't help but laugh. She fell back on her bed, feeling really and truly "besieged." Flanked by the devil on one side and a besotted puppy on the other, with her nosy, meddling family in between, she'd be fit for Bedlam by the end of the Season.

The Somerset ball was the perfect place to launch a second campaign.

She had chosen her armor with care, and wore pale, corn-flower-blue silk traced with delicate silver embroidery embellished with tiny pearls—and the lowest décolletage her mother would tolerate. The gazes tracking her progress told her she'd chosen well: the men's were satisfyingly appreciative, the women's satisfyingly not.

Her pleasure dissolved as she spied Chadwick, who appeared to be anxiously searching for someone.

Please don't see me! she thought, trying in vain to hurry her mother along.

No such luck. He managed to join them just before they were announced, making them appear a trio. Mortification filled her at the resulting flurry of whipping necks and wagging chins. She wanted to run and hide. Instead, she forced herself to walk on with head held high, looking everywhere but at her impromptu escort.

Inadvertently, her gaze lit upon Lord Montgomery. Impotent rage swept through her at the sight of his knowing smile. She turned to look elsewhere, anywhere but at him, and caught sight of Miss Bidewell and her mother. Both were staring at her and Chadwick with naked hostility.

Lady Bidewell's flaring nostrils made her look like a bull ready to charge. Before she could stop it, a smile spread across Sabrina's face.

Lady Bidewell's ample breast heaved and her cheeks darkened further.

Damn! thought Sabrina. Why, oh *why* couldn't she behave herself? What devil prodded her to such constant impertinence? Forcing a neutral expression to her face, she looked at Chadwick out of a desperate need to find something safe upon which to rest her gaze.

Fortunately, Chadwick appeared not to have noticed. He was too busy strutting at her side like a bloody peacock, nodding to passersby as if he were King George himself on promenade.

The nightmare worsened as she caught sight of Fairford—staring right at her.

The bottom fell out of her stomach.

At that same moment, Lord Montgomery appeared before her. Faint strangling noises issued from her escort as Montgomery bowed and made a display of taking up and kissing both of her hands. "My lady, such loveliness as yours must make the stars themselves grow dim with shame," he said—loudly.

She froze, her gut immediately tying itself into a complicated knot. Whether the reaction was due to mortification or because his thumb was grazing her palm, she could not tell. Somewhere amid the half-formed thoughts flitting through her mind, she registered the fact that his thumb bore a callus. The slight roughness felt rather oddly pleasant as he traced small, slow circles, filling her palm with liquid fire.

Chadwick was not to be put aside so easily. He shot Montgomery a sour look. "Indeed, my lady. One can only agree, and add that such beauty as yours inspires neither rest nor peace in a man's heart. Yet, one smile from your lips, and I am instantly restored. I long for your smiles, as one longs for the *sunrise* after a long, dark night."

The reference to his own awkward prose fell on deaf ears, however, as Montgomery came closer. "If your beauty disturbs one's repose, my lady, it certainly doesn't make one long for the sunrise." His gaze dropped to her mouth, and her pulse began to hammer. "And though it is indeed a most potent restorative, no smile can cure that with which you have afflicted me. I believe I would require something far more tangible from your lips to cure *my* ailment."

The scathing retort she'd been formulating dried up. His lazily circling thumb now grazed the base of her wrist, sparking feather brushings of unspeakable heat between her legs.

"Would you care to dance?"

"I would be delighted," she answered automatically, the huskiness of her own voice surprising her as much as the speed of her response. *Why did I agree to dance with him?*

Leaving a dumbfounded Chadwick behind, she let Montgomery lead her away.

Chapter Five

*L*OUNGING AGAINST THE MANTELPIECE, HENRY REFLECTED upon his good fortune. Obliging Sabrina's urgent request to leave the ballroom immediately after their dance, he'd led her here, to Somerset's library.

Somerset's otherwise *unoccupied* library.

After visiting Aylesford, he'd made a decision. Sabrina interested him. She was by far the loveliest woman he'd ever seen, but it was more than that. Being near her made him feel...different. It made him feel as though something that had been asleep in him had awakened.

She had matured into a fascinating woman. Intelligent, outspoken, a bit impudent. He didn't mind. Too many times he'd been introduced to women trained to meekly agree with every word that came from his mouth. Not Sabrina—or at least not with him.

She paced the room, picking up figurines and replacing them, poking about in the corners, looking at the books on the shelves—anything to avoid looking at him, it seemed.

He walked over to where she stood fiddling with the bric-a-brac. "It's been ten minutes and you've not said a word."

She fidgeted with the little porcelain shepherdess in her hands and glanced at him apprehensively. "I'm not a gifted story-teller like you," she snapped.

"In order to tell a good story, one must have an interesting subject. I could tell a hundred stories about you, Pest," he said, chuckling. He knew he ought not to goad her—but he just couldn't seem to resist.

Her brows lowered. "Yes, well, I would appreciate it if you didn't. And don't call me that."

"Oh, come now. You cannot possibly still think I mean it as an insult," he said. Still, she did not soften. "Why are you so angry with me? I just rescued you from that buffoon out there, after all."

"Rescued me?"

"Were you *not* happy to be rid of your escort?"

He knew he had her when she bit her lip guiltily.

"He doesn't mean to be—"

"An oblivious ass?"

The corner of her mouth twitched. "I was going to say thoughtless."

"Well, I don't blame him for forgetting his manners."

"What is *that* supposed to mean?" she said, glaring.

"Will you relax?" he laughed. "I meant to imply that the way you look tonight would make any man forget his good manners."

Her cheeks pinkened. "Oh." She looked down at the carpet, obviously flustered.

"Is it so very surprising that I might say such a thing?" he asked, taking a step closer. She was so beautiful in the candlelight.

"A bit," she admitted warily. "I wouldn't expect *you* to pay me any sort of compliment."

"I forgave you for the snake and all the other nasty things you did to me long ago," he said with a grin. "As long as you don't put anything living in my pockets from this point forward…"

"That *isn't* funny!"

"I beg to differ. It's hilarious."

She let out a frustrated huff and turned to leave.

Without thinking, he reached out to stop her. She stared up at him, her hazel eyes wide, her bottom lip trembling ever so slightly. On impulse he extended a finger and tipped her chin up.

"Why is it that whenever I'm with you, I can never say the right thing? Perhaps I ought to give up trying to say anything at all."

He bent and claimed her mouth. She tasted just as sweet as he'd imagined, and he suddenly realized he'd wanted to do this ever since seeing her again tonight. Teasing and worrying her pouting bottom lip, he savored the plump fruit. The nape of her neck fit his hand perfectly. He threaded his fingers through her hair, dragging her closer. She felt so right in his arms.

Her response was quite unpracticed, and he knew without having to ask that she'd never been kissed before. Thus, her protest when he tried to withdraw came as a pleasant surprise.

His already aching erection hardened. Animal lust commanded him to claim her—at once—but good sense said otherwise. She hardly knew what she was doing, after all.

Still, it was hard to resist the temptation.

For all that it saved him from committing an exceedingly rash act, the gentle creak of hinges was an unwelcome intrusion.

He opened his eyes just enough to see Lady Carrington, London's biggest gossip, standing there in the doorway, looking on with undisguised glee as she took in what was no doubt a torrid tableau.

"Henry?" Sabrina's voice sounded drugged. Her eyes were still closed, lashes fluttering against her cheeks as wildly as the pulse hammering at her throat. "Don't...don't stop. Please."

Lady Carrington's garish, rouged lips formed a little *O* of shock.

In that moment, Henry knew there was nothing for it but to play the cards he'd been dealt. Even if he pulled away and stopped right then, it was already too late. The damage was done. Not unhappily, he obliged Sabrina's request. After a few seconds, he heard their spectator fleeing back down the hall.

In approximately five minutes every person of consequence in the Somerset ballroom would be informed that one Lady Sabrina Grayson had been caught in flagrante delicto with one Lord Henry Montgomery.

This must be what it feels like to drown…

Sabrina cataloged the differences between this kiss and the first. They were quite distinct. The first had been an exploration. This one tasted of pure hunger.

Montgomery's hands were everywhere, trailing fire across her body wherever they made contact. Had he not been holding her so fiercely, she would have collapsed to the floor when his thumb dipped beneath the edge of her bodice to graze a nipple.

He pulled away just in time.

"Given adequate time and a more appropriate setting, I can show you such pleasures as you have never even imagined," he murmured.

His words registered, filling her with mortification. Tearing loose, she bolted for the door.

But he was one step ahead. "Sabrina, wait, listen to m—"

"Let me go!" Shrugging off the now too-familiar hands that grasped her shoulders, she backed away, furious. Her anger was directed more at herself than at him, but she'd be damned if she'd let him know it.

"Not until you hear what I have to say."

"Say it then, you...you unspeakable bastard! And then let me go!" she spat, backing as far away from him as possible.

"I know this must be a bit of a shock." He took an unsteady breath. "It certainly is for me. Taking liberties with women in libraries is not a regular practice of mine. In fact, I can say in all honesty that this is the very first time I have ever done such a thing."

Even in her upset, she found it within herself to lift a sardonic brow.

"You must believe me," he insisted. "I did not come here intent on your ravishment."

"I don't *care* about your intentions! You'll not touch me again! Not ever!"

Defying her words, he reached out. "Sabrina, please—"

She flinched away, warding him off with raised hands. "If you come any closer, I shall scream the roof down and to hell with the consequences. I am not some, some...*strumpet* for you to, to—"

"Damn it all, Sabrina! I only wished to spend time with you, to get to know you better!"

"Yes, well, you certainly achieved your purpose, didn't you?"

"You know that isn't what I meant."

"Then what *do* you mean?"

"I should *like* to court you," he all but shouted.

Stunned, she stood there, mouth agape for several seconds. "Court me? *Me*? You cannot possibly..." An incredulous laugh burst forth from her lungs. "This is some sort of elaborate jest, isn't it? You *are* getting back at me for all of those pranks..." She searched his face, but he appeared to be perfectly serious. "If it isn't that, then you're daft."

"Perhaps just a bit," he admitted with a slanty grin. "But if I've lost my head, it's because ever since the moment I saw you again, you've been all I can think about."

An electric sensation washed over her skin on hearing his words, the same feeling she experienced just before a thunderstorm. Alarmed, she drew herself up as she'd seen her mother do so many times and put on her sternest face. "Lord Montgomery, I am afraid I must refuse. Now, please let me pass."

His brows drew together. "On what grounds do you refuse my suit?"

"Because I...you...because..."

"We are perfectly matched, Sabrina." It was a silken promise. "You know it in your blood."

"This is preposterous!" But her heart began to pound again.

"You asked me not to stop just now."

The quietly spoken condemnation rang in her ears. She had indeed.

"Is it so preposterous to think we might make a good match?" he added softly.

Her trembling was uncontrollable now and spreading to the rest of her body, inside and out. Whether it was caused by fear or temptation, she could not discern. "You, sir, belong in Bedlam!"

"Why? Why is it insanity to know what I want?" he laughed, apparently not understanding why she was being so difficult.

After all, wasn't it every woman's desire to marry? And he was no paltry catch. To entertain such thoughts, however, was very dangerous. "You'd have to be insane to even *think* I'd ever agree to such a thing! I want no part of this lunacy."

"Are you so certain?" The corner of his mouth curled, eliciting another pull of desire within her. "I want you, Sabrina. And you, if you'll admit it, desire me. Let me court you."

Fire licked through her. Yes, she wanted him. Which was why she had to get out now. Quick as lightning, she turned and ran to the door, not daring to look back as she propelled herself through it and into the blessedly empty hall.

Damn him. And damn me for not having better sense! She had to go home. At once. But on entering the ballroom, she immediately sensed that something was terribly wrong.

One by one, the stares settled on her like strange, leaden butterflies. Silence fell as she neared, followed by whispers after she'd passed. The sibilant echoes of the softly murmured word "kiss" were repeated over and over.

Embarrassment seared her like a winter frost. They knew. Somehow, they all knew.

The icy dread lasted only a brief instant, however, before the flames of wrath burned it away. Devil take them all for hypocrites! Especially that horrid, smirking Regina Cunningham! Why, just last Season, the little harlot had been caught with Lord Ludlow—a married man twice her age! Her enormous dowry was the *only* thing standing between her and spinsterhood.

Straightening her spine, Sabrina lifted her chin and ran the gauntlet. Let them gawk. It was only a kiss, after all. She'd done nothing most of the girls in this room hadn't done a dozen or more times, at least. Her thoughts turned angrily to Henr—*Lord Montgomery!* she corrected herself. He was to blame for this.

Though she tried to smother it into silence, her conscience pricked her. No. This was her fault entirely. She'd tempted Fate, knowing the risks involved.

Another titter sounded as she passed, and she heard: "*Lady Carrington said she saw them, and that the Grayson girl practically had her skirts tossed over her head, she was so thoroughly...*"

Sabrina turned toward the source of the chatter, and the speaker looked away guiltily. So! Lady *Carrington* had witnessed their kiss—and had obviously greatly embellished the event in the telling.

Her temper rose. She'd intended to find Mama and go home at once, but now it appeared she had no choice but to face down her accuser and correct her gross exaggeration. It had to be done, and quickly. Lady Carrington had sent many a poor girl running, her reputation in shreds regardless of whether or not she was actually guilty of the alleged act.

She knew if she disappeared now, she would be ruined. She could not let that happen.

After all, she *was* innocent. Sort of. Certainly, she'd not done anything to merit the slander she'd just heard.

Anger made her brave as she searched the crowd. At the center of a gathering of eagerly listening people stood her enemy, her jaws working at the speed of lightning. *Prune-faced old dragon!* Someone spotted her. A hush fell as Carrington's audience fell back.

A malicious smile curved the gossipmongers' loose lips as Sabrina approached, and a frisson of apprehension brushed her spine. Everything depended on her holding her ground here. She crossed her arms and fixed the woman with angry, accusing eyes.

Chapter Six

ENRY LOOKED ON THE SCENE BELOW WITH ASTONISHMENT and admiration. Sabrina had more courage than many a man in his acquaintance—nobody crossed Lady Carrington. They wouldn't dare.

And yet there she was, facing the woman down.

Words were exchanged between the two women. He couldn't hear anything from his vantage point, but whatever Sabrina had said, it was certainly effective—Lady Carrington flushed a most unbecoming shade of red and looked down.

Henry blinked to be sure he wasn't imagining things as Sabrina walked away, chin raised, eyes flashing with righteous indignation. In her wake, the crowd's chatter returned.

She'd done it. She'd won. What a woman the little "Pest" had become! No battle-hardened general could have done better against such an enemy.

That a woman with her kind of spunk had run from *him* in a panic spoke volumes. His effect on her must be truly remarkable. He shifted his stance, grimacing slightly. Her effect on him was certainly powerful. Even now, he felt another pull of desire at the sight of her.

"My God, she's actually pulled the fangs of the beast," said a droll voice behind him.

Startled, Henry turned to see Percy standing there watching over his shoulder. He'd been so preoccupied he hadn't even noticed him approach. "I take it you heard about—"

"The kiss?" interrupted Percy, grinning. "Oh, indeed. Within moments of Lady Carrington's rather flustered arrival. Good job! When's the wedding date?"

"Don't get ahead of yourself. She won't even allow me to court her yet."

Percy looked shocked. "She's rejected you? Must have been a dreadful kiss. I told you you ought to get in a bit more practice. My offer to escort you along the primrose path still stands, you know."

"Funny," Henry muttered. "It was a perfectly good kiss, I'll have you know," he said softly. "Trouble is, she doesn't seem to think I'm serious."

"You? You're one of the most serious people I know. The only serious one, in fact. Far too serious, in my opinion."

"Not everything is a joke, Percy."

"It is when you're me," answered his friend. "Do you really wish to pursue a woman who doesn't wish to be pursued? Why, when there are so many others who would give their left leg to bag the illustrious heir of Pembroke?"

Henry kept his face neutral. "It would be a very convenient union. I've known her and her family a long time."

"I see. Are you certain that is the only reason?"

"I'm also damned attracted to her, if you must know."

"Ah, now we get down to the truth of it!" Percy's eyes lit. "Perhaps you're *not* quite withering away. Excellent!" He coughed a little. "May I assume that the problem lies in that the lady is not likewise attracted?"

"She is." His answer was short, as was his patience. Normally, he wouldn't mind sharing his thoughts with his old friend, but Percy had a habit of playing devil's advocate, and he had no desire to endure such discussions at the moment.

"But?" persisted the other man.

Damn. "I'm not certain why she seems so bent on rebuffing me. But I intend to find out and overcome the objection."

"There's the spirit!" exclaimed Percy, slapping him on the shoulder. "Don't take no for an answer. Just be certain you're not making a mistake by seeking her hand."

Henry closed his eyes and quietly sighed.

"Marriage is rather permanent, you know," continued Percy. "You don't want to be forever tied to a woman who doesn't want you. Though there is always the pleasant diversion here and there, should the shackles become unpalatable. I should know. I provide such diversion to a number of lovely ladies."

"Percy…" Now he truly wished he'd kept silent on the matter.

"Yes, yes. I know. I'm incorrigible. It's part of my charm, so I'm told."

"Can we discuss this another time?"

Percy's grin broadened. "She's really got you all in a dither, this one. Fine. I'll let you brood in silence and solitude. If you need help—or rescuing, should she turn out to be a harpy—you know where to find me." He departed, making a beeline for the nearest cluster of ladies, who greeted him with fluttering lashes and coy smiles.

Shaking his head, Henry returned to watching Sabrina. She was dancing with Lord Sheffield and behaving quite as though nothing untoward had occurred only moments prior. He laughed to himself. She might have removed her head from between the lion's jaws, but she had not escaped unscathed. No matter how much she wanted to erase the incident, everyone would now think of them as a pair.

And they would be watching to see what happened next.

The music ended and she and Sheffield disappeared into the crush. He turned away, and his gaze lit upon Chadwick and his lady mother coming in his direction. The pair seemed to be in the midst of a quiet, heated debate.

Quickly, Henry moved to stand at the outer edge of a nearby cluster of guests and waited for them to pass. He had no desire for a confrontation with the lad.

But the mother and son did not pass by. They stopped—almost directly behind him.

Lady Chadwick's voice was a reptilian hiss: "Apparently, they were so enthralled with one another they didn't even take notice when she opened the door."

What she said next surprised Henry.

"You've *lost* her, you fool! If you were less incompetent and more of a man, it would have been *you* in there instead of him!"

The lad did not answer, and Henry thought that would be the end of it, but then Chadwick broke his silence with evident fury. "Allow me to remind you that I am a man full grown *and* heir to my father's estate in its entirety. Your future comfort is dependent upon my goodwill, and I will not tolerate being berated in public like a child!"

Good for him! thought Henry.

Lady Chadwick sucked in an audible breath, but her son cut her off before she could vent her spleen. "We both know I'm not destined for an earl's daughter, though saints know I tried my damndest," he said. "But neither am I willing to be sold to the likes of Miss Bidewell. I can hardly stand to be in the same room with her."

"That is entirely beside the point!" honked Lady Chadwick. "That girl comes with a substantial dowry. It is an excellent match, and you would do well to put aside your foolish notions of l—"

"I will bloody well choose my own wife!" the young man snapped. "And it will *not* be Miss Bidewell, or anyone like her!"

"I suppose you want someone like your fine Lady Sabrina, is that it?" taunted the matron. "A shameless little harlot who'll cuckold you the instant you turn your back? Tell me, have you come completely unhinged?"

Her words angered Henry, but he knew he could say nothing, lest he put Sabrina at further risk. She'd already faced down enough censure tonight because of him. He listened as Chadwick took up the gauntlet.

"I should keep my viper's tongue behind my teeth if I were you, Mother. This is Montgomery's doing! Sabrina is innocent of any duplicity, an unwitting victim of his cruel manipulation."

Cruel manipulation? Henry nearly chuckled. He was only *half* responsible for that kiss.

"Yes, well, according to Lady Carrington, your precious *innocent* practically had her skirts hiked up to her ears!" Lady Chadwick shot back. "Perhaps you'd better leave the judgment of a woman's character to one who knows women better than you."

Henry couldn't help himself. He turned just enough to see them out of the corner of his eye.

Chadwick towered over his mother, his face hard. "If I may be so bold as to remind you, Mother, less than an hour ago you were quite pleased to welcome her into our family. Clearly, your opinion is utter bollocks."

Henry turned away and clapped a hand over his mouth to cover a surprised laugh.

"Be warned," continued Chadwick, "for if I find you've spoken one ill word against her to anyone, I'll have you packed off to the country for the remainder of the Season. Do I make myself clear?"

Henry heard her mouth shut with an audible *pop.* Obviously, the threat carried some weight.

"I shall be in the smoking room for the remainder of the evening," Chadwick announced. "I would leave this very instant, but if I am to ever show my face in public again, I've no choice but to face this with dignity. Should you wish to leave, you may take the carriage. I shall find my own way home tonight."

Henry looked down as Chadwick walked past. He contemplated the interchange. Likely, he would be questioned by his own father regarding tonight's petite scandal, just as Lady Aylesford would no doubt question Sabrina. He had a perfect explanation for his behavior—one that would be immensely pleasing to his marriage-minded father. He could not help but wonder what excuse Sabrina would give.

I suppose I'll discover that soon enough...

"I am astounded at your lack of propriety, Sabrina," said her mother the instant the serving girl left. "You know how fragile a young lady's reputation is."

Sabrina repressed a weary sigh. She'd been expecting it all morning. Mama had been simply too upset to speak of it last night on the way home. "Yes, Mama," she answered. "And I assure you that it was not my intention to grant him liberties of any sort."

Her mother's gaze remained fastened on the plate before her. "Yes, well. From the way I heard it told, you were not exactly protesting. I need to know every detail—and I expect the truth. Was it indeed only a kiss?"

"Yes, Mama."

"How long were you alone together?"

"Less than half an hour. Perhaps twenty minutes?"

Her mother frowned, clearly unhappy. "Not long enough for ruination, given the short amount of time that passed between Lady Carrington's announcement and your reappearance."

Sabrina twisted the napkin in her lap. She simply could not let it alone. "If I didn't know better, I'd say you were displeased."

"I won't say I wouldn't have been happy to pair you with Henry, but I would much rather it be under better circumstances," replied her mother. "You are absolutely certain she was the only one to see you?"

"Yes." It came out angry. "I thought *I* was to choose my husband?"

Now her mother looked her in the eye. "That promise is only as good as your restraint. If you allow yourself to be ruined out of recklessness, you'll have no choice but to marry your accomplice—because no other man will have you." She sawed viciously at a piece of ham. "Your behavior last night was enough to jeopardize your good name. You cannot afford to let it happen again. Have I made myself perfectly clear?"

"Yes, Mama." She waited, expecting the tirade to continue, but it appeared her mother was finished—at least for the moment. Her stomach growled, and she looked to the food on the table with renewed anticipation.

The butler appeared in the doorway. "Pardon the intrusion, your ladyship, but Lord Montgomery has arrived."

The savory bacon in her mouth turned to ash.

"What? At this hour? Show him in here," said her mother.

It was all Sabrina could do to swallow past the knot in her throat. Did the man possess no compassion whatsoever? For him to show up on the heels of her interrogation was not to be borne. She jumped up to flee before his blasted lordship appeared— only to find the exit blocked by the broad chest of her nemesis. A colorful oath slipped out before she could shut her teeth on it.

"And good morning to you, my spicy little sailor," murmured Montgomery sotto voce. "Sleep well?"

Furious, she hissed back at him, "I'm sure *that* is none of y—"

"How lovely of you to surprise us with a visit so soon, Henry," said her mother. "Sabrina, ring for another setting."

"Yes, Mama," she answered, stalking over to the table and doing her level best to separate the bell's clapper from its mooring. She slapped it back down and sat, glowering at the food growing cold on her plate, her appetite gone.

"What brings you here?" asked her mother.

After a moment's hesitation, he answered. "Father has decided to have a small celebration in honor of Rebecca's sixteenth birthday." He withdrew a creamy envelope from his pocket. "I came to personally deliver the invitation."

Sabrina looked at him with suspicion. *That's not what he was going to say.*

"Henry, how wonderful!" her mother exclaimed as she took it. "I can hardly believe your baby sister is old enough to be coming out."

Sabrina gritted her teeth and fumed in silence. Apparently, Mama had forgiven *him* everything!

"Rebecca is a baby no more, I'm afraid." A soft light entered his eyes. "There will be a small family gathering that afternoon, if you'd like to join us early. I know she would love to see you."

"We wouldn't miss it for the world!"

Sabrina's heart stopped. When Montgomery turned to give the servant his breakfast order, she waved her hands at her mother, signaling frantic disagreement.

But Mama merely continued as though unaware. "You simply must tell us her likes and dislikes, Henry, so that we may select an appropriate gift."

By all rights, Sabrina's glare should have roasted the hide right off her, but Mama, having borne six girls, had long ago become impervious to filial ire. Montgomery wasn't paying her the least bit of mind at all, either. He'd become deeply engrossed in discussing his sister's preference for all things yellow.

Her gaze was drawn to him against her will. The afternoon sun slanted through the breakfast room windows, illuminating motes of dust hanging in the air and surrounding him in a nimbus of light. It was a contradiction, that golden halo. He ought to be surrounded by night's velvet darkness.

Setting her jaw, she tried to put him out of her mind. It was no use.

Though she could not have repeated what he said, every word Montgomery uttered seemed to seep into her flesh like warm honey. Each syllable was a tangible touch whispering against her senses.

Her hands shook so badly that she almost upset her cup when a servant came to refill it. She set it down after just one sip, hoping no one had noticed. Folding her hands in her lap, she gazed out across the gardens, searching for some distraction.

"Sabrina, don't be rude!"

The sharp rebuke jerked her back to the present. Heat tingled in her cheeks. "I'm terribly sorry, Mama. What did you say?"

"*Do* pay attention," chided her mother. "Henry asked whether or not you remembered Rebecca."

"I'm afraid I do not. After all, I was still very young when she was born," Sabrina answered, deliberately reminding everyone of their ages.

Montgomery's eyes twinkled. "No matter. I have every confidence you'll become the greatest of friends. I wonder"—he paused for a moment—"perhaps you'd be kind enough to share some of your wisdom with her as she enters the fray. She is quite naive and has not the benefit of an experienced older woman to guide her. I would be most appreciative if you would consider taking her under your wing."

Experienced older woman? She felt her cheeks tingling again. Knowing he'd only returned her fire in kind made it no easier to bear an insult that was far too close to the truth. She would have let her tongue have free run, but the presence of Mama and the servants prevented it. She had no choice but to swallow the insult.

"Indeed, I shall be glad to do so," she said with a sugary smile. "Better for her to learn it from a member of her fellow sex than from some self-serving blackguard." *There!*

He merely smiled. "Excellent. I shall convey to her your eagerness to become acquainted. She has been beside herself with excitement over the prospect of meeting you, so I know my news will please her greatly."

She wanted to throttle him.

To kiss him.

Concentrate!

So, he'd spoken to his sister about her, then. She wondered what he had told her. Despite her having bested Lady Carrington last night, the papers this morning were rife with gossip, most of it not flattering.

"Oh, I almost forgot," said Montgomery. "I've a box for the premier of *Giulio Cesare* next Friday, if you ladies would care to join me. Father isn't much for the opera, so I have it all to myself."

"We'd be delighted to accompany you, of course," said her mother with enthusiasm.

Sabrina held back a scream of pure frustration.

It was long after he'd gone before she worked up the courage to speak with her mother and beg her to leave off any further matchmaking.

"Oh, there you are! *Giulio Cesare*—isn't it wonderful?" asked her mother the moment she saw her standing in the doorway. "Henry was always a dear boy. It is *such* a joy to see what a fine young man he's become."

Sabrina hadn't seen her so cheery in years. Her determination wavered. Mama had suffered enough disappointment in life. For her sake, she would bear Montgomery's odious company a bit longer. It might slow her plans to conquer Fairford, but it would certainly not stop her.

"I must say, *you* were not yourself this afternoon, young lady," her mother continued. "You are not feeling ill, I hope?"

"I'm perfectly fine, Mama. Just tired."

"Did you not sleep well?"

Why is everyone so concerned with the quality of my sleep?

"Well, I suppose there *was* a lot of excitement last night," her mother answered herself lightly.

Sabrina's patience finally frayed. "It was only a kiss, Mama!"

"I was not speaking of your indiscretion," replied her mother without missing a beat. "The world does not revolve solely around you, my dear."

Her cheeks warmed. "I'm sorry, Mama," she muttered.

"Quite all right. I suspect your attention was taken up by… *other* things." She smiled wickedly, and Sabrina's face heated a bit more. "Colonel Blake offered for Cassandra Mayfield's hand. The boy dropped knee right there in the ballroom. But you would know that, had you been where you were supposed to be."

She ignored the barb. "They only met but a fortnight ago—she's mad if she accepts!"

"Why? Many marriages begin with the bride and groom meeting for the first time on their wedding day. I've spoken with her mother, and she feels they're very well suited. Cassandra is overjoyed."

"Cassandra is bereft of all good sense!" Sabrina said, scoffing, unwilling to give over. "How can anyone possibly be certain of their feelings for someone after only a fortnight?"

Her mother shot her a knowing glance. "I agree with Lady Mayfield and believe it to be a fine match. I saw them dancing last night, and I feel they will be very happy together. They are announcing the engagement next week."

Sabrina crossed her arms and set her jaw. "Well, *I* certainly shan't accept the first fellow to claim a tender sentiment for me. In fact, I should prefer it if the man I marry never speaks to me of love at all."

"Pish tosh, girl! You'll be grateful if your husband harbors warm feelings for you, I assure you."

"Of all people, how can *you* possibly say such a—" Sabrina stopped, aghast. "I'm sorry, Mama, I didn't mean—it's just that I remember..." She looked down. "I know how things were between you. How they really were."

"This has been coming for a long time," said her mother calmly. "I thought that perhaps you might have grown to understand without my having to explain. I see now that I was wrong." She patted the bed beside her. "Come and sit, my dear."

Numbly, Sabrina did as requested.

"Your father had mistresses out of necessity, Sabrina. I nearly died giving birth to you, and the doctor told us it would be too dangerous for me to go through it again." She bowed her head, her voice growing soft and sad. "Your father was still young, still full of vigor. He did the best he could under the circumstances. Out of respect for me, he kept a proper mistress rather than shaming me with the household servants like so many men do. And he never kept the same one for more than a year, to prevent any undue attachments from forming."

Her mother blushed to the tips of her ears. "I can't believe I'm telling you these things, but it's time you know the truth."

"Mama, I really don't think this is—"

"It is absolutely necessary!" snapped her mother. "You need not fear your husband's affections."

"I'm *not* afraid of—"

"Shh! Let me finish." Her mother clasped her hand. "There are ways to prevent conceiving, Sabrina. Ways I didn't know about until it was too late. Your father was already quite ill by the time I learned of the herbs and the"—her voice sank to a whisper—"the French sheath."

Sabrina squirmed. Augusta and she had talked about such things in whispers a few times. Never had she expected to hear of it from Mama!

"I asked him about it just before he died," continued her mother. "I asked him why he'd never suggested that we—"

"Mama!" Sabrina exclaimed, mortified.

Her mother let out a frustrated sigh. "I can see you aren't ready for this yet. But you *will* be one day. And when that day comes, I want you to know you can talk to me, Sabrina. I have knowledge that could save your marriage. I'm only trying to help you, darling."

Sabrina remained silent, hoping, praying that this uncomfortable conversation would end. Mama had it *all* wrong. She wasn't afraid of her husband losing his desire for her. Such was only to be expected.

"I'll tell you another thing," continued her mother, "I'm considering marrying again."

"*What?*"

"Lord Sheffield has asked for my hand. Again."

"Lord *Sheffield*? But mother, he's, he's—"

"A bit older than me, I know, but still spry enough. He was quite the handsome buck when we first met. I actually quite fancied him. In fact, I almost accepted his first proposal. But then I met your father, and I was so attracted, I knew I could marry no other man. Sheffield was crushed—begged me not to do it. Swore he'd run Harry through and then kill himself if I did. But I'd already made my choice. Because of me, they didn't speak to each other for many years."

It was as if the laws of reality had simply unraveled. Men had *vied* for her mother's hand, threatening violence and suicide over the loss of her affections.

"We were mad for each other, Harry and I," her mother said softly. "Simply mad. We married as soon as decency allowed. Life isn't always going to follow the neat little plans we've laid out, Sabrina. I fully intended to marry Sheffield all those years ago, but I was so drawn to your father after I met him that I could think of no one else. It was very romantic."

Immediately, the spirit of rebellion arose in Sabrina's breast. Romance. What useless drivel! Her mother seemed determined to place her faith in illusions. Papa had not taken a mistress as a last resort, he'd simply done what *all* young married men did after a few years. Papa had been faithful to her longer than most husbands, in fact.

Given her own dreadful experience, Mama ought to understand her point of view regarding sentiment—especially now that she herself was marrying for more sensible reasons. Sheffield would make a much better companion for her than Papa had been. Not only were they good friends, but it was unlikely the man had any interest in passion at his age. Theirs was an eminently sensible arrangement. Saying such things, however, would earn her no favors with her romantic mother. "I understand, Mama," she said quietly.

"I don't think you do understand," said her mother. "Your sisters all married for love, and look how happy they are. I'd hoped you would marry happily as well."

"I will," she assured her. Mama did not know everything, apparently. Her sister Victoria had recently written to Georgiana, who had in turn shared with her in confidence that Victoria suspected that her husband had taken a lover. Having "married for love," she'd been devastated. No. Her way was better. "But for me, happiness means a sensible arrangement, Mama. Please try to understand."

Her mother stared at her for a long moment, her face inscrutable. "Though I disagree with it, I respect your choice. But beware, for one day you may find that your heart has been given away without you even knowing it, my girl. And then you will have two choices: follow it, or learn to live without it. I would not advise the latter."

Sabrina did not intend to ever be faced with that choice. Passion and desire seemed to lead to misplaced affection; therefore, she would avoid them.

Which meant avoiding Montgomery at all costs.

Chapter Seven

THE SUN SHONE BRIGHTLY AS SABRINA MOUNTED HER mare. The sky was a deep cerulean unmarred by clouds, the air crisp and clean. It was a perfect day for a hunt. Draping her skirts just so, she lifted her head proudly, tilting her chin up to show her profile to its best advantage. Prim and proper from her lace collar down to the shining toes of her polished boots, she knew it would be hard to believe she'd been caught kissing anyone in a library.

Such was her hope, anyway.

Fairford, who was mounting his horse just beside her, looked splendid in his pinks, a perfect example of refined English elegance.

At last, she saw him turn toward her. Immediately, she twisted away. The motion was a practiced one that deliberately exposed the sweep of her neck while emphasizing her miniscule waist. Her sister Georgiana had taught her that one.

Unfortunately, before she could turn back to him, another horse came up beside her. "Good day, Lady Sabrina. Fine morning, is it not?"

She looked up and nearly fell from her saddle. "In...indeed it is, my lord."

Chadwick patted his mount's neck, and it nickered softly, pawing the ground in anticipation. "I love riding on days like this. Good horse, lovely weather, excellent company. What more could anyone ask?"

His smile was benign and friendly—and completely bewildering. Her mind raced to come up with a reason why he would deliberately seek her out after having been so publicly humiliated. If London's gossips had come down hard on her, they had been incredibly unkind to him. "I—I know of nothing better," she replied, feeling awkward and praying she wasn't about to be the center of a scene.

"Fairford." Chadwick acknowledged the man behind her with a nod. "Are you for the paw or just enjoying the ride today?"

Fairford's lip curled. "What is the point, if not to win?"

"Why, the pursuit itself, of course," said Chadwick. "The excitement lies in the chase, does it not?"

"So speaks one who cares not whether he wins or loses," answered Fairford. He flicked a glance at her. "One should never accept less than a win, if indeed the prize is worthy of pursuit."

She knew Fairford was no longer discussing the hunt. It seemed she finally had his attention.

Chadwick's smile tightened. "Defeat is a part of life, sir. A man who cannot accept this truth will soon be buried beneath the rubble of his broken pride." He turned to her, his expression softening. "And yet, fear of losing should never stop a man from pursuing his heart's desire."

Oh, not again! She could actually feel the blood draining from her cheeks.

"True," replied Fairford. "However, one man's jewel is but a common stone to another."

The blood returned all in a rush as she absorbed his words. Had he just called her...*common*?

"When it comes to determining the value of a thing, I'm afraid I have a higher standard than most," Fairford went on, his gaze now lingering on her. "To merit my interest, the prize in question must be truly impressive."

She released the breath she'd drawn in preparation, biting back a nasty retort. Of course, he meant not to insult her, but to challenge her. He was absolutely right to be selective. Any potential husband of hers would certainly have to pass a barrage of tests before she accepted his offer, so why should it be any different for him?

Chadwick, however, took umbrage at Fairford's statement. "It has been *my* experience that one only belittles something when one feels the challenge to attain it is too difficult."

"No one here is belittling anything." A passing rider greeted them, temporarily forcing the conversation to a halt. Fairford's blue gaze was icy when it swung back to regard Chadwick. "While I find our philosophical differences fascinating, I'm afraid I must now join my party. Enjoy the hunt"—again his gaze flicked over her—"and may the best man win."

Kicking his horse into motion, he left them both staring at his retreating back.

"I remain uncertain as to which is the bigger ass—that horse's rear or the man riding it," muttered Chadwick. "He had no right to insult you so."

A hot coal of shame burned in Sabrina's gut. This man had every reason to give her the cut direct, but instead he'd thought only of coming to her defense over a perceived insult. Surprised by a sudden stinging in her eyes, she looked at him. "You are a true gentleman, my lord."

Instantly, Chadwick's expression changed to one of compassion.

She hesitated, not wanting to give him hope, yet not wanting to crush him, either. "I'm so sorry for what happened at the Somerset ball. I assure you, I never intended any—"

"I know," he cut her off. "But what is done is done, and now we have little choice but to deal with the consequences. Though my heart breaks in saying it, I can no longer court you."

Again, the unexpected pricking of unshed tears assaulted her composure.

"I expect you'll be announcing your engagement soon, anyway."

Her head snapped up. "I beg your pardon?"

"Well, naturally, Montgomery must have asked for your hand by now."

"It…it was only a kiss!"

His brows lowered ominously. "Do you mean to tell me that he hasn't had the decency to ask you to marry him? I should have asked your mother the next morning, if not that very night, were I in his place. That he hasn't only proves what a complete scoundrel he is. Lady Sabrina, you must demand that he marry you at once."

Heaven help her, she almost laughed aloud. "He did ask permission to court me. And I refused him."

The look he gave her was one of utter astonishment. "You refused him?"

"I did," she said stubbornly.

Chadwick looked uncomfortable. "Sabrina, if you hope to earn the favor of another gentleman, I should tell you that upon hearing of the incident, my own father forbade me from further pursuing your hand. You would do well to reconsider his suit."

Feeling oddly disappointed, Sabrina could only nod. If he'd really loved her, fear of his family's disapproval would not have stopped him. The knowledge stung, even though she wasn't the least bit interested in becoming his wife—*or interested in love.*

To make matters worse, Montgomery chose that moment to appear. "Good day, friends!"

"Good day, Lord Montgomery," she returned stiffly. *Go away, Lord Montgomery!*

The easy smile that stretched his lips made her toes curl. "It feels so awkward, your insisting on such formality while your mother calls me by my Christian name," he said. "I do wish you'd call me Henry, as she does."

She cast him a withering look. "My mother may have known you in your infancy, my lord, but *I* did not. Therefore, I am uncomfortable with such familiarity."

"Ah, yes—I forget you've only known me as an *adult*."

The barb hit its intended mark, and she felt her ears grow hot. "I'm afraid I find the status of your adulthood somewhat questionable, my lord," she shot back in her iciest tone.

"You didn't seem to doubt my maturity at the Somerset ball."

Even more infuriating than his smug expression was the dangerous spark of heat elicited by his insinuation. Every insult she knew gathered on the tip of her tongue, but none of them made it past her lips before he again assaulted her dignity.

"Temper, temper, Pest," he tutted with a meaningful nod at her clenched fists.

The dam broke. "You black-hearted son of the devil! How *dare* you even speak to me after...after—"

"After...?"

The way he said it set her cheeks aflame. "I told you I never wished to see you again," she hissed. "Stop calling under the pretense of visiting my mother. Just go away!"

"Why? So you can lure some other poor, unsuspecting fool into your nets?" His gaze slid toward Chadwick.

Sabrina fumed. That was *exactly* what she was planning to do—if he would ever leave her in peace to do it. "I refuse to speak to you until you can keep a civil tongue." She made to turn her horse, but he wasn't finished yet.

"I find it entirely amusing that my tongue, civil or otherwise, is now viewed with such hostility," he said lightly. "Such was certainly not the case when last we met, you and I."

Again the blood ran hot to her face. Beside her, Chadwick's mouth hung open.

Damn.

She grappled once more with the impulse to hurl invectives at Montgomery's head. It would be infinitely satisfying to give him a good public dressing down, but the risk of it turning against her was too great. Thus, she kept her curses behind her teeth and urged her horse on.

He was making every effort to sabotage her. He'd as much as admitted it, the rotten scoundrel! And now, once again, he'd made it appear to everyone present that they were—she swallowed her rage, blinking back tears—together. Fairford would *never* look at her once word of their little tête-à-tête made the rounds.

If she'd disliked Montgomery before, she positively loathed him now. Unfortunately, her animosity did nothing to quell the desire she felt on hearing his low, intimate laughter behind her.

Henry's gaze remained fastened on Sabrina's retreating figure. He'd simply been unable to resist provoking her.

"Why in heaven's name do you deliberately incite her wrath?" asked the young man beside him. "If you wish to gain a lady's favor, should you not instead ply her with gifts and soft words?"

"Soft words will never work with that one," Henry said with a laugh.

Confusion puckered the lad's brow, and Henry smiled. "You'll understand one day. If you're very lucky."

He joined Sabrina's group just as they rode out, and silently kept pace with her as she worked her way to the fore. She rode as if the devil himself were on her heels. He matched her pace, stride for stride.

Glancing back at him, she urged her mount on and shot ahead, taking the first fence at full tilt.

Damn her for a fool, she'll break her bloody neck! He followed a heartbeat after her mount cleared it, but when he saw she wasn't going to let up, he finally backed off.

She tore across the fields, and he marked how she kept looking back over her shoulder—making sure he wasn't too close.

She was angry, he knew. But there was something else. She was obviously terribly upset over their little sparring session, more upset than she should be. He'd embarrassed her, certainly, but there was more to it than that. She'd been embarrassed before and had not reacted in this manner. He turned the conversation over in his mind, reviewing it, looking for clues.

Any other woman would have laughed off his insinuations and played along, deflecting his comments—such was the nature of flirtation—but she hadn't. She'd taken the bait and sunk her teeth into it with a vengeance, in turn provoking him to do the same.

She'd been shaken by their encounter too. He could see it in her eyes when she looked at him. It was most satisfying to know she was no more immune to the attraction between them than he was himself. But whereas he felt drawn to her and craved nearness, she seemed to want the opposite.

It struck him suddenly that she was afraid. Terrified. Terrified enough to refuse his suit, terrified enough to run from him now. But why? He'd given her no reason to fear him.

It stung that she would distrust him so without just cause. He'd shown great restraint in *only* kissing her. Granted, it had been her first, but still. A girl with as many sisters as she had couldn't possibly be afraid of something so benign as a kiss. *And* he'd asked to court her. He had behaved with honor where many other men would not.

Somewhere along the way, he'd missed something. Something vital. If he did not find that missing piece of the puzzle, he would never be able to get close to her. And he wanted to. Very much.

Chapter Eight

TARING INTO THE HEARTH, SABRINA CONTEMPLATED THE events of the day with chagrin.

The whole of the afternoon had been spent trying to avoid Montgomery to no avail.

Dinner had been a catastrophe. Their hostess had seated her beside Fairford—and opposite Montgomery. Her shining opportunity to impress Fairford had been utterly ruined. Their discourse had been stilted and lifeless, devoid of any wit or substance. It was damned difficult to converse politely with a gentleman when another man was disassembling your gown with his eyes.

She buried her face in her hands and groaned.

When the water in her bath had cooled enough to be uncomfortable, she dried off and poured herself a large glass of mulled wine. It served to drive away the chill and warm her somewhat, but it did absolutely nothing to relax her. Nothing would bring her relief save Montgomery's removal from this house.

She knew he slept somewhere in the opposite wing, but that mattered not. He might as well have been in the next room, as far as she was concerned.

It was going to be a long night.

A faint rustle at the door drew her attention, and she watched as something slid beneath it. The moment the messenger's footsteps retreated, she tiptoed over and snatched up the note. She frowned. It was probably another hideous poem from Chadwick.

"I should never have come to this damned house party," she muttered sourly as she tore off the wax and opened it. The writing jumped at her from the page:

I've been an ass. Please forgive me. H.

Her traitorous heart pounded as she refolded it. Padding to the desk, she picked up a quill, hesitating, uncertain whether to respond or to simply ignore the communication.

Nib touched paper.

Forgiven. Now, I beg you to leave me alone! S.

Half an hour later, she still lay awake, unable to sleep after having sent her reply. A soft knock startled her from her reverie. Flinging off the coverlet, she rushed across the room, hoping to catch the messenger and tell him to bear the letter back to its author unopened. She jerked open the door and gasped in surprise.

"May I come in?" asked Montgomery.

"Did you not read my note? No."

"Sabri—"

"No!" She tried to close the door, but his foot was wedged in the opening.

"Sabrina, I must speak with you."

"Do you think I've forgotten what happened the *last* time you managed to get me alone?" she hissed, pushing against the door in vain.

"I swear I shall not lay a hand upon you. Upon my honor."

She snorted, unable to contain her censure. "What honor?"

"I wish only to speak with you, and then I shall trouble you no more this night. You have my word."

After a moment, she reluctantly stepped aside, allowing him to slip past. She followed, deliberately leaving the door unlocked. As long as he didn't get between her and that door, she was safe. Shivering, she moved to the fire's warmth. "Have your say, then, and begone," she commanded.

With a strangled curse, he strode over to her bed and yanked off the heavy down quilt. Coming back, he held it out to her. When she made no move to take it, he shook it, ignoring her maidenly squeak of fright. "Take it—or I won't be responsible for what happens."

The shriek she'd been preparing to release died in her throat, suffocated by mortification. Snatching the blanket, she quickly pulled it around herself, grateful for the warmth as well as the concealment it provided.

With a sigh, he sank into one of the chairs before the hearth, gesturing for her to do the same.

She perched on the very edge of the seat opposite him and waited, terrified of the heat already unfurling in her belly.

"I wasn't going to come here tonight, but I could not rest after receiving your reply. I think we need to discuss what is between us."

"There is nothing between us, my lord. A kiss does not constitute an obligation."

He smiled wryly. "No, it does not. But I won't deny my desire for you, Sabrina. Why you choose to deny yours for me I cannot understand. It isn't as if I've asked you to have an *affaire*—I approached you honorably and offered suit. I have not changed my mind."

"I cannot accept," she managed.

"Why?"

"Because…" Her parched tongue would not form the words. Every fevered dream she'd had this past week was sitting right here in front of her, living and breathing. In her room. He wore his shirtsleeves with the neck open, and she could see his throat as it worked when he spoke. Her fingers longed to trace the line of it, to feel his voice vibrating beneath them.

Sweet heaven help me…

"Why?" he again demanded. "Why won't you consider me?"

"Because you're not the right man!" *There, I said it.*

One brow rose. "And might I inquire as to whom you think that man might be?"

She answered him with stubborn silence.

"Who, Sabrina?"

"I don't know—but it *isn't* you!" She saw him flinch, and shame gnawed at her. "I'm sorry!" she wailed. "I just…" She took a deep, steadying breath. Perhaps if he knew the truth, he would have mercy and leave her alone. "It was like this between my parents, and my mother was miserable because of it. I cannot endure what she suffered. Please understand."

"We are not our parents."

"No, but I'm not so foolish as to think history cannot repeat itself. I want a marriage that does not include this sort of emotional upheaval."

"I can assure y—"

"No!" she yelped, jumping up to put her chair between them as he rose. "And you swore you wouldn't touch me and that you'd leave me alone once you said your piece. Well, now you've spoken. Please go. Now. Before something terrible happens."

"And by *terrible*, I suppose you mean my making love to you?"

Sabrina looked down to where her toes curled into the rug. Heat suffused her at his bold words. Her reactions to him were both humiliating and utterly debilitating. He had to leave. Immediately.

Her head snapped up, alarm filling her as Montgomery slowly advanced toward her. She took a hasty step back.

"I swore not to lay a hand on you, and I shan't," he said. "I never break my word, Sabrina."

Even so, the look in his eyes made her take another step back. Panic fluttered in her stomach as her backside bumped into something behind her. Fumbling behind her, she searched for the edge of the obstacle, not daring to take her eyes off him.

"I promised I'd leave you alone for the remainder of the night when I was done," he continued.

"Yes, you did—now leave!"

"Ah, but I'm not finished, Sabrina."

Moving with astonishing swiftness for so large a man, he trapped her in the corner between the wardrobe and the wall, bracing his hands on either side of her, blocking her escape.

She prepared to scream. But instead of kissing her as she'd anticipated, he merely stared down at her. The heat of his nearness twisted her insides. What he was waiting for?

She watched as he slowly clasped his hands behind his back.

The scream died in her throat, lost along with the breath that rushed from her lungs, as he leaned in to trace the delicate line of her jaw with a feather brushing of his lips.

"Kiss me, Sabrina," he whispered, the ache in his voice tearing at her defenses.

All at once, longing exploded across every inch of her flesh. Without thinking, she turned her face upward, shuddering with hunger as he took the offering.

All rational thought scattered like ashes in the wind as she pressed into him, the chill of the room forgotten in the presence of his life and heat. The dark velvet of his tongue worked its magic, sapping the strength from her legs. She leaned back until she rested against the wall, twining her arms about his neck and pulling him with her.

Relinquishing her lips, he bent and tugged at the ribbon holding her nightgown closed with his teeth.

Shrugging the garment down from her shoulders, she sucked in a burning breath and moaned as his mouth closed over her pebbled nipple. A damp, aching heat blossomed between her thighs.

With every swirl and flick of his tongue, she spun further out of control. When he moved to her other breast, she arched up and tightened her arms around his neck, pulling him down.

Hands still clasped behind him, he slowly stood.

Unwilling to be parted from the source of her pleasure, she clung to him as he rose and walked over to the bed. When her buttocks bumped the mattress, she froze. *What am I doing?* She put her feet on the floor.

Before she could move any farther, however, he dipped again and drew upon a throbbing, rose-tipped crest.

All inclination to put a stop to this madness was instantly driven from her mind. Instead, she wriggled until her nightgown fell the rest of the way to the floor.

Montgomery proceeded to anoint this newly exposed flesh with featherlight kisses, first her neck and shoulders, then the hollow between her breasts. Again he tormented a nipple until she cried out softly. Then he sank to his knees before her and kissed her navel.

She didn't even have the time or presence of mind to be shocked when he ran his tongue along the crease between her thighs, nudging the plump mound at their juncture. Groaning aloud, she leaned back against the bed for support and sat, her liquefied knees falling apart to expose her most secret place.

He left her no time for maidenly objections.

A soft, keening cry escaped her when his hot mouth closed over her swollen flesh, as his tongue plunged between her slick folds to tease the sensitive jewel nestled within.

Poised in an arc of ecstasy, she alternately gasped and held her breath as he took her to the chasm's edge and danced back, as each time she moved a little closer to the precipice, until at last her body clenched in a paroxysm of undiluted bliss.

Limp and dewed with sweat, she lay before him, still filled with want. She wanted more. She wanted *him*.

All of him.

He rose, again bracing his hands on either side of her prone body.

An odd peace settled over her. In that moment she was ready to surrender. He would take her now. And she would let him. He would enter her willing body and bring her to the heights of pleasure, and that would be the end of it. She would be his wife within the month.

But he did not. Instead, he hovered above her, watching her with his dark eyes until she squirmed with disquiet.

"Always remember that I kept my word," he murmured. "I did not lay a hand on you, not even a finger. Not once."

He hauled himself up just enough to brush her lips in a soft kiss.

She tasted herself on his mouth, and another pang of cruel desire stabbed her to the core. *Now it comes...*

He pushed off and stood. When he failed to begin removing his clothing, however, she stared at him, confused.

"You may rest assured that I will trouble you no more this night," he said softly. "But understand that this is far from over."

Turning, he departed. For one heart-stopping instant, he paused on the threshold, but then he moved forward and closed the door behind him.

The chill in the room crept into her bones as she lay there listening to his fading footsteps, the sweat cooling uncomfortably on her skin. Blessed darkness welcomed her tears and muffled the sounds of her rage and despair.

Henry flung himself through his chamber door, still shaking with the effort it had taken to leave her like that. He'd come so close to ruining everything just now, but had pulled back just in time. Or so he hoped.

Damn you, Aylesford.

It wasn't fair that she compared him to her father, but there was nothing he could do about it except prove to her that he was a different sort of man. A man worthy of her heart and her trust.

It would be no small task.

Aylesford had tilled and planted London thoroughly, with little thought to discretion. And as so many wives did, Lady Aylesford had publicly endured his *affaires* with graceful nonchalance. She'd had no choice. Had she denounced him, London's appetite for sensation would never have allowed her a moment's peace.

But Sabrina had seen the truth. Her mother *had* cared a great deal, and her heart had been broken time and again with each of her husband's betrayals. His final one had been his worst; he'd died of the pox. He doubted Sabrina knew that little detail, but even so, she'd certainly seen enough of her mother's pain to wish to avoid it herself.

No wonder she was terrified of her own desires.

He ran his hands through his hair, disheveling it. Why couldn't he want someone without all these difficulties? It would be so easy to walk away now. To find some innocent girl fresh on the market. To forget the Pest.

Such thoughts were a lie, he knew. He couldn't forget her. And he couldn't stand the thought of her entering a cold marriage out of needless fear.

He needed to earn her trust, to show her that passion didn't always lead to tragedy and betrayal. The problem was that every time he got near her, his blood simply ignited. That, he could not change any more than he could change when the sun rose and set.

He cast himself on the bed, groaning. Even now, he was filled with lust. But if he was to gain her confidence, he'd have to exercise the utmost self-control.

It would be a challenge—God knew how she inflamed him— but if he wanted her hand, he would have to meet that challenge.

Chapter Nine

I F ANYONE AT THE HOUSE PARTY NOTICED THAT SHE appeared a bit wan and tired this morning, they didn't comment on it. She ate her breakfast in silence until interrupted by a familiar voice.

"Sabrina?"

Looking up, she met Chadwick's soft, brown eyes. "My lord?" She lowered her voice. "I thought you didn't—"

"I came to ask if you'd reconsidered Montgomery's offer."

Her mouth went dry. "No, I have not," she answered sharply. Just the mention of his name was enough to upset the calm she'd worked so hard to restore.

Nearby, heads turned and brows began to rise. She didn't care.

Chadwick leaned closer, visibly trembling. "I know you dislike him. I've witnessed firsthand how he vexes you. If you do not wish to marry him, then I beg you to reconsider my offer."

Horror filled her at the thought. "But your father—"

"My father can keep his bloody money," he said, surprising her. "I'll earn a living on my own. A gentleman isn't supposed to soil his hands with trade—but I'm no gentleman, not really." He hung his head for a moment. "My father, though he'd die before admitting it openly now, was once a merchant. He won a lady's hand. Why cannot history happily repeat itself?"

So complete was her shock that her tongue cleaved to the roof of her mouth.

"As for Montgomery, if he objects, I shall happily challenge him. I know I probably don't look it, but I'm quite skilled with a blade," he added. "I've bested all of my instructors and feel quite confident in my abilities. Say you'll have me and I'll rid you of him forever. And I swear I shall never provoke you as he does. A man should have more respect for the woman he wishes to become his wife."

For a moment, Sabrina feared she might actually faint.

Smiling tenderly, he placed a hand atop hers. "I quite forgive you for your momentary lapse in the"—he looked around and then again lowered his voice—"in the library. Montgomery is an experienced seducer, and you in your innocence could not help but be overwhelmed." His eyes grew hard with disapproval. "I would never embarrass you so. And"—his voice sank even lower—"I vow only to touch you when *you* wish it."

Her thoughts crystallized. "Come with me," she said, grabbing his hand.

"What? Now?"

She rose. "Now."

He remained seated, staring up at her in bewilderment. "Are you certain you're feeling quite well?"

She looked down at him. No. She was most certainly not well. But if she did not do this now, *right* now, she might lose her one chance to discover whether or not her fate was truly sealed. She had to know. "If you do not come with me this instant, then you may marry Miss Bidewell, and I shall wish you joy on your wedding day." Pulling her hand free, she walked away.

He caught up with her just as she strode through the french doors. "Have I said something to anger you?"

"Not at all, my lord."

"Has Montgomery said something, then? Shall I challenge him? Really, I am not afraid, you know."

The quiver in his voice betrayed the truth, but she admired his bravery, nonetheless. Into the gardens she led him until, entering the deep shade of a rose arbor, she spun on her heel. "The only challenge you need face is the one standing before you now. Kiss me."

His eyes widened and he stumbled back, lumbering into one of the arbor's posts.

She advanced and pressed him against it, ignoring his hard flinch at the contact. He wriggled and squirmed, his hands flailing at his sides, as though he was unsure where to put them. When he clutched at the latticework behind him for support, his left thumb caught on the thorns of the climbing roses adorning it. Wincing, he snatched it away.

A fine line of scarlet beads formed on his flesh as they both stared at it.

Sabrina took his wrist and slowly pulled his hand up to her mouth, placing his thumb between her lips. She drew gently upon it, and his soft moan—half protest, half desire—told her she was successful in stirring him.

All she needed was to break his restraint and unleash his passion, as well as her own. If she could just feel *something* akin to what she'd felt last night, even the tiniest twinge of desire, she would know it was possible to want someone else, and Montgomery's hold on her would be broken.

Releasing his thumb, she stretched up to meet his lips. This time, though he still jerked violently, he did not attempt to evade her. But though she employed every trick she'd learned from listening to her sisters—and, ironically, her limited experience with her enemy—she remained utterly unmoved. Infuriated by her own lack of response, she rubbed her breasts against his chest, hoping…

Chadwick's muffled yelp of protest was like a bucket of cold water dashed in her face.

She broke away.

Breathless, he lay back against the sharp thorns, uncaring that his jacket was being shredded. The look in his eyes was much like that of a cornered rabbit facing a hungry fox.

Turning away, she sat on a little stone bench beneath the arbor's shade, defeated.

The rustling of leaves followed by several soft curses told her that her victim had at last managed to extricate himself from his botanical prison. "I suppose you must think me a shameless wanton," she said woodenly.

"No, no, I—I don't."

She looked up at him in disbelief. "Tell me, then, what *are* you thinking?"

"I suppose…" His throat bobbed as he swallowed compulsively. "I suppose I'm wondering *why* you kissed me," he said lamely.

Hot tears slid down her equally heated cheeks.

He mistook her reaction, naturally. "I'm sorry if I bungled it. It's just that, until now, no woman has ever shown the slightest interest in kissing me. If I'm not everything I should be, I'll—I'll learn," he stammered, flushing an impossible shade of red. "I'm no fool, Sabrina. I know you've kissed Montgomery. And I know he's kissed more women than I—many more, I'm certain. You're my first, actually. I may be inexperienced, but I will make every attempt to please—"

"It's not that." Never had she felt so ashamed.

He knelt beside her. "Then, what is it?"

An inexplicable sadness filled her. It was so stupid, really. "If you really wanted me, you'd have tried to kiss me back."

He blinked.

"You wouldn't have tried to back away. You'd have taken me in your arms and—"

"You *wanted* me to ravish you?"

The look on his face was one of such comic astonishment that Sabrina, unable to help herself, giggled through her tears. "I only wanted to know if you felt any passion for me," she said at last.

His eyes grew round with comprehension. "My darling, of course I do! How could I not? You're so lovely, so incomparable—"

"Then *show* me," she demanded, standing. Perhaps if he were more forceful this time, she might feel something.

Chadwick stood, but he made no move toward her.

"You see?" she laughed, swiping at her eyes. "You've been thinking you're in love with me. But if you were, you'd do more than just stand there."

His shoulders sagged. "Sabrina, I'm not a seducer of women. I'm not *capable* of—"

"Liar," she interrupted, her eyes drifting down to rest upon the telltale bulge in his breeches.

He flushed again, and this time, the purple reached his ears. "Well, I—I…of course I'm *capable*, but it isn't pr—"

"I don't care about being proper anymore. *Touch* me, Tristan," she commanded, deliberately using his Christian name. Closing her eyes, she tilted her face up in offering.

Something inside him must have broken free, because there was plenty of ardor in *this* kiss. Yet she remained unaffected as his lips moved over hers in a patent mimicry of what she herself had done to him only moments ago.

Nothing. Not one heartbeat out of time, not one frisson of desire.

Chadwick withdrew. "It's no use, is it?"

She remained silent, numbed by the truth.

Releasing her, he ran a shaky hand through his hopelessly mussed hair. "Perhaps if I'd been bolder in the beginning and won your heart..." His lips compressed with resignation. "You should accept Montgomery's offer. It would be for the best."

"But you said—"

"I would have loved you, Sabrina. I would have dedicated my whole life to making you happy. But it's too late for that now." His brown eyes were infinitely sad and wise.

"I'm so sorry," she whispered, filled with regret for having hurt him.

"Don't apologize, please, or you'll break my heart all over again," he said, taking a deep breath and squaring his shoulders. "I've learned a valuable lesson. If ever I find my heart's desire again, I won't hesitate to reach out for it and make it mine."

Standing on tiptoe, she placed a gentle kiss on his cheek. He didn't flinch this time. "How I wish things had been different," she said, looking up at him through a shimmer of fresh tears.

From behind the screen where he'd been reading the papers and drinking what was now his frigid morning tea, Henry fumed.

Miss Woodbine had returned in haste from her morning constitutional to relay the news: she'd just now seen Lord Chadwick and Lady Sabrina kissing beneath the arbor—with *great* enthusiasm. Everyone was scandalized. Young Chadwick, it seemed, had rallied and retaken the lead for the lady's hand.

Fists clenched into white-knuckled balls, Henry listened as friendly bets were placed amid the jesting.

"There'll be a duel before the Season's out," one man chuckled. "I'll put myself down at White's tomorrow. Fifteen pounds on Montgomery."

"One can't really blame her indecision, poor girl," remarked a sultry, French-accented female voice. "Choosing between two confections can be difficult, after all. Which will she take, I wonder? The sweet or the spice? I prefer spice, myself—far more interesting to the palate."

"Perhaps. But not everyone has your appetite for it, my dear," added a voice that Henry recognized as Fairford's. "I wouldn't put my money on either of them, if you want my opinion. Neither seems to be to her taste, or she'd have settled by now."

"Well, I think it's all terribly romantic," a high, girlish voice sighed.

"I'll warrant 'romance' has little to do with it, Regina!" the first man guffawed.

"Indeed. I must agree with you, Cunningham. Perhaps young Chadwick isn't such a duffer, after all," another gentleman commented wryly. "Ten pounds says the redheads wind up married—and a passel of fiery-haired babes to follow."

There was a grunt of disagreement from another gentleman. "Montgomery'll never stand for that, my lad. He'll retaliate, mark my words. Ten pounds says Montgomery takes the wench."

Henry knew exactly why she'd done it, and he also knew that no amount of kissing other men would erase last night from Sabrina's memory. Loath to provide the gossips with further grist, he stayed out of sight until they moved on, and then he went to his chambers to pack. It was time to leave.

"Montgomery!"

He stopped short, his hand on the latch. How he longed to punch the owner of that voice. He quashed the impulse. It wasn't really the lad's fault. Chadwick would have to be bloody well dead not to respond to the advances of a woman as beautiful as Sabrina. There was no doubt but that she'd cornered him and instigated their little romantic interlude.

The thought did nothing to improve his mood.

"I've just spoken with Lady Sabrina," said Chadwick. "I came to tell you that I'm withdrawing my suit."

It was certainly not what Henry had expected him to say. "I beg your pardon?"

"We've agreed we are not a good match for one another."

Then, to Henry's further astonishment, Chadwick did the unthinkable. "Please forgive my presumption when I say that I—I hope you two come to an understanding quickly, before she does something foolish. She's a very headstrong young woman. But then, I think you already know that," he added awkwardly. "I wish you the best of luck."

Henry looked him in the eye for a long moment. Perhaps the lad wasn't as naive or foolish as he'd thought. If nothing else, he was certainly one of the most decent fellows he'd met in a long time. And courageous. Not many men would have been brave enough to face him, even to give over the field, much less offer strategic advice on how to win the battle. Most would have simply withdrawn in silence, hoping to avoid conflict.

"Thank you," he managed, though it sounded more gruff than grateful.

Chadwick, who had begun to look exceedingly uncomfortable, acknowledged him with a relieved nod. Turning, he departed.

Lifting the latch, Henry entered his room and closed the door.

So, her plan had gone awry. What would she try next?

Chapter Ten

TUDYING HER REFLECTION WITH A CRITICAL EYE, SABRINA carefully smoothed the pale-lemon silk of her skirts.

Speculation ran wild regarding which man she would choose. Would it be Montgomery or Chadwick? Eugenia had said that her husband had seen with his own eyes that the book at White's had three whole pages filled with wagers on the topic.

The problem lay in that she didn't wish to marry either of them.

She applied a light floral scent to her wrists and neck.

Her mother swept into the room. "You'd best break publicly with Chadwick, and quickly," she advised. "It was a damned daft thing you did, Sabrina. Had his family approached me, you would have been forced to accept the offer. To be quite honest, I'm still not certain whether to be grateful or angry that he decided not to pursue the matter."

Sabrina gave no reply. It was a moot point.

"I can't tell you how disappointed I am in you," continued her mother. "And I don't care if you *have* rejected Henry's offer, you will be civil this afternoon. Have I made myself clear?"

Keeping her gaze on the mirror, Sabrina made a minor adjustment to her hair. "I won't embarrass you, Mother," she sighed, doing her best to sound as if she meant it.

Oh, she'd go to the party, but she'd sooner be damned than play nice with Montgomery. She'd never forgive him for what he'd done. Not a night had gone by since the hunt without her waking in the dark, her whole body coiled tight with need, every part of her stricken with the sickness of longing.

The simple act of getting dressed this morning had been a torment. Every time her aching nipples had brushed against the fabric of her chemise, she was reminded of the delicious feel of his mouth on her flesh. She was beginning to doubt her own sanity. And it was all his fault.

"Embarrassment has nothing to do with it," snapped her mother. "Your reputation is at stake, girl. If you are to obtain a husband, *any* husband, you'd best do it soon—before it suffers any further damage!"

It was the last straw. "Mama, wasn't it you who told me that men once fought for your affections?"

The older woman sniffed and began picking at the lace on her sleeve. "Those duels were purely the result of idiotic male rivalry. They were *not* in defense of my honor. My virtue was never in question. Certainly, no one ever saw me kissing anyone until my wedding day."

Sabrina smiled as her mother abruptly left. No one had *seen* her. That didn't mean she hadn't done it.

To her surprise, Sabrina received a warm greeting at Pembroke, Montgomery's family home. "Thank you for your most gracious invitation, my lord," she gushed, dipping an overly deep curtsey. She experienced a malicious sense of glee as her mother's smile grew strained.

"We are honored to have you as our guest," replied the Earl of Pembroke.

She couldn't help but mark the unnerving similarity between father and son. Eyes the exact same peculiar shade of violet weighed and measured her. She knew what he must think. What they *all* must think.

The entire evening was spent in tense awareness of her nemesis. Montgomery was everywhere. No matter where she looked, his mocking stare met her. By the time the dancing began, her nerves were as raw as butcher's beef and tight as a hangman's noose.

After an uneventful hour had passed, her gut began to untangle itself. Perhaps he might not harry her tonight. After all, he wouldn't want to risk a scandal being associated with his sister's coming out.

As though the very thought had summoned him, she turned to see him heading straight for her. The knots returned all at once. Before he reached her, however, he stopped and offered his arm to another young lady.

A thoroughly delighted young lady.

"Sabrina?"

Yelping, she spun about. "What are *you* doing here?" she blurted. Immediately, she regretted her words, aware of how rude she must sound.

Chadwick's laugh was relaxed. "I was invited ages ago, before you and I even met. I considered not attending but thought it might provide an opportunity to close things properly between us."

"Then…you have not yet told anyone?"

"As a gentleman, I leave the manner of officially ending our courtship to you," he whispered. "I ask only that you have a modicum of mercy on my poor, battered reputation. We had best do this quickly," he added, looking pointedly over her shoulder.

Sneaking a sidelong peek, Sabrina saw the countless pairs of eyes watching them. Among them were Montgomery's. Trembling, she looked away.

Chadwick offered his arm, commanding her with an infinitesimal shake of his head to refuse it.

"Truly, you are a gentleman among lesser men," she murmured for him alone. Filled with remorse, she did as the sacrificial lamb before her intended and took one small but very significant step backward.

"I must refuse, my lord," she said loud enough for those nearest to hear. "For reasons of my own, I cannot accept your invitation."

She knew that he had prepared for this moment for days, yet she could see that in his heart he'd harbored a tiny spark of hope, the stubborn belief that she might change her mind.

That hope had just been forever extinguished.

"I accept your decision, my lady, and bear you no ill will. I bid you a pleasant evening." Bowing formally, he withdrew.

Though it had been handled in a very civilized manner, she felt as though she'd just been dragged across a field of broken glass. The look in his eyes as she'd dashed his heart to pieces was something she'd never forget.

Guilt and rage boiled over within her, a toxic potion that ate at her vitals. The guilt was too painful to deal with here. To the anger, however, she gave free rein.

She sought out Montgomery, the source of her displeasure. *This is all his fault!* Her anger doubled when her gaze found him lounging against a column, grinning down at a pretty young woman with dark hair and flirtatious eyes.

Like an animal scenting danger, Montgomery's head lifted, and he met her gaze.

By all rights, he should have been struck dead where he stood, incinerated on the spot. Instead, to her great dissatisfaction, he merely turned his attention back to the woman, eliciting a smile.

Fingers of dread crept in to extinguish her anger, quickly replacing it with jealousy so intense it made her physically ill.

She despised what he represented: the very weakness that had steered her mother wrong. And yet Sabrina's hands begged to touch him. As if drawn by some devilish incantation, she took a step in his direction.

His gaze flicked up once more, and her body heated at the unmistakable flare of desire in his eyes.

Titters broke out among a group of young ladies standing nearby, and the spell was broken. Disgusted by her lack of self-control, she did the only thing she could under the circumstances and fled.

Before she could reach the safety of the powder room, however, she caught sight of Fairford and hesitated. When had he arrived?

He was turning about as though looking for someone. Then he spotted her and, to her surprise, came over at once. "I crave your pardon for my regretful behavior at the hunt, my lady. I'm afraid I was in a foul mood that morning. I was on a borrowed mount, you see, mine having stepped in a hole on the journey there. Still, one has no excuse for ill manners, and I feel I must apologize."

His smile was nice, or it would have been had it been genuine. His eyes were too cool, too assessing. This was a test. "I remember nothing untoward in your demeanor, my lord," she lied prettily. "I found your company quite pleasant."

He extended an arm and smiled back. "Will you dance with me, Lady Sabrina?"

Henry watched Sabrina flirt with Fairford and wondered who the hell had invited him. He looked to his father with suspicion, vowing to have a private word later.

His hands began to ache, and he realized they were clenched into fists. Slowly, he released them to allow the blood back in.

He stared at the couple, unable to help himself. Her act was flawless, her manner demure yet inviting. Fairford, to all appearances, seemed to be taken in by it.

But Henry knew better. Not a week prior at White's, he'd heard the man laughingly deny any interest in trying for her. If he'd changed his mind, there had to be a reason.

He waited until Sabrina partnered with another gentleman and then approached Fairford. "I heard you tell Pendleton you weren't interested in Sabrina Grayson."

Fairford continued to stare into the crowd. "Upon reflection, I thought it worthwhile to reconsider."

"I wouldn't," Henry said bluntly.

"I believe the lady has made her feelings toward you quite clear," replied Fairford.

"Do you intend to pursue her hand?"

The blond man shrugged. "I don't see why I shouldn't."

*I can think of one very damned good reason...*Henry held his tongue in check and focused on finding answers. "Why have you suddenly changed your mind? Have you begun to harbor a *tendre* for her?"

The other man snorted. "Marriage is a business arrangement first and foremost. She is a wise investment, being from a decent family and having a substantial dowry. Marrying her will silence my father's constant harping on the subject and provide me a measure of peace. The fact that she is attractive is merely a windfall." His eyes, which had been full of avarice, now gleamed with lust. "One I shall certainly enjoy to the fullest extent possible—at least until my heir swells her belly."

Henry's reaction was swift and angry. "You'll never reach the end of the aisle."

After a tense moment, Fairford laughed. "You surprise me, Montgomery. I never thought you the sort to play the fool over a silly woman." The smile vanished. "If I wish to attempt to win the lady's hand, it is within my rights. Until she accepts someone's offer, she is fair game. Don't get in my way." Without further conversation, he departed.

Henry let him go unhindered. For now.

About that time, he saw Percy. He went and stopped him. "Have you a moment?"

"For you? Always."

Quickly, Henry ushered him into a salon.

"This is about the redhead, isn't it?" said Percy as soon as the door was shut. He grinned. "First she spurns you and Chadwick, and now she bats her eyes at Fairford; I must say I'm rather surprised he was invited, actually. I thought you didn't like him much."

"I'm fairly certain he wasn't invited, and I like him even less now. Every instinct tells me something isn't right about him."

"Oh, come now. Are you certain this isn't just a bit of jealousy on your part? You can't fault the man for admiring the lady."

Henry glared at him. "I've no reason to be jealous. What do you know about him?" he asked, ignoring the dubious expression on the other man's face.

"Well, it's common knowledge that he went to live in Paris after leaving university," answered Percy. "He returned three years ago and took up with the Childers woman almost immediately…must've developed a taste for more than cognac brandy while across the channel."

"Why was he there to begin with, I wonder?" mused Henry.

"Does a man need an excuse for Paris?" said Percy with humor that quickly sobered under Henry's gaze. "I assumed that, like you, he must have been there on the Crown's business."

"No." Henry shook his head. "I have knowledge of the king's objectives in France and the names of those who've been assigned there. Fairford has never served England in such a capacity. What of attachments?" he prompted, moving on. "He's been here long enough to have formed friendships and alliances."

Percy shrugged. "Other than the Childers woman, his father, and a few country cousins—you remember young Thomas from university? Very decent fellow, that one—I don't know of any. His father is very social, but from what I can tell his son isn't the chummy sort. Though he's been seen hanging about with Fenton of late, but that's a new development." He paused, his brows puckering. "I really know very little about him, which is rather curious, considering I know nearly everything about everyone." He grinned and bounced on the balls of his feet. "I hear quite a lot of gossip. The ladies are ever so eager to inform."

"Let us stay focused, shall we?" Henry interjected before the man could begin elaborating on his favorite pastime. "It seems Fairford is adept at making acquaintances and just as skilled at preventing them from progressing beyond that point. He joined my circle for a bit, just long enough for everyone to know his name, but then he drifted on." *Until tonight...*

"He did the same with mine," said Percy, frowning. "I didn't think anything of it until now. I noted at the time that he wasn't one for talk. Never initiated the conversation, always seemed more keen on listening, though he did contribute the occasional comment here and there."

"He's trying to build standing without letting anyone get too close," Henry muttered. "Can you recommend someone reliable and discreet to have an eye on him?"

"That serious, is it?" said Percy, lifting a brow. "She must be a real Helen of Troy to have you launching an investigation on the man."

"This is more serious than that. While it is true that I wish to protect Sabrina, my duty to England comes first." He knew Percy would jump to conclusions and hated to deliberately mislead him, but he needed his help and didn't wish to suffer constant interrogation about his personal affairs.

"You suspect he is spying for the French?" whispered Percy, all traces of humor gone.

Henry neither affirmed nor denied the supposition. "It might be nothing. I would have the guard watch him, but I do not wish to alarm the king or cast suspicion on the man without just cause. If evidence of subversion is found, I will have him arrested immediately."

"I know several good people," said Percy. "Shall I have them contact you?"

"As soon as possible."

"Done. Now, all of this intrigue is giving me a headache. If that is all, I should like to return to the festivities at once and attempt to drown it. Lady Boswell is leading a merry chase this evening, and I am in the fore."

They returned, and Henry resumed his vigil. Fairford, thankfully, seemed to have disappeared back beneath the rock from under which he'd crept.

When the master of ceremonies announced the final dance of the evening, Henry's eyes immediately sought out Sabrina.

Striding up, he claimed her, ignoring the fact that she'd already accepted another gentleman's arm. The young man gaped at the flagrant breach of etiquette, but wisely chose the better part of valor and let his host tow her away without further protest.

Sabrina, however, was not so easily cowed. "How *dare* you?" she hissed, struggling to keep pace with his long stride.

He ignored her efforts to free herself and tightened his grip.

The moment they faced one another on the ballroom floor, their eyes locked in battle.

"You cannot simply drag me off as if you're some savage! You've no right to behave in such a—"

"I saw you with Fairford."

"What of it?" she retorted. "Am I not allowed to dance with whom I please?"

He bit his tongue, knowing she was deliberately trying to provoke him. "I don't trust him," he said as calmly as possible.

A bitter smile crossed her lips. "And I don't trust you."

The dance separated them momentarily. Her answer was nothing he hadn't expected, but at least now he could address the issue openly. "I hope to change your opinion of me, Sabrina," he said when they rejoined.

"Do you? Well, you can begin by not embarrassing me the way you did just now!" Yanking her hand loose, she left him standing there.

Bloody hell.

Chapter Eleven

TWO DAYS LATER

ER MOTHER'S BROWS LOWERED AS SHE READ THE CARD presented to her by the footman. "It appears we have a caller. Lord Fairford is here."

Sabrina had to work hard to keep a triumphant grin from spreading across her face. He *had* come!

"I hope you know what you're doing, Sabrina."

"Oh, Mama! He's perfect, I tell you," she whispered excitedly. "Just give him a chance, and you'll see."

"My lady, I thank you for receiving me," said Fairford, bowing elegantly upon entering. "I do hope I have not caused any inconvenience."

"Not at all. We were just having tea, if you would care to join us." Not waiting for his reply, her mother signaled the attending servant.

Sabrina waited with anticipation as Fairford sat across from her.

"What brings you here?" asked her mother.

"I was in the area on business." He smiled crookedly and looked down. "The truth is that, although I sent an invitation this morning, I wanted to personally invite you to a ball I'm hosting next month. I do hope you'll both attend."

"We'd be delighted, of course," came her mother's polite reply.

The breath Sabrina had been holding was released.

"Wonderful. Naturally, I do hope to visit again much sooner," he added.

Sabrina smiled. He'd said it while looking right at her. *This is it. It's now or never.* "Are you planning to attend the opening of *Giulio Cesare* next week? We shall be there," she said, ignoring her mother's sharp glare.

"I had not planned to do so, but if you wish it—"

"Lord Montgomery has invited us to share his family's box for the event," her mother cut in cheerfully. "We're *so* looking forward to it. Ah, Susette!" she greeted the servant pushing the tea tray. "Come in and help me pour."

Sabrina sat with growing impatience as her mother spent the next several minutes determining everyone's preference for cream and sugar, informing her guest that this particular tea was her favorite, and elaborating on its history and fine qualities ad nauseam.

"I can hardly wait to hear the aria. It's been described as utterly magnificent," continued her mother, switching back to the initial subject without preamble. "Such a thrill to have fresh, new entertainment."

Sabrina did her best to keep a cool head, projecting calm and dignity. There Mama sat, chirping like a magpie—and sabotaging her efforts to gain Fairford's interest.

Luckily, he seemed not to notice. Cool, pleasant, and above all humble, he remained the perfect antidote for Montgomery.

As her thoughts turned to him, her stomach tightened. He would be wroth when he learned of Fairford's visit. She breathed deeply and forced herself to return to calm nonchalance. There was no reason to worry, after all. She'd made no commitment, no promises. Any anger on his part was purely his own problem, not hers.

"More tea?" she asked Fairford, encouraging him with a smile.

"How is your father?" asked her mother. "Sheffield tells me he has not seen Lord Middleton in some time. He used to play chess with him almost weekly."

"He is well," said Fairford, setting down his cup. "A fever he contracted years ago has left him with a weakness of the lungs that has held him prisoner in the house all winter, but the warmer weather we've had of late seems to be doing wonders. I shall tell him Sheffield craves a match. Perhaps that will speed his recovery."

"Please give him my felicitations as well," her mother added. "Though it is many years since I have seen him, I remember him well."

"Of course, your ladyship. I expect he will be delighted to greet you at our little soiree."

"Tell me, my lord, do you play chess?" Sabrina asked.

"Indeed, I am a proficient player," answered Fairford even as her mother frowned at her from beside him. "And you?"

"It is one of my chief enjoyments," she replied, happy to finally be establishing common ground with him. "I should very much like a match when next you visit."

Mama was now shaking her head slightly in warning, but Sabrina needed to know whether Fairford sought a companion or merely an ornamental vessel for his heirs. She would modify her approach according to her observations today.

"Of course, my lady," he answered. "Your pleasure is mine."

"Sabrina is quite an accomplished young lady," her mother interjected. "She excels at *all* of the arts and is especially gifted in music. I hired the finest teachers in England to tutor all of my girls."

"Is that so?" said Fairford, seeming genuinely interested. He turned to face her. "What instruments do you play?"

"I am skilled at both the spinet and the flute," Sabrina responded. "I've written several original compositions as well," she added. "Perhaps you might like to—"

"They really are quite pretty, considering she is an amateur," cut in her mother, giving her another quelling look.

"I should very much enjoy a recital," he said. "After our match, of course."

His answer pleased Sabrina, even though she noted that his smile did not quite reach his eyes. "I would be delighted, my lord."

When he departed, it was with the promise to call again soon.

"Sabrina, you took a foolish risk, revealing your bluestocking tendencies to a man like him," said her mother. "You ought to know by now that not every man appreciates a woman's skill beyond that which is required to keep his home. You're very lucky it didn't put him off."

"I thought you didn't approve of him?"

"Though his rank is less than I'd hoped, I favor him more than others and less than some," her mother replied. "At least he isn't the son of a merchant."

Well, that's a mercy, thought Sabrina, relieved. She knew who her mother meant by "some," of course. Montgomery. But as long as she didn't disapprove of Fairford, that meant she had a chance. If he came to scratch, that is.

The night of the opera had finally arrived, and she readied herself with great anticipation. The green velvet gown she'd selected would be just right to offset the frilly confection she'd worn the last time Fairford had seen her. Tonight, he would learn she could be sophisticated as well as virtuous.

Donning the lovely thing, she surveyed her reflection, determining that her hair was nowhere near what it should be for a gown this elegant. She bade her maid redo it in a higher style to accentuate the low décolletage. She must look her very best.

Just as it was finished, she heard a commotion below. Montgomery had arrived.

She sighed. There was no point in waiting here, stewing in her own bile. He would only take it as a sign of cowardice. So, with one final adjustment to her hair, she went to face the enemy head-on.

I shall be cordial and sweet, she resolved. *After all, I can afford to be nice. Only a little while longer, and I'll be free of him forever.* The moment she saw him, however, she wanted to throttle him, for he looked her up and down with deliberate slowness.

"How enchanting you look this evening."

"Thank you, my lord." *Leave it. Say nothing more!*

"The shade quite becomes you," he added softly, igniting her with his gaze.

The look, along with his compliment, made her pulse jump. "My mother selected the fabric," she lied.

His lips lifted in that slanted smile, the one that sent heat down the backs of her thighs. "She must have known how fetching you would look in it."

Thankfully, her mother swept in at that precise moment, preventing her from having to reply.

Sabrina tried her best to ignore Montgomery as the carriage rolled along toward their destination, and prayed she would not be required to make conversation with him, polite or otherwise. Unfortunately, heaven seemed not to be listening to her at the moment.

"I hear Fairford called last week," he said.

Damn. "Indeed. He was in the area and stopped by to pay his respects." She hoped she sounded nonchalant.

"I hear he also paid a visit to Miss Bidewell," he added.

She had *not* heard about that. "May not a gentleman call upon a lady without the immediate assumption of impending nuptials?"

"Well, certainly," answered her mother before Montgomery could speak. "He called upon you, didn't he? However, Lady Sotheby told me yesterday that his visit to the Bidewells was a bit more than a simple social call. Apparently, Lady Bidewell has reason to hope for a match."

Sabrina looked at her suspiciously. She'd known about this since yesterday and had not breathed a word of it to her. How convenient that she'd waited until *now* to mention it! Her gaze swung over to Montgomery. Were they collaborating, she wondered?

It didn't matter. She would see Fairford tonight and discern his intent for herself. "If he has decided to court Miss Bidewell, then I wish him—and her—the very best, of course."

They arrived at the theater and made it to Montgomery's box without further discussion on the matter. She would have liked a bit more distance between herself and their escort along the way. Everyone who saw them smiled *that* smile—the one that said, "We expect a wedding invitation!" They would indeed receive an invitation, but the groom would *not* be the man beside her now.

Once seated, she began to scan the crush for familiar faces, searching for one in particular. When she at last espied Fairford, she was most displeased indeed, for Lady Bidewell and her daughter flanked him. She watched as he offered Miss Bidewell his opera glasses.

"If I didn't know better, I'd think you were setting out to seduce someone tonight," Montgomery murmured at her ear. "Tell me, did you wear that luscious velvet for me?"

A wave of gooseflesh rippled across her skin, causing her to shiver. Taking a deep breath, she struggled for composure. "I did not."

He leaned closer. "Then for whom, might I ask, did you wear it? Certainly not for a man sitting all the way across the theater? A man who can hardly appreciate it at such a distance? A man sitting with another woman?"

"I wore it to please myself!" she hissed, glancing at her mother, who appeared oblivious to the goings-on a mere pace away.

Again he chuckled, once more raising the hair on her neck. "I think not. A woman always dresses to be admired, Sabrina, and not by her mirror. Therefore, it would be rude of me not to comply with your wishes and...*admire* you."

The lights dimmed and the opera commenced.

She spent the next half hour painfully aware of the man beside her. His clean scent acted on her senses like an intoxicant. Every detail seemed to jump out at her: the way his jacket's sleeve tightened across his arm and shoulder when he moved, the strong tendons in his hand as he adjusted his opera glasses. She found herself wishing he would touch her, giving her a reason to slap him silly and run away.

But he did not. He behaved like a perfect gentleman, save for the way his gaze caressed her from time to time. Each time it roved across her skin, heat suffused her flesh as if it were a physical touch. When the curtain fell for intermission, she fairly leaped from her seat.

The hall was filled with people, the stifling, warm air redolent with every perfume known to womankind. Escaping both the crush and the miasma, she made for the outside steps. To her delight, Lord Fairford was there, enjoying a pipe and taking in the night air.

His eyes lit at her approach. "Good evening, Lady Sabrina. A pleasure to see you once again."

"Likewise," she said, meaning it. After the disturbance upstairs, his presence was like a cool bath to her raw, heated nerves. "Are you enjoying the opera?"

"I am now."

The blatant flattery earned him a saucy smile.

Just then, she spied Miss Bidewell. Sweeping in, the woman took possession of Fairford's arm. "There you are, my lord. I—oh! Lady Sabrina. I didn't know you enjoyed the theater."

"I'm here at my mother's behest. While I can appreciate the skill of the performers, opera is her passion, not mine," Sabrina replied, having quickly picked up on Fairford's aversion to it.

Miss Bidewell sniffed in disdain. "I see. Then pray tell us, what *is* your passion?"

"I quite enjoy politics, philosophy, chess, and most literature," Sabrina replied.

The other girl's smile tightened, her eyes glittering with malice. "Yes, your love of books *is* well known."

Sabrina knew she was expected to take umbrage at the blatant inference, but she refused to give the little serpent the satisfaction of seeing her react.

No woman with older sisters grew up without learning what to expect from a hostile rival. The proper way to counter an attack on one's character was to gracefully redirect it back at the source. If she had earned a certain reputation for naughtiness, then she would bloody well use it to make her opponent appear a prudish bore!

"Oh, I'm not *completely* cerebral in nature," she laughed mischievously. "I enjoy the outdoors well enough when the weather is fine. I am inordinately fond of gardening." Here she paused for effect, looking her enemy directly in the eye. "Roses are my particular favorite," she added. "Although, I admit the thorns can be somewhat, shall we say...inconvenient?"

Miss Bidewell's face turned ashen, save for two bright-red splotches on her cheeks.

Sabrina noted that Fairford's expression had turned to one of amused appreciation.

He acknowledged her triumph with a slight nod. "A woman of diverse interests is like a many-faceted jewel."

She allowed a smile to curve her lips—just a small one, the sort one gives a fellow conspirator when the prank has been played to its humorous end.

But the butt of the joke wasn't quite ready to concede just yet. "I understand you are sharing a box with Lord Montgomery this evening," said Miss Bidewell, her voice filled with venom. "I hear he has visited Aylesford quite frequently over the past several weeks."

Sabrina's smile remained unshaken. "His mother and mine were favorite companions in their youth. Mama has known him since he was born."

"How delightful for you to share such an intimate association," said Miss Bidewell. "One must assume he *also* adores books, given his similar propensity for lurking in libraries," she said pointedly. "Although I'm afraid he doesn't seem quite the gardening type—"

"Actually, I quite enjoy it," answered Montgomery, stepping out of the shadows and walking down the steps to join them. "Sabrina, your mother is looking for you. I told her I thought you might have come out for a breath of air."

She started in surprise. How long had he been listening?

"Indeed, we are dear friends," he continued jovially. He turned to her, his eyes dancing with humor. "We share a great many interests, including horticulture. I've yet to show her my own garden, but I have every intention of doing so at the earliest possible opportunity."

Her heart sank. His insinuation could not be more clear. She winced inwardly as she looked to Fairford, expecting to see irritation. She was surprised, however, to see that his cheery smile remained.

"Perhaps, Lady Sabrina, you would like to visit Wollaton Park?" the man calmly inquired. "The king himself has named it a veritable paradise on earth. I should be most pleased to share my bit of paradise with a fellow enthusiast."

"I should be delighted, of course," she answered, jumping at the chance.

"Then, naturally, you must visit anytime you like. I leave you with an open invitation."

She could feel the animosity emanating from Montgomery, though his face was cast into shadow by the lamplight. She knew that, given half a chance, he would run Fairford through in an instant.

"Sabrina?" All heads turned to see the Dowager Countess of Aylesford approaching. "Ah, there you are! And Henry. Lord Fairford and Miss Bidewell, a delight, as always."

Miss Bidewell curtseyed, as was proper, though it clearly galled her to do so.

"No need for that, my dear," said the countess. "When next you see her, do tell your mother that I have relayed to Lady Buxton the latest news regarding the ladies' charity circle. Hadn't we better all return to our seats? I believe the program is about to resume."

For once, Sabrina was glad for her mother's interference—until Montgomery took her arm to lead her back into the theater. The crowd pressed in on all sides, forcing them into close contact. To her further annoyance, his fingers kept brushing hers as they lay atop his sleeve, sending little sparks of heat throughout her body.

It was with great relief that Sabrina at last took her seat, grateful for the scant few inches of separation provided by the wooden arm of her chair.

The lights dimmed, the curtain rose, and the music welled forth once again.

Five minutes later, her mother quietly excused herself. Before Sabrina could rise to follow, Montgomery clamped a hand around her wrist. "The devil always promises paradise, Pest," he whispered. "Just beware the snake in the garden." He smirked. "I can almost guarantee that if you seek to pocket Fairford, you will most certainly be bitten."

"The only snake I see here is you," she hissed back, struggling to wrench free.

He grinned, coming closer. "My blood is anything but cold, as you well know. You should know that Fairford is out for conquest. He has no tender feelings for you."

"Then it is well that I am not even remotely interested in sentimental foolishness, as I've told you before," she replied frostily, scooting as far away as possible. The arms of her chair, formerly looked upon as friends, now imprisoned her. "And he is not 'cold,' as you imply. He is quite nice. You simply fail to understand that a lady actually prefers a man's demeanor to be proper and dignified. Unlike you, *he* knows how to behave like a gentleman."

"But you don't want a gentleman, not really," murmured Montgomery, his breath stirring the hair at her temple.

The desire she'd been so carefully keeping at bay broke loose to flood her with disturbing sensation.

"And you should be *very* interested in whether or not your future husband cares for you," he continued, nuzzling her neck. "I think you are—only you're too stubborn to admit it to yourself."

She turned away, but the action only served to expose more of her neck to his predations. There in the darkness, his warm lips gently caressed her flesh. Her whole body screamed at her to meet them and kiss away the terrible ache. Instead she shut her eyes tight, resisting the urge, while at the same time prolonging the pleasure of his touch.

When she at last opened them, her gaze fell by chance on Fairford's box. Fairford was watching the scene below, looking bored. Miss Bidewell, however, was not. The girl's eyes were focused directly on her.

Sabrina elbowed Montgomery firmly in the ribs. "Stop that at once!" she commanded softly, squirming away.

He chuckled, a low, intimate sound meant only for her ears. The deep rumble melted into her bones. "I don't like the idea of you visiting any garden but *mine*, Sabrina. It puts me in a most disagreeable mood."

She froze, pleasure sweeping through her at his confession. She'd known he was jealous, but this was the first time he'd said so openly. The atmosphere suddenly felt charged, as before a lightning strike. On one level, such possessiveness was frightening. On another, it was completely exhilarating.

Reason quickly took over, cooling her excitement. What did it matter? She could not seriously consider him.

In direct opposition to all of her instincts, she deliberately stiffened and pulled away. "Then I'm afraid you'll have to be in a disagreeable mood for a very long time, my lord."

"Don't make me raise the stakes," growled Montgomery, running a hand down her thigh. "I already told you, I *won't* give up." He gripped the material of her skirt, dragging the heavy velvet upward.

She grabbed his hand and tried to force it back down, but he was too strong. Slowly, he exposed her stockinged ankles, then her calves, and then her knees. Her nails dug into the back of his hand, but still he soldiered on.

"If you try to get up, I promise you that you'll leave half your clothes behind," he chuckled wickedly, caressing her now naked thigh.

She gasped as he grazed the moist, heated flesh at their juncture. Moaning softly as he parted her delicate folds, she closed her eyes, shutting out the world. Tingles radiated from the point where his hand made delicious contact with her body.

"You were made for me, Sabrina."

Just as she drew near the breaking point, Montgomery withdrew, tugging her skirt back down.

Dazed, she turned to see his laughing, dark eyes. Emotions rioted in an aftershock of longing and disappointment—and rage.

He bent until they were nearly nose to nose. "If you are to visit any garden, Sabrina, let it be mine. I assure you the blooms are never so sweet anywhere else."

His lips swept down in a light wisp of a kiss that, for all its brevity, managed to fuel the fire in her loins to a roaring conflagration. It was all she could do not to follow him when he suddenly rose and excused himself.

Her mother came through just as he pushed aside the drape. "Henry, where are you going?"

"Just visiting the gentlemen's lounge for a pipe. I'll be back soon."

Sabrina was left with no choice but to fume in stony silence. Refusing to look at her mother for fear she would be unable to contain her ire at having been deliberately left alone with *that man*, she took up her opera glasses and pretended to focus on the scene below.

Her gaze soon strayed across the theater. With a start, she realized she was again being watched—only this time, it *wasn't* by Miss Bidewell.

Fairford was staring right at her. Horror flooded through her as the corners of his mouth slowly curled and he cocked his head in acknowledgment. His expression made it plain that, despite the dim lighting, he knew or at least guessed at what had transpired.

Her gut twisted. What must he think of her? Raising her glasses again, she observed him carefully, looking for any sign of disapproval. But his smile only widened, further confusing her. Perhaps he *hadn't* seen?

Her mother cleared her throat, making her jump. Sabrina kept her eyes on the stage for the remainder of the evening, ignoring Montgomery when he returned—and ignoring Fairford as well.

He hadn't seen anything. Surely he hadn't. And if he *had*, then apparently her behavior had not displeased him. Quite the contrary, if his smile was any indication.

That thought disturbed her more than a little. She'd heard of men who enjoyed sharing their women. He hadn't struck her as the sort, but then again…

No. She had to assume that he had simply not seen anything. Therefore, she must continue with her plan. He'd professed a love of winning. Therefore, she must continue to present a challenge. But how?

Montgomery was too dangerous to use as a foil to draw him out. The risk of becoming the victim of her own trap was too great. No. She had to find someone else. With him sitting beside her, however, it was impossible for her to think of any candidates for the job.

His clean scent assaulted her with every breath. Soap. Leather. Boot polish. *Him.*

Strategizing would have to wait until her mind—and body—settled down. It was with immense relief that she at last applauded the singers.

As they waited for their carriage, she spotted a familiar shock of ginger hair amid the crowd and smiled to herself. At Chadwick's side was a lovely, sweet-faced young lady who looked positively aglow with adoration.

By chance, he happened to glance up at that same moment.

Sabrina nodded her approval, and his lips parted in a familiar grin. Gladness filled her heart. *Good for him!* Quickly, she turned away lest his companion notice her and become upset.

And there was Montgomery, staring at her with a most knowing expression.

Her gaze dropped before he could read her thoughts in that uncanny manner of his. How she *wished* he would just go away. Her conscience pricked her sharply for the dishonest thought. The truth of the matter was that she wished he would snatch her up in his arms.

All the way home, the memory of his touch haunted her, and with it, a craving for more. Her mother nattered on endlessly about trivial things until she thought she would go mad. And he, *he* responded just as easily as if he hadn't had his hand on, on her—where it didn't belong, less than an hour before.

It was unjust in the extreme that he should even be able to speak coherently, while she herself was a bundle of raw nerves. She excused herself the moment they arrived, claiming exhaustion.

Montgomery caught her as she passed. "Pleasant dreams, Pest."

She shot him a murderous glare. He knew bloody well he'd condemned her to a night of torment. Again, she wanted to strangle him with her bare hands. If she could only manage to do so without touching him.

Chapter Twelve

HENRY DRUMMED HIS FINGERTIPS ON THE DESK, AGITATED. "You're certain it was him?"

"Yes, my lord," answered the man. "I was assigned to watch Childers's residence. He visits her almost daily, straight there and back—or so we thought. I suppose someone didn't do their job properly this time, because the curtains weren't drawn when his carriage left, and I could see the vehicle was empty. So I went back and hid 'round the carriage house where I could see everything. Half an hour after his own carriage had left, I watched Fairford get into another unmarked carriage. I followed it to Boucher's and saw him get out and go in. He was wearing a mask, but it was him. He had the same pale-blond hair."

Hell. A wave of acute distaste washed over Henry. He looked at Percy and marked that he seemed to find the news just as disturbing.

Had it been an ordinary brothel, he would not be so alarmed, but the nature of the services provided at Madam Boucher's were legendary. That particular establishment catered to the worst sort of debauchers, and the things that happened behind those doors defied all morality, not to mention several laws.

"Do you want me to keep watching him, my lord?"

"Yes," Henry answered. "I want to know how often he frequents that establishment. And if anything else turns up, you are to let me know immediately."

"Yes, my lord."

"You may go now," said Percy, opening the door.

"If Fairford has been keeping an unmarked carriage at Mrs. Childers's so that he can send his own back empty and then later depart in the other one, that means he knows he's being watched," Henry said softly after the door closed.

"Not necessarily," said Percy. He went to the tray and took up a decanter of brandy, poured two large glasses, and brought one to him. "It may just be that he doesn't wish all of London to know the details of his personal affairs. After all, it *is* Boucher's. I wonder if it is as bad as they say."

"It is far worse, I can assure you. Have you never been there?"

"What sort of man do you think I am?" asked Percy with a snort of disgust. "I may be jaded, old friend, but I'm not one of *that* sort. But you sound as though you've experienced the place firsthand." He sat down and lifted an expectant brow.

"Yes. I've been there. Once. I was invited along once by one of my fellows at university." Being young and randy, he'd accepted on a lark, thinking it a grand adventure. But what he saw and heard there had sickened him. In the end, he'd paid the poor girl selected for him without utilizing her services and had never returned. In fact, the experience had put him off brothels entirely.

"You look as if you need another drink," said Percy, topping off his glass for him.

"Thanks," he answered, downing the liquor.

Boucher's was the most infamous whorehouse in all of London. For a price, the proprietress offered her clientele a variety of forbidden perversions—and the security of complete confidentiality. Anyone wishing to enter the premises had to be an established client or personally escorted by one, and patrons often wore masks to protect their identity.

It was a miracle Fairford had been caught.

"What is the plan now?" asked Percy. "Nothing of your French intrigue seems to have turned up—I don't suppose the king will care that the man is frequenting a whorehouse?"

Henry coughed and cleared his throat. "For the time being, we wait for more information—and make certain he doesn't make any progress with Sabrina. Now that we know where he's been spending his time, it is vital that his suit fails."

"My, my, how the delinquent have reformed," teased his friend. "What is it about this woman that has you suddenly donning a halo and wings?"

"I told you, I wish to protect her. Her mother and mine were close friends, and I've known her since she was a child."

"Is that your only justification?" asked Percy with a piercing gaze. "She certainly isn't a child now. Surely she can—"

"It's all the justification I need," Henry cut in, fixing him with a hard stare. "She has no father to look out for her, and Fairford has recently informed me of his intent to court her. I cannot in good conscience allow her to marry him if he frequents that place."

A shrug lifted his friend's shoulders. "Very well, if you say so. I take it this means the rumors of your pursuit of her are greatly exaggerated?"

"She continues to hold a grudge against me for my having courted her sister Eugenia, who was in love with someone else at the time. I was perceived as an enemy to her sibling's happiness," Henry told him, hoping to close the subject. "She hated me so much that she once put a live serpent in my pocket."

Percy's brows rose in surprise, and he burst into laughter. "I *like* her! Tell me more about this virago."

Relieved to be back on safer ground, Henry gladly obliged. God knew he had enough Sabrina stories to keep his friend laughing for at least a solid hour. Hopefully, Percy would forget his astute suspicions and let the matter of his motivations for seeking to discredit Fairford lie unexplored.

It was purely out of desperation that Sabrina finally decided to confront Montgomery. If Fairford was ignoring her in favor of Miss Bidewell, it could only be due to his interference. At the Wilbourne picnic, she worked up her courage and asked Montgomery to escort her to the pond to see the swans.

"I've asked you repeatedly to leave me alone," she said once they were out of earshot. "I'm asking you one final time to stop harassing me."

His lips twisted. "You'd do well to rethink your decision to bag Fairford. Whatever his interest in you, I can guarantee it isn't to your good."

"And yours is? You've all but driven me to Bedlam!"

"Such was not my inten—"

She rounded on him. "Your *intentions* seem to be misplaced frequently. Why are you doing this to me?" she asked. "Why can you not simply leave me in peace?"

"Because I have no peace without you."

The softly spoken words stopped her in her tracks. A surge of desire rocketed through her.

No. To give in would be to lose herself.

"You have deluded yourself into believing you love me," she said at last. "But the truth, if you will only admit it, is that you are"—she took a deep breath and admitted it—"*we* are attracted to one another. That is all. And attraction is the last thing one should base a marriage upon."

"You are indeed lovely," he agreed, the corner of his mouth lifting a little. "But that isn't what draws me to you. It's what's inside you. I know the real Sabrina you try so hard to hide. You've shown her to me, whether or not such was your intent."

"When?" she squeaked.

"Your dealings with Chadwick have been most telling. I know you never intended to hurt him. I know you feel terrible for having done so. I could see it in your face that night at my sister's party."

"You are correct in that I regret my part in his pain," she replied. "But none of that would have happened had you done as I have repeatedly asked."

"You blame me for his heartbreak? I was not the one who used him as a convenient means of escape. I was not the one who encouraged him to think he had a real chance with you. And I *certainly* was not the one kissing him in the garden that morning."

"You *know* why I—" Horrified, she clamped her mouth shut.

He took a step closer. "Yes, Sabrina. I know exactly why you did it. And I know why you run from me at every turn." He reached out and touched her cheek. "But I am not like him."

What she saw in his eyes made her quake inside and out. She backed away. "I said far too much that night. I made the mistake of being honest with you, of hoping that you would have the decency to—"

"Hallo! I say, Lady Sabrina!"

The jovial greeting startled her, and she turned to see Lord Fairford striding toward them across the lawn.

Montgomery frowned as he drew near. "What are you doing here?"

Ignoring his rudeness, Fairford smiled. "Like you, I received an invitation to the event. I would have arrived sooner, but I was detained by a business matter."

Again, Sabrina noted that his smile didn't quite reach his eyes. "Is Miss Bidewell not with you today?" she inquired politely.

"I'm afraid I've had to come on my own, as she is indisposed. A shame, really. Such a perfect day for a picnic. Couldn't ask for better. But I'm glad to see you out and about." His smile changed to a look of reproach. "I cannot tell you how disappointed I've been over the fact that you've yet to visit Wollaton Park, my lady. I do recall inviting you."

Such was the awkwardness of the moment with the two men facing each other that she was at a loss for words. Her heart sank right down to the toes of her silk slippers. Montgomery would surely make some insinuating remark.

But he only stared at her inscrutably for a long moment before bowing. "If you will excuse me, I must find Sheffield. I promised him a game of bowls."

She didn't bother to disguise her shock as he turned and walked away, his step as jaunty as if he hadn't a care in the world, as if he hadn't just been rebuffed. The breeze carried back the fading strains of a cheerful melody—he was whistling!

Bewildered, she turned to her new companion.

"Shall we rejoin the festivities?" offered Fairford, holding out his arm.

Chapter Thirteen

ONTGOMERY DID NOT CALL THE FOLLOWING DAY.
Nor the day after that.

For an entire week, there was nothing. No notes, no messages, no surprise visits.

Nothing.

Sabrina's eyes sought him everywhere, but he was nowhere to be found. Finally, she humbled herself enough to inquire of her mother.

"He's gone to his estate to take care of some important business."

"He has left London?"

Her mother smiled archly. "Interesting that you should ask after his whereabouts."

"I merely wondered at his sudden absence. After all, he's practically spent his every waking moment here until only recently. I'm surprised he didn't start receiving his daily post at our address," she said with all the sarcasm she could muster.

Fairford must have gotten wind of his rival's seeming abdication as well, for she soon began receiving invitations to social gatherings from him.

And on the third day, gifts began arriving. The first was a book of French poetry, the second a quarter-scale, hand-carved, ivory-and-onyx chess set. Nestled in a carved mahogany case inlaid with pearl and precious stones, it was a present worthy of royalty. *For traveling*, the accompanying note said.

At her mother's insistence, the gifts, along with polite regrets, were returned. An invitation to a garden party to be held in three days' time at Wollaton Park, however, was deemed acceptable.

The days passed at a snail's pace, the hands on the clock seeming to creep through the hours with unbearable slowness. The sound of carriage wheels on the drive caused Sabrina to rush to the window each time, only to be disappointed. Though she told herself that it was the anticipation of the party that slowed time's progress, and that she looked for Fairford's carriage, in her heart she knew the awful truth.

Why should I care that he's gone? she thought angrily, vowing to leave the curtains untouched the next time. *He's only doing as I requested. I told him to leave me be, and he is. I ought to be grateful.*

The only reprieve from limbo was another letter from Georgiana expressing outrage over their sister Victoria's situation. Having grown suspicious after too long a silence, Georgiana had gone for a surprise visit. What she'd found was their sister essentially held hostage in her own home. Victoria had threatened to petition for a divorce over her husband's infidelity. He'd countered by threatening to have her declared mad and put away in an asylum.

She was utterly miserable.

Victoria followed her heart, and look where it landed her. All the more reason to welcome Montgomery's absence.

The day of the garden party finally arrived, prompting a fit of feminine nerves. She could not tell whether she was anxious about her planned seduction of Fairford or hoping that Montgomery would show up. If he did…

Don't be daft. Fairford would never invite him. Stiffening her resolve, she donned her selection: a gown of finest mint silk and creamy lace, its bodice exquisitely embroidered with birds, vines, and tiny jeweled flowers. Her hair was piled in curls atop her head with a few left loose to spill artfully over one shoulder. Designed for wear before tea, the gown's décolletage was wide and shallow, displaying breadth of shoulders rather than depth of cleavage. It was modest, yet still somewhat provocative for the sheer amount of bare flesh it revealed.

In a word: perfect.

Her wayward thoughts drifted back to the night of the opera, reliving briefly her last conversation with Montgomery. It haunted her still.

If only *he* could see her in this gown, his dark eyes would fill with desire...

The image in the looking glass blushed, and she shook herself, furious. It was no use thinking such things! What was the matter with her? He was gone, and there was a conquest to be made.

Upon reaching Wollaton, they were welcomed by Fairford and his father, an elderly and kindly gentleman—just the sort of father-in-law she'd always pictured herself having.

Wollaton was beautiful and orderly. Perfection lay in every direction. She could easily imagine herself mistress of this place. She would have her own little section of the garden. Her children would play on the green beneath the spreading trees.

The vision was so vivid.

A moment later she realized that nowhere in it had she placed Fairford. *And that is as it ought to be*, she reasoned. Naturally, he would have business to attend to.

The party was typical of its kind: tea in the garden and plenty of inane chatter. She quickly learned that Miss Bidewell was again not in attendance. As Fairford was still officially courting her, the lady would no doubt be most unhappy to learn of her rival's attendance. She wondered if Miss Bidewell knew her suitor was sending gifts to another woman. Perhaps her absence today was a protest?

Regardless of the reason for her not being here, Sabrina was relieved. It was much better to avoid another confrontation with her, if at all possible.

It wasn't long, however, before her relief was replaced by irritation. Fairford had barely paid her any attention at all since his initial greeting. Keeping up her smile, she nattered on politely with the other guests until at long last, she felt a light touch on her shoulder.

"I can't begin to tell you how delighted I am that you have at last come to my home," said Fairford. "When you sent back all of my gifts along with so many refusals, I feared I'd somehow offended you."

"Not at all, my lord. Though the thought was appreciated, I simply couldn't accept them for fear of giving the wrong impression," she replied, her appropriately prim words at odds with the siren's smile she deliberately wore.

"And what impression would that be?"

"Why, that I had accepted your suit, of course."

"Would you not?"

"You have not asked."

"And if I did? Would you then accept my gifts?"

She gave him a long, steady look before allowing one corner of her mouth to curl ever so slightly. "Perhaps."

She turned and began walking.

He followed. "You must have a look at my latest acquisition, a rare blossom from the jungles of the Americas. I procured it from a man who barely survived an encounter with savage natives in order to obtain it."

She smiled prettily. She would have been far more impressed had *he* been the one to face the jungle savages, rather than merely being the man who'd purchased a silly plant. She bit her tongue, wondering when she'd become so critical. He was a gentleman! Of course he wouldn't be tramping about in the wilds of the world hunting plants, or anything else for that matter.

She could see Hen—*Montgomery* doing something like that, though, for all he was a gentleman from the top of his head to the soles of his feet…A small, strangled sound escaped her throat, and Fairford looked askance. She coughed a little and smiled sweetly, wroth at herself for thinking about *him* again.

They sauntered down the path, feet crunching in the carefully raked gravel, until around a corner there appeared a glass structure.

"A hothouse," she murmured. Through the misted windows, she could just make out the colorful reds, pinks, and yellows of the blooms within.

"Indeed. I keep the tropicals here. Come." He produced a key and opened the door.

A rush of warm, moist air flowed over her, bearing the scent of earth and flowers.

"As I said at the opera, my little slice of paradise." He closed the door behind them. "And now, with you here, the most beautiful blossom of all has joined these, and my heaven is complete." He approached her slowly, holding out his arm. "My latest treasure lies this way."

She allowed him to guide her past perfect blossoms of jasmine and hibiscus. Orchids of all varieties painted a riot of color all around, and the tinkling of water played a merry tune from some hidden place. When they reached its source, a small decorative fountain, Fairford stopped.

Reaching out, he gently lifted a trailing vine bearing bright, golden flowers the color of new butter. The bell-like blooms emitted a heady cloud of scent, enveloping them in a cocoon of sweetness. "Here is a flower that has had no name given it—until now," he said, turning toward her. "I named it after you, hoping it would make amends for my treatment of you when we first met. I sent in the petition to the Royal Botanical Society weeks ago. They sent the approval yesterday, just in time." Plucking an envelope from his coat pocket, he presented it to her.

Opening it, she scanned the enclosed paper until she saw it: *Jasminum-Sabrinus Floridum.*

He'd named a bloody flower after her.

What did one say in response to such a thing? "I—I'm not… what I mean to say is…"

Stepping forward, he gently grasped her shoulders. "Sabrina, since the day we met, I've been able to think of little else but you. I've come to adore you, to long for you, my darling."

It was all she could do not to burst into laughter. For all its naïveté, Chadwick's heartfelt declaration had been much more inspiring. Fairford's was nothing more than a pretty phrase concocted to dupe her into believing the lie of his regard. There was no true feeling behind it whatsoever. Still, that was what she wanted, wasn't it?

Telling herself it was the right decision, she slowly lowered her lashes, giving him the smoldering stare she'd learned from watching her sisters, the same one she had practiced in the mirror since the age of nine.

Emboldened, Fairford ran a single finger along her shoulder where it merged into the column of her neck.

Closing her eyes, she obliged, bending her neck to accommodate.

Bending, he ran the tip of his tongue along the line of her collarbone.

She expected a rush of pleasant sensation to flood through her the way it had before. The way it had with Henry. But there was nothing. Nothing but mild irritation at the rasp of his stubble against her delicate skin and a shudder of distaste. She quashed it and made herself bring her hands up to his shoulders.

Bending her back, Fairford flicked his tongue across the hollow at her throat, then took her chin in his hand and claimed her mouth.

She wanted to scream in frustration. It was revolting! She felt as if he were trying to suffocate her with his tongue—and he tasted all wrong. Where was the lightning in her veins? Where was the familiar pull in her belly?

Where was Henry?

Stubbornly, she silenced the thought and tried to concentrate on the moment, on *making* her body feel passion.

It was impossible. Memories of Henry kept intruding, until finally she could take no more. Pulling away suddenly, she turned so Fairford wouldn't see the truth in her eyes—that she was repulsed by him. Her hands trembled as she brought them to her face.

"Sabrina, darling," said Fairford, lust making his voice rough. "I shall speak with my father tonight. No doubt he'll be thrilled with my selection. You'll make a fine baroness."

Her hackles rose at his peremptory attitude. His "selection" indeed! Why, the arrogance of the man! Who did he think he was? She was an earl's daughter, and he a mere baron's son. And to assume that she would marry him without even the preamble of courtship?

Her next act was impetuous, born of swift, hot anger.

"I…oh, dear me, how awkward!" she gasped, casting her eyes down as though stricken with embarrassment. "I think I must have misunderstood your intent. I did not take your declaration as a proposal of marriage, but of courtship. I feel I must inform you that Lord Montgomery has *also* declared his devotion to me, and as I was unaware of your interest at the time, I've already permitted him to press his suit."

Fairford froze, his smile fading. "You'll tell him he must withdraw it at once, naturally."

She looked him directly in the eye. "A lady may have as many suitors as she pleases until she becomes engaged, my lord. Since I hardly know you well enough to agree to such a serious commitment, I should like a bit of time to become better acquainted before making *my* decision."

His smug expression evaporated. As quickly as she'd seen it flicker across his face, however, the momentary flare of ire was hidden behind a contrite mask.

"Forgive my gross assumption. I suppose I'd rather hoped you'd set your heart on having me to the exclusion of all others."

The corner of her mouth lifted. "Perhaps I also misunderstood *your* intent, my lord. Are you not also currently paying court to Miss Gertrude Bidewell?" *Touché!*

"It was my father's wish that I court Miss Bidewell," he replied. "Given the situation between you and me, however, I intend to withdraw my suit immediately. I'm certain he will agree. Ours is the more advantageous match, after all."

Had she been the romantic sort, his statement would have been extremely offensive. *But I am not*, she told herself, wrestling her bruised pride into submission. This was merely the preliminary to marital negotiations between them, nothing more. And a perfect opportunity to set the tone for the future.

With an eloquent shrug, she turned to the bright flowers that now bore her name. "It would be unfair of me to expect you to give up your options while I have no inclination to do the same. I assure you, it will bother me not at all if you continue to pay court to Miss Bidewell until such a time as a mutual understanding is reached between us, if ever. You'll find I'm not the jealous or possessive sort."

There! Now he knew she would tolerate his having a mistress. She glanced at him over her shoulder as she plucked a flower and tucked it into her curls.

Fairford's eyes widened, and he nodded slowly. "As you say, then. I shall leave matters as they stand until you decide which of us to accept as your betrothed. But I warn you, I shall not make it easy to choose my competitor." He stepped forward and placed a kiss on the nape of her neck.

She allowed him to touch her for an instant longer and then sauntered away. She could barely breathe and wanted nothing more than to run from this place. With an iron will, she maintained her leisurely pace as she moved to the exit.

Fairford followed a few steps behind, his presence making her skin prickle unpleasantly.

He wanted her, but he didn't love her. That much was clear.

And I'll never be hurt by it because I'll never love him. It was exactly the kind of arrangement she'd planned. But now that it came down to it, she questioned the wisdom of such a plan.

Plans…

Frustration filled her. All her careful plans had gone awry in the worst way. She'd certainly put her foot in it, telling Fairford that she had accepted Henry's suit. Now she had no choice but to follow through and make that lie a reality.

Strangely, the idea was not as disheartening as she thought it ought to be.

Chapter Fourteen

ENRY WANTED TO HIT SOMETHING, TO PULVERIZE IT TO bits. To make it feel like his heart did at the moment. He'd arrived home only to be immediately informed by his father that Fairford was now officially courting Sabrina.

To find out like this, with nary a personal word from her? How could she?

The very next morning, a servant entered bearing a letter addressed to him in an achingly familiar hand. Snatching it off the tray, Henry crumpled the missive unopened, intending to toss it into the fire and forget all about Sabrina Grayson. But his hand was stayed by the monstrous pain in his heart. Dismissing the bewildered servant, he flattened out the envelope as best he could, tore it open, and scanned its contents.

It was an invitation to tea. Today. He tossed the letter into the hearth and watched it flare orange for a moment before disintegrating into ash. He would see her one last time.

Upon arrival at Aylesford House, he was shown into the parlor where Sabrina waited. The sight of her standing in the sunlight at the window was like a physical blow.

Still facing the glass, she spoke without inflection. "I am allowing Fairford to court me, but I will also accept your suit as well, if you still wish it."

In two strides he was across the room. "I swear to you that you will not regret it." He felt her arms tighten around him briefly before she stiffened and pulled away.

"I am only doing this out of kindness to my mother. She wishes me to give you a chance."

His hands fell to his sides. "If you truly have no real desire to marry me, then why should I bother?"

"Because"—she hesitated, as though debating whether to continue—"because in addition, of late, I have begun to question my chosen path."

"Fairford is not turning out quite to your taste, I take it?" he said, immediately biting his tongue as her green eyes flashed.

"I simply wish to know whether or not you and I can, in fact, coexist peaceably as adults—something I very seriously doubt," she snapped.

He watched as she stopped and struggled for calm.

Her eyes were on the carpet as she continued. "I admit that I have perhaps been unfairly biased against you due to a child-hood animosity. That, and the fact that I did not wish to allow my desires to lead me astray. I am willing to put aside past differences, if you will do the same," she stressed with a sharp look, "and stop constantly trying to provoking me."

"Agreed," he said. He would try his best. "And as for your latter ex…reason?"

She blushed. "As I said, I have recently come to debate whether or not my chosen course is the best. Regardless, my mother wishes me to give you a fair chance, and I cannot deny her."

Henry sent a prayer of thanks to heaven. She might think she was only doing this at her mother's command, but he knew better. She was finally beginning to come to her senses. He took her face between his hands and kissed her gently. He felt the trembling of her lips, and he breathed in her soft sigh. "Sabrina,

I promise you that I will never give you any reason to—" Sounds from the hall outside signaled the arrival of Lady Aylesford and tea, and Sabrina moved away.

Damn.

By the time he left, a plan had begun to form. He needed to expose Fairford's perfidy, but Sabrina would never believe a word of it from him. He needed help…

Sabrina went to her room utterly drained. Closing the door, she lay on her bed, her heart galloping like a horse gone mad.

All of her careful plans had gone awry in the worst way. She should *never* have sent Henry that note, but nagging doubts had forced her to reconsider him. The sensible choice just didn't make as much sense anymore. Or was it just her body's—or worse, her heart's—demands interfering?

But the feeling of being in his arms again…all the fire that had been so utterly lacking in Fairford's kiss had been there with Henry. It was no use denying her desire for him. Coupled with the emotional attachment beginning to form between them, it was a disaster waiting to happen.

Urgency filled her. Though she had misgivings, she must give Fairford a fair chance as well. The thought of him touching her was still repugnant, but she chose to ignore it. After all, her gut reaction was what had gotten her into so much trouble with Henry. She dare not trust something as fallacious as instinct, whether it pointed in the direction she wanted or not, to make her decision for her.

The chess set and poetry book Fairford had again sent caught her eye. She'd accepted them the second time. It still surprised her that he'd remembered their conversation at the opera.

He'd also invited her to a literary-club meeting this week. His thoughtfulness and consideration pleased her enormously.

With passion erased from the equation, Fairford made perfect sense. She could never love him, but she could get along with him just fine. And she was certain she'd be able to tolerate him in the marriage bed.

Eventually.

The thought made her squirm as memories of Henry again intruded. His hands, his mouth…

Devil take it!

Her only chance for sanity lay in exposing Henry's faults. She had to prove to herself once and for all that he was unequivocally the wrong man for her.

And that was something she couldn't do if he wasn't around. She resigned herself to enduring the torment for a little while longer.

A knock intruded upon her thoughts. "My lady, a courier has just arrived with a message for you," the butler stiffly announced.

She looked up expectantly, but there was no tray in the servant's hand. "Well, where is it?"

"Apologies, my lady," the flummoxed man replied. "He refused to deliver the message to anyone but your ladyship."

"Who sent him?"

"He would not say, my lady."

Mystified, she put aside her book and followed the indignant servant down to the foyer. A young man awaited her, a parcel wrapped in black velvet and tied with scarlet silk ribbons in his hands.

With a bow, the young man presented the gift. "My lady, I was instructed to place this only into your hands and to tell you to open it in privacy," he said, withdrawing an envelope from his pocket. "This accompanies it."

Within the crinkly parchment, her fingers discerned the shape of a key. She immediately recognized the handwriting on the envelope. Thanking the courier, she turned toward the stairs.

The butler practically leaped to head her off. "My lady, hadn't you best open it here, in case something dangerous lies within?"

"It's quite all right. I know the sender's hand," she told him with a smile. Leaving the curious man behind, she continued her march up the steps to her room. Once there, she locked her door and placed the package on her bed. For a long moment, she just stared at it.

Henry's first courtship gift. What could it be?

Taking a deep breath, she removed the ribbons and pulled back the cloth to reveal an intricately carved wooden box. A floral motif decorated its dark, polished surface, each leaf and bloom crafted of precious gems and joined to its sisters by vines of hair-fine silver inlay. The box alone was a gift worthy of royalty, yet she could feel that something else lay inside.

The envelope beckoned. Tearing it open, she inserted the strange little key into the lock and turned it. The tumblers aligned with a soft *snick*, and she lifted the lid. Inside lay a leather-bound book. A note slipped out as she held up the tome to more closely examine the elaborate tooling on its cover.

Sabrina,

Please accept these gifts as tokens of my great affection and regard. For my lady: Murshidabad silk from the looms of Bengal and an ancient, sacred Hindi text.

Yours,
H.

Silk? She looked to the box and there, beneath where the book had lain, was another packet, this one a soft, featherlight parcel wrapped in chambray. Opening it, she shook out a swath of palest pink silk so fine it was practically transparent.

It was a night rail.

Fingers trembling, she held out the delicate wisp of fabric, her exhalation of reverence causing it to ripple like water. The thing looked as if made for some exotic princess, its neckline embroidered in satin threads and lavishly encrusted with seed pearls, beads of silver, and tiny, sparkling jewels—diamonds and rubies, to be precise.

She gasped in astonishment. A royal gift, indeed! It was worth an absolute fortune.

No doubt Henry meant for her to wear it on their first night as husband and wife. Unbidden, a wicked curl crept across her lips, and her heart began to pound. So delicate a garment would likely be ruined within seconds of his seeing it on her.

Carefully laying it aside, she returned her attention to the book in her lap. Page after page was filled with curious, curling script that, while interesting, was also utterly unintelligible. The next leaf she turned, however, revealed a beautifully inked, color illustration depicting lovers engaged in a passionate embrace.

Naked lovers. And they were...

Her face caught fire as she stared, mesmerized.

Years ago, while clandestinely poking about in the servants' quarters, she'd chanced upon some naughty leaflets hidden beneath a bed. This image looked *nothing* like those, however. Those had been crude and demeaning. This was not. This was beautiful. The couple appeared utterly enraptured with each other. She flipped through the remaining pages, stopping to absorb each illustration. Each pane had been drawn with exquisite attention to detail.

She swallowed. *Every* detail. Not all were sexually explicit, though the ones that were made her blush. Henry had said it was an ancient, sacred Hindi text. Obviously, it was a treatise on love.

If Mama found out about it, it would surely be ample cause for her to end his suit.

Or demand that they marry at once.

Was it worth the risk?

Her heart nearly leaped out of her throat at the sound of a knock on her door.

"My lady?" called a muffled voice from the other side.

Sabrina panicked. "A moment, if you please." The book and gown she quickly put back into the box, which she then hid in the darkest corner of her wardrobe.

Cheeks still aflame, she went to the door and opened it.

"Your mother has returned and requests your presence downstairs at once, my lady," the servant informed her.

As Sabrina turned to leave, her eye fell on the chess set Fairford had given her. Somehow it wasn't very inspiring anymore. And the little book of French poetry he'd given her suddenly seemed trite and full of sentimental drivel—none of which, she knew, echoed his feelings for her. He was only satisfying the conventions of courtship.

Chapter Fifteen

SEVERAL DAYS LATER

"SABRINA TOLD ME HOW YOU'VE NAMED A NEW FLOWER after her," said Mama with a bright smile as Fairford entered the room. Sabrina was glad to see she'd begun to warm toward him. "You simply must send over a cutting, so that we may grow it here in our gardens and be eternally reminded of your thoughtfulness."

"Of course. I shall be delighted to oblige."

"Excellent. Now, then. I hope you don't mind, my lord, but I've invited over a few friends to join us for a small gathering this afternoon. Sheffield will be here at any moment, as well as the Hesterfields and the Darlingtons and a few others," she said, waving a hand vaguely. "With the weather being so very lovely, I've decided we shall take to the outdoors. I do hope you'll join us."

Even as he nodded amiably, Sabrina once more wrestled down a powerful urge to swear. She'd counted on having time *alone* with him. How could she begin to accustom herself to his manner while being forced to natter over cards and stale tea cakes with a bunch of their friends?

Just then, the butler announced Sheffield's arrival.

Mama rose. "You'll have to excuse me, my lord. My other guests are beginning to arrive."

He bowed before her. "Lady Sabrina, always a pleasure."

"I must apologize," she began after allowing him to kiss her hand. Though he hid it well, she could tell he was disappointed.

He shrugged. "No harm done. But I did wish to speak to you in pr—"

"Ah! There you are. I see that I am not the first of your admirers to arrive," teased Lord Sheffield from the doorway. He crossed the room to kiss her cheek in fatherly fashion. "I do hope you'll join me in a game of chess, my dear. I've yet to ease the sting of your having beaten me last week."

Sabrina flicked a nervous glance in Fairford's direction. "Ah…yes, of course, my lord." She'd lied to him regarding her skill at the game, for Georgiana had once told her a man did not like to think his woman was more intelligent than himself. It might be off-putting if he discovered she was good enough to beat the likes of Sheffield, who was a player of some renown.

"Excellent! Then I hereby claim a match," said Sheffield.

"I don't suppose you've heard the news," interjected Lady Aylesford as she came up behind Sheffield with a group of guests. "Our Sabrina has had a newly discovered flower named after her by the Royal Society, thanks to Lord Fairford!"

After an hour or so, Sabrina thought she'd go mad if she had to retell the story one more time. As if a silly flower mattered in the least. It had been a ploy to win her affections, nothing more. She longed for peace and quiet, but the din only rose as more people arrived. Obviously, Mama's idea of a "small gathering" was everyone else's idea of a large, noisy throng.

By the time they finally moved outdoors, she was extremely grateful. Fairford now lay on a blanket across from her, watching while she set up the chessboard again. They had played four rounds thus far, and she'd purposely lost two of them. Two moves ago, she had deliberately put her queen in jeopardy, ensuring his win.

She gazed at the others out enjoying the day and spied her mother and Sheffield strolling across the lawn, chatting amiably. Her mother was smiling, her face filled with contentment. There was not a hint of any passion between them whatsoever, not even the faintest whiff of the kind of insanity she experienced with Henry.

They have exactly what I desire.

"Checkmate," Fairford murmured, tipping her king. He arose and stretched. "I believe I'm ready for a constitutional."

"Of course, my lord," she said, rising to join him. "The orchards should be particularly fine on a day like this."

Sauntering past manicured lawns and bordered gardens, they entered the lush green of the orchards. Spring had at last arrived, and every twig was swollen with fat, fuzzy green buds.

Stopping beneath the spreading branches of a gnarled old apple tree, he turned to her. Before he could so much as utter a word, however, she stepped right up to him and kissed him firmly on the mouth. In the conservatory, she'd been timid, reticent. It was time to see if she could bring herself to feel some sort of attraction for him.

At first, it was gentle and not entirely unpleasant. The moment she brushed her tongue against his lips, however, everything changed. With a groan, he backed her up against the bole of a tree and ground his pelvis into her belly.

She refrained from rolling her eyes. All men seemed to be led by the beast between their legs. She tolerated it—until his hands began fumbling at her breasts. Without thinking, she sank her teeth into his bottom lip in protest. The salty tang of blood touched her tongue, and she shoved him away just as he moaned in pain.

She'd felt no reciprocal desire whatsoever. No tingles, no flashes of liquid heat, no shivers of pleasure. Only revulsion. "Please accept my apologies, my lord. I—I don't know what possessed me."

He moved in behind her and grasped her shoulders lightly. "You need not apologize, my dear. Not to me. The truth of the matter is that you only barely beat me to the mark. I fully intended to kiss you the moment we were out of view," he murmured, caressing the tip of her ear with his lips.

She shrank away from his touch. "I think we had better return." She could not seem to overcome her reaction to him.

His hands tightened on her shoulders. "I think not. Not just yet."

Turning her around, he hauled her close and dug his fingers into the hair at the base of her skull, preventing any escape. Startled, she began to struggle as his tongue delved deep into her mouth. She pushed at him with her other hand, but he only grabbed her wrist in a viselike grip. She gasped and kicked at him as the delicate bones rubbed together painfully. It was to little effect, however, for her heavy skirts prevented any real contact.

A chuckle escaped him as she squirmed, and his fingers tightened in her hair, wresting a whimper from her throat. The tiny sound seemed to satisfy some need in him, and he broke away. She stood there, shaking. Disgust filled her. She'd heard of men who enjoyed violent love play.

He smiled benevolently. "Forgive me, my darling," he said, caressing her cheek. She flinched. "You simply bring out the beast in me. How can any man hope to maintain his self-control with you?"

She forced out a flirtatious chuckle, unwilling to let him see that he had upset her. "Surely not *you*, my lord? A man of the world such as yourself has probably lost count of the number of ladies he's kissed."

"None so inspiring as you," he answered smoothly. "They were a mere candle to your bright sun. I cannot remember a single name in your presence, other than your own sweet syllables. You drive me mad with your charms."

She concentrated on the grass at her feet. "You flatter me, my lord."

He moved in behind her. "I never offer an insincere compliment." She forced down her panic as he reached around to caress the side of her breast and then moved lower, flattening his palm against her belly. "And when I say you drive me to madness, I truly mean it." He pressed himself against her buttocks for emphasis. "I want you," he whispered at her ear. "*Now.*"

She stepped away. "I am no lightskirt, my lord. I shan't give myself to any man but my lawful husband."

"Then marry me, and let's have done with this ridiculous game."

Her brows lifted in response to his tone. "If it is a game, then surely you understand that the stakes are highest for me."

He addressed her in a more conciliatory manner. "I'm ready to make a commitment here and now. I'll make a fine husband, Sabrina. I'm wealthy, titled, decent looking." He smiled boyishly. "Marry me, and I'll make you the envy of all women."

Such arrogance! No woman ever brought up the competition during a marriage proposal, but she did not hesitate. "I should be the envy of all women if I married Lord Montgomery as well. Why should I choose you over him?"

Fairford stood there, stunned into silence for a moment. "Why should you choose...? Well, because—because I...because I can give you what you want," he blurted, clearly confused.

"Exactly what is it that you think I want?" She cocked her head to one side and waited.

"Why, what every woman wants: a passionate, devoted husband. Not to mention a fine home for you a...and our children," he added quickly. "I can provide a life of comfort and security. You will never lack for anything. Name it, and it will be yours."

"And what of Mrs. Childers, your mistress?"

Once more, he was taken aback. "I—I beg your pardon?"

LIANA LEFEY

"If I choose to accept your offer, I expect you to keep to my bed—and my bed *alone*—until two males are born of the union. After that, what you do is a matter of supreme indifference to me. I ask only that you are discreet and that you leave me in peace."

"So much for sentimentality," he said with unexpected bitterness. "What you propose is a business arrangement, not a marriage."

She laughed softly. It was regretful that she had to be so blunt, but he had to understand where she stood on the matter if they were to agree to marry. "Perhaps it is, at that. A husband must provide for his wife's safety and comfort, and in return she must provide him with heirs and care for their family and home. I should like the relationship to be an amiable one, of course, but unlike the majority of my sex, I don't delude myself. The lies of 'true love' and 'happily ever after' are the stuff of children's stories. I prefer to be pragmatic. Life becomes far less disappointing when one's expectations are within reason."

"I should think you'd want to keep such unconventional opinions to yourself, lest you drive away your *mark*," he replied indignantly. "After all, a man likes to at least *think* he's wanted for more than his purse!"

"I see. Does my honesty wound your heart, then, my lord?" She knew he didn't love her. But desire would be enough.

"No. But it certainly doesn't fill me with delight, either." He peered at her curiously. "You truly have no interest in love?"

"Love is for little girls and sentimentalists. Not for me."

"Why marry at all, then?"

"I suppose I could take care of my mother until she dies, after which I could choose to live with relatives or become a teacher or governess. But there is no security, no happiness in such a life. I want a home of my own, children to raise, and above all, peace."

"And in return?"

"My bloodline and dowry, my body to bear your children, and my considerable skills as hostess and chatelaine. Your life as my husband will be a pleasant and comfortable one, my lord. There shall be no contention in your home with me as its keeper."

"And what of your loyalty?" he asked. "What would bind you to me, if not love? How could I be certain of your fidelity?"

"Rest assured I shall keep my wedding vows. I've no interest in romantic entanglements."

"But what of passion? Has desire no impact on your decision at all?"

She decided to be completely candid. "If it did, I should already be married to Lord Montgomery and we would not be having this conversation. But I am not so foolish as to allow myself to be led by the nose into making a bad decision over a purely physical reaction."

Her answer gave him pause. "Not many women have such self-discipline," he said softly, surprising her. "Sentimentality I can live without, but not passion," he said, edging closer. "And passion is what I feel for you, Sabrina. I'll admit I didn't want to feel it, but it exists, nonetheless. I would want it returned in some measure, at least for a while."

"I should think that over time, it would come of its own volition, my lord. Familiarity should eventually overcome reticence," she demurred. She would never feel any kind of passion for this man. But she would make certain he never knew it.

"And when will you arrive at your decision?" he asked.

"Selecting a husband is the most important decision of any woman's life. My choice is one I must live with for the rest of it; therefore, I must decide carefully."

"Indeed, I could not agree more. But know that I, too, have other options and a choice to make—and I will not wait forever."

She smiled faintly. "Miss Bidewell."

LIANA LEFEY

"Many women would be more than pleased to accept my offer," he snarled. "She is certainly *not* my only other choice."

"Of course, you must do whatever you think is best," she said, keeping her face neutral. She'd pricked his pride, apparently. The look in his eyes was cold and ugly. "If you feel someone else will make a better wife, then you must marry her, naturally." Turning, she began to walk back to the house, forcing her feet to move at a steady march, rather than running.

An arrogant man like him would be unable to resist the need to prove her wrong. And he truly *wanted* her now. She could have him with a word. But his was a savage desire, untempered by any sort of tenderness. She shivered with the knowledge that he truly wouldn't care whether or not she loved him, so long as she belonged to him.

Once he'd had his fill of her and she'd done her duty as a broodmare, he would indeed set her aside and pursue his pleasure elsewhere. It was what she'd wanted, wasn't it? But could she really marry such a man?

The path that had seemed so certain to her before now seemed fraught with pitfalls. Only one other remained untried. But could she actually do it?

Chapter Sixteen

"**I** DON'T SEE HOW YOU CAN POSSIBLY GET OUT OF IT, Sabrina," whispered Augusta. "You'll have to accept one of them."

"No, I don't," Sabrina told her sister. She looked to the doorway with apprehension. Mama had gone to speak with cook about dinner before Montgomery and his sister arrived, but she could return at any moment. "I've a plan to avoid all of this unpleasantness."

Her sister's expression turned incredulous. "You call it 'unpleasant' to have men competing for your hand?"

"If you'd endured what *I* have, you'd agree with me," Sabrina replied sourly. "But you had it easy."

"Philip is a dear." Augusta smiled, her gaze softening.

Sabrina snorted to herself. Philip was an unsophisticated country squire who'd inherited his title by the sheer grace of a cousin's stupidity. To put it plainly, he was a bumpkin, and she suspected that Augusta visited London so rarely mainly in order to keep him that way. The variety of temptations offered here corrupted men all too easily. Victoria's husband had certainly fallen prey to its lures. Augusta was extremely wise to cling so closely to her husband's side when they visited.

"It's a shame you didn't pay mind to his brother," continued Augusta. "Peter would have made an excellent husband. And don't make that face! You *always* make that face whenever I speak of Peter," she complained. "He's a good man, and he would have come to scratch if you'd shown any interest at all."

"Oh, Augusta! Must we revisit this every time you come home? Peter never showed the slightest interest in me. It's a moot point, anyway, since he's gone for the church, isn't it?"

"He could still marry," said Augusta. "He'd be here in a shot if you wrote to him with even the least amount of encouragement."

"I doubt it. Even if he did harbor an unrequited *tendre* for me, he has a reputation to uphold now. His parishioners would likely start piling wood at the stake if he brought me home," she added stubbornly. "Now, enough about Saint Peter."

"Oh, all right. I was only trying to offer a solution to your problem," grumbled Augusta. "Tell me about this grand plan of yours, then."

She took a deep breath. "I'm going to find another suitor."

"That's your plan?" exclaimed Augusta. "Add to the 'unpleasantness' further? How many suitors does a girl need?"

"Just one. The right one. And don't you dare lecture me! Half a dozen of the ladies in your own circle entertained several suitors before they settled."

"Yes, but *they* weren't in *your* situation," said Augusta, pointing an accusing finger. "You really ought to reconsider. You can't afford to take chances, not after the sort of scan—"

"I can, and I shall. I will not fall prey to the same tragedy as our mother and our sister. I assume Georgiana has told you about Victoria?"

"Yes. I received a letter from her two days ago," said Augusta, her voice sinking to a whisper. Now she, too, glanced at the door anxiously. "Does Mama know anything yet?"

Sabrina shook her head. "She does not. She is afraid that if Mama finds out, she will come storm the castle and cause a complete uproar. What do you think she ought to do?"

Augusta cast her gaze to the carpet. "I don't think there is much she can do, to tell the truth. You know menfolk hold all of the power. She has no recourse, no choice but to put up with his indiscretions quietly."

"Just as Mama did," Sabrina murmured sadly. "My plan will work, Augusta. It must."

Their mother sailed into the room with Henry and Rebecca in tow, effectively curtailing the conversation.

"Sabrina, it's happened!" the girl squealed happily, extending her hand and waggling her fingers.

"You didn't!" Sabrina gasped, snatching up the girl's hand to get a better look at the sparkling jewel.

Rebecca's grin broadened. "Charles gave it to me yesterday."

"I'm so pleased for you," said Sabrina, forcing a happy smile. How could she be engaged after only knowing the man for a few weeks? "Rebecca, this is my sister, Lady Billingsly," she told her, introducing them.

"Congratulations—and please, call me Augusta," said her sister.

Sabrina listened numbly while Rebecca regaled them with her fairy tale of an engagement. "Are you not in the least bit concerned about how quickly this has all happened?" she interjected, unable to stand it any longer.

"Absolutely not. I love him, Sabrina. And he adores me!"

"But how can you know that after such a short time?" she argued.

Rebecca shrugged and sighed. "I just know. When he's near, I can't think of anything else. And when he's away, it's the same." She looked guiltily over at her brother and lowered her voice to a whisper. "And when he kisses me—oh, it's shameful, Sabrina! But I can't help myself. I'll *die* if I don't marry him."

Sabrina's heart began to pound. Just the sound of Henry's voice was enough to make her tremble inside. Even now, as he chuckled at something her mother had said, she felt it like a physical touch. She pushed him from her mind. "You would risk your life's happiness on a mere infatuation?"

"Oh, it's more than that," answered Rebecca. "Far more! I simply cannot live without him."

"But you hardly know him."

"I know him well enough."

Sabrina shook her head. It just didn't make sense. "Well, at least you'll have until next spring before it becomes final. You can still change your mind."

"I won't," said Rebecca. "And we're not waiting until next spring. We are to marry at the beginning of June. Father is going to announce it next week."

"*June?* But—"

"Father has given consent for us to wed as soon as decency allows, lest the matter end in a Scottish scandal," interrupted Rebecca. A rosy blush stained her cheeks.

"Rebecca!"

"Well, it's true! We can barely be in the same room together."

Again, Sabrina's heart clenched. Augusta's sharp elbow in her ribs finally forced her to drop her argument. "You will do as you please, I suppose," she trailed off. The girl was obviously not using her head at all.

Folly. Pure folly. Her heart, however, insisted on maintaining the hope that Rebecca would be just as blindingly happy in five years' time.

From across the room where he sat with Mama, Henry's gaze pierced her. How was it that he could create such chaos within her, while others did absolutely nothing—or worse, repulsed her?

"I came as quickly as I could," said Percy as he entered Pembroke's estate office.

"Thank you. You may go now," Henry said to Watkins, handing him a sheaf of documents and then gestured for Percy to make himself at home. Naturally, he went straight over to the brandy decanter.

"It's barely even midday."

"What are you, my maiden aunt?" groused Percy. "If you'd had the sort of night I did, you'd be having a drink, too. Now, tell me why in heaven's name I dragged myself out of bed to come here. And why are we in *this* musty old room? Not that I'm complaining," he added, lifting his glass to admire the rich amber fluid in it. "Your father's personal stock is quite fine."

"We are here because no one ever comes in here uninvited, and there is no way for anyone to approach this room without being heard coming down the hall," Henry said, keeping his voice low. "There has been a disturbing turn in the investigation."

"Oh?"

"Our man found a girl who'd run away from Madam Boucher. She said she and the others there are frightened and directed him to visit a friend who used to work there."

"Used to work?"

"A patron paid Boucher to remove her, in order to make her his private plaything."

"I was unaware one could do such a thing."

"This woman was one of Boucher's established girls, who'd been fortunate enough to secure the affections of her patron. She said that there had been changes in the way things were being run at her former employer's. Boucher has recently begun having her bullies approach families in the poorer districts with offers to buy their untouched girls, and then grooming them to be sold, not rented."

"That smells of slavery," said Percy, wrinkling his nose.

"Indeed. And I was told several pleasure houses have begun doing it to cater to patrons who fear the pox. It's quite profitable, apparently. In return for her relatively small investment in a virgin, Boucher receives quite a sum. And there is an agreement between her and the client that if he ever tires of his purchase, he returns the girl. Thus, she can begin 'regular' service and earn her further profits."

"Quite the entrepreneur, isn't she?"

"There is more. This woman told our man that two months ago, Fairford bought a girl from Boucher and that she has not been seen or heard from since. She said that, like her patron, many of Boucher's clients decide to keep their 'bought' girls and set them up as proper mistresses, but that Fairford has purchased girls from Boucher twice while she was there. To her knowledge, he has not returned either of them, and no one has heard of his setting up a new mistress anywhere in London."

"They simply disappeared?"

Henry nodded. If the idea of Sabrina marrying Fairford had been unacceptable before, it was truly terrifying now. "There is no evidence to prove that he has brought them to harm, but..."

"I agree. With all his secrecy, it does not bode well," said Percy. "What of Childers? Is she somehow involved?"

"The man said he didn't think so. She knows Fairford often goes somewhere besides his own home when he leaves her, but we think he keeps her ignorant of the details. One thing is certain. If he has bought girls from Boucher, he must be keeping another house somewhere in London. Thus far, he has not gone directly from Childers to visit it, which leads me to think he is switching carriages again—at Boucher's."

"In the front door and out through the back immediately after," said Percy, nodding. "How do we go about proving it and finding this hideaway?"

"I've hired more men, enough to have one follow every carriage that departs Boucher's from the time Fairford arrives. It's the only way to catch him at his final destination."

"Good lord, man," gasped Percy. "Do you have any idea how many people visit that place a night? The expense of it! I certainly hope she is worth it."

"Which leads me to the point of bringing you here. I need another favor, Percy. Sabrina won't listen to me if I try to tell her anything about Fairford, but she might listen to someone else."

"But she'll know immediately that it comes from y—"

"I've said nothing of our association to her, and her mother and sisters would know nothing of it, either. Few people knew we were close friends before I left for India, and I haven't been in London long enough for it to have become widely known. I need you to get close to her, gain her confidence so that when you let slip about Fairford, she becomes curious."

"And then you wish me to spoon-feed her the information we've obtained."

"Just so."

"The moment she learns we are friends, it will be over. Everything I will have said will be discredited."

"Yes, but by then she'll hopefully be curious enough to continue digging on her own and perhaps start asking questions."

"Do you really believe this will work?"

"There is only one way to know, and that is to try," said Henry.

Chapter Seventeen

THE RUTLAND BALL

*S*ABRINA KNEW *EXACTLY* WHY FAIRFORD HAD BROKEN OFF with Miss Bidewell—and she refused to be pressured into making a premature decision.

Her plan to obtain another suitor had to be implemented, and soon. It had to be someone she could like well enough, without there being a danger of further emotional attachment. And it had to be someone her current suitors would never perceive as a threat.

She searched the room and had selected a likely target when, much to her surprise, Lord Falloure approached her.

"My lady, how delightful to see you again. And how charming you look this evening."

Confusion filled her. For five years every marriageable female's mother had salivated over the possibility of a match with Falloure, yet none had succeeded in so much as getting him to come to tea. And here he stood before her, waiting with what looked like anticipation.

Had her name become *that* infamous? She eyed him with careful consideration. No one would ever imagine that he would come to scratch. Therefore neither Fairford or Henry would see him as a threat. Did she dare attempt the impossible? "Oh, dear! You gave me a start, Lord...?"

Though his smile remained, his nostrils pinched. "Falloure, my lady. We were introduced at the Westfield ball. I partnered you in a minuet."

"Did you? I've attended so many balls and danced with so many gentlemen, you must forgive me if I do not recall."

"You wound me to the heart." He grinned, and his voice lowered suggestively. "Rare is the lady who doesn't remember dancing with me."

Suppressing a laugh, Sabrina appraised the man before her. Dressed fit to rival the king, the tall, slender dandy wore an exquisite jacket of violet silk embroidered with silver thread and embellished with jewels. Polished silver buttons marched in long, gleaming rows down his chest, and the long, elegant fingers peeking from beneath the frothy lace at his cuffs were heavy with rings. Even his shoes glittered with gems.

"Well, to be fair, I was likely a bit distracted," she said at last.

"Oh?" He frowned. "And what, pray tell, could possibly distract you so?"

"I'm sure you've heard of my current predicament," she finally said. Might as well lay all of the cards out in the open. Well, most of them.

"Who has not?" he asked, with a twinkle in his eye.

She decided to take a gamble. "And what think you?"

"I think you must be a truly fascinating woman to have attracted offers from three such vastly different men in so short a time." He reached out and lifted her face. "And I think you would already be engaged to one of them had he been what you desired."

Miracles do happen! "You are correct in your estimation," she told him as calmly as possible. "I am looking for something different."

He gave her the smile that she knew had melted the knees of countless women. It was very pretty, but she found herself unmoved. *Excellent.*

"I beg you to tell me all, only promise me your next dance," he said, offering his arm. "And I vow to prove myself more worthy of recollection this time."

By the time the dance was over and a glass of champagne had been shared in a quiet corner, Sabrina had firmly attached him. When he suggested they take a breath of air outside, she knew she had him hooked.

They walked along the gravel path for a bit in silence.

"Now that the moon has set, one can see them quite clearly," he said, gazing up at the stars. "Such beauty is hard to parallel. Like jewels they are. And look, there is the brightest of them all, Venus." He pointed at one particularly brilliant point. "Named for the goddess of love, 'tis said the sight of her is a blessing to all lovers."

"Better Venus than Mars, I suppose," she chuckled. "I should think the auspices of that particular deity must be avoided by lovers at all costs."

"Ah, but Mars was the lover of Venus," he murmured back, coming a little closer. "He would never dare to cause strife where his beloved walked. Every man should follow his example and be content to worship at his lady's feet, denying her nothing her heart desires."

What utter rubbish! she thought, rolling her eyes under the cover of darkness. He was almost as bad as Chadwick. "My heart desires only peace. I do not know if I can take much more of this rivalry. I apologize, my lord. I fear I shall bore you with such talk."

"Nonsense," he said, patting her hand where it rested on his sleeve. "You may lay the burdens of your heart upon my ears and know that your secret is safe with me."

"My, but you *are* sweet to sympathize so. None of my other friends have such a generous heart."

"Such callous treatment!" he exclaimed with mock alarm. "I wonder that you still name them friends."

She shot him a sidelong look. "Flatterer! Think not that I am fooled, my lord. I am well aware of your reputation."

"Then you know that I have no ulterior motives lurking beneath my counsel," he told her. "You are safe from my wicked predations—so long as you remain undecorated by a wedding ring."

"Shame on you, my lord!" she laughed, caught off guard. "You truly *are* the devil they say you are."

"I give him a run for his money every now and then," he confessed. "But you may rest assured that this old devil is on your side, dear lady. As charming as you are, I've no interest in ravishing you. At least not for the moment," he added, lifting a wry brow. "Once you've gone and shackled yourself to some poor fool, however, I may change my mind. Beware the day you wed."

She pointed her nose skyward. "I'm afraid you will be sorely disappointed, for I intend to be quite loyal to my husband, whoever he may be."

"Your announcement inspires the gravest disappointment, my lady. The kind of disappointment that might make any other man reconsider his wickedness and contemplate reform."

"But not you, I take it?"

"Me? Reform?" He gave a theatrical show of horror, eliciting a giggle. "I shudder to even think what life would be like if morals suddenly became manifest in my constitution. I should be a most dull man if I ever decided to walk the straight and narrow."

"Then my intent to honor my vows makes me dull?"

He stared at her for a moment. "Not in the least. What makes for dullness in a man makes for virtue in a woman, and womanly virtue is a thing to be admired, not mocked. It has become all too rare, these days."

Her smile slipped. "You are one of the few who think me virtuous, I'm afraid."

"Bah! What are a few stolen kisses? Nothing, that's what. If you want my opinion, any man who chooses the perfect paragon of chastity for a wife is only asking for trouble."

"You'd rather marry a woman with a tarnished reputation?"

"Good heavens no!" he laughed. "The family name must be preserved, after all. I'm merely saying that I would never wish to marry a complete innocent."

"Every man wishes to be the first," she argued.

"My dear, I have been a willing participant in more *affaires* than I care to count, and they have taught me much. I can say with confidence that wives who cuckold their husbands most often came into their marriages completely ignorant. By contrast, the women I've found most frustratingly loyal to their vows are those who married after having sampled passion's delights."

Sabrina stared at him, incredulous. It was unconscionable that he should speak so candidly to a young lady. She should by all rights be appalled, but she simply couldn't find it within herself to be such a hypocrite. She rapped him on the arm with her fan, taking a playful approach to relieve the tension. "You, sir, are trying to corrupt me!"

"I? Corrupt you?"

She nodded her head emphatically. "Everyone knows that a female light in the skirt before her wedding is only likely to remain so afterward."

"I see. Everyone knows this?"

"Everyone who matters."

"Ah, yes. *Society*," he supplied with a curl of his lip. "And whom do you believe? The blackguard who speaks from many years of happy experience—or some shriveled-up old matron who's never known a moment of passion in her life?"

"Then what would you advise? Ought I to kiss every gentleman I meet before I dance my way down the aisle?"

"Certainly not!" he said with horror. "A woman should only kiss those truly skilled in the art. Otherwise, she'll learn nothing."

Though she couldn't say it, she knew exactly what he meant. Kissing Chadwick had been like kissing an awkward scarecrow, and meeting Fairford's lips was a lesson in overcoming repulsion. But kissing Henry...

Her skin began to heat.

"Then I should only kiss rakes?" she said, pushing away the thought.

Percy turned and answered in a velvety voice: "Only the ones you trust implicitly. Tell me, whom do you trust?"

She favored him with a gimlet stare, knowing full well that its effect was ruined by the twitching of her lips. "None that I have met thus far."

She laughed with delight as he clutched his chest in a comic pantomime of having been shot. She'd handled him just right.

Henry chuckled as his friend flopped into the chair opposite him. "The look on your face...Well? What did you think of her?"

Percy's grin was easy. "I have indeed met the formidable Lady Sabrina. Sherry," he murmured to the servant who'd come to attend him. "I can certainly understand why Chadwick was so eager to put on the leg irons."

Henry nearly dropped his drink. "I beg your pardon?" Such a comment from the man was unprecedented.

"A fascinating specimen, is she not?"

"My God, don't tell me she's rooked *you*?"

The other man looked at him over the rim of his goblet with merry eyes. "Me? Rooked? Nonsense! There isn't an unwed female alive who isn't out to bag me. I saw what she was on about the moment she pretended not to know me."

Henry relaxed.

"She's shopping for another suitor," continued Percy. "If I'm to succeed in this little deception, Henry, I'm afraid I shall have no choice but to put myself on the market."

"You're not serious?" Henry wasn't sure he liked the direction this was headed. Sabrina was as safe with Percy as she was with her own mother, but...

Percy shrugged. "You asked me to help you watch her and keep her safe from Fairford—well, here is the perfect opportunity. Well? What say you? Shall I cast my lot in?"

Though his face remained impassive, Henry's heart burned. "I suppose, if it is the only way," he said reluctantly.

His friend leaned forward, eyes alight with curiosity. "And what if through this ruse of yours I should actually succeed in persuading her to marry me? Ought I go through with it, do you think? I know my parents would be delighted to strengthen ties between our families."

"She's not your kind of woman," Henry answered sharply. He calmed his tone. "Your standards are far more sophisticated. Sabrina is an innocent."

Percy only laughed. "Any woman who would put a living snake in your pocket is certainly up to my standards by merit of sheer mischief. Besides, my father has been after me to find a decent girl." He peered at him, sobering. "By George, you aren't bothered by the idea, are you? I know you've kissed her, but I thought that was just—"

"Of course not. It's only that I know Sabrina would never seriously consider you," Henry said, deliberately doing his best to appear nonchalant. "You are far too much like her father." *Which is the problem.*

The impudent grin returned. "I can certainly remedy that little misperception. You're, ah, quite certain you aren't interested in her yourself?"

Henry wanted to hurl the decanter at his friend's head. Instead, he gripped the handle a bit tighter and poured himself another glass. "Do as you please—only don't come running to me in a panic when the hellion takes you up on it," he said with nearly perfect equanimity. Nearly.

The other man stared at him for a long moment. "Very well, then. I shall shock the masses tomorrow and put myself forth. I would only do this for you, you know. I've spent years cultivating my reputation as an impossible fish to catch. I hope you appreciate my sacrifice."

Henry forced a smile to his lips. "She hasn't accepted you yet."

"She will," promised Percy, laughing. "I can be very persuasive, and I've never yet had a woman turn me down."

God.

His head began to pound. It was time to face the truth. If she accepted Percy's proposal, it would mean he'd never had a chance at all. Not really.

He made the decision to try one more time. If he could not convince her to marry him for the right reasons, then he would rather her have a measure of what she took for happiness with Percy. At least with him, she'd be safe from Fairford.

It was the lesser of two evils. He doubted very much whether he would be able to wish them well, but if she persisted in her blind prejudice against him, it might be the only viable alternative.

There is always abduction, his thoughts whispered. He could. He could compromise her and force the issue. But she would never trust him again for as long as she lived, and that was no marriage. He wanted her to choose him.

Chapter Eighteen

ONDON WAS ABUZZ WITH THE ASTONISHING NEWS: LORD Falloure, the man long hailed as "The Terror of the Ton," had at last succumbed and was paying earnest court to the increasingly outrageous Lady Sabrina.

And there was more. News had reached Henry that Percy had put aside his latest mistress.

Today, as he and Sabrina walked along the edge of the woods at Belleford, Henry decided to take the bull by the horns. "I wish to discuss the matter of you and Falloure," he began quietly, staring at the reflected sunlight dancing on the river's surface.

"What is there to discuss?"

"Are you planning on accepting his offer?"

She shifted, the nervous motion betraying her. "What offer? He hasn't made one."

"He will."

"Are you so certain of another man's intent?" she inquired lightly. "I've already told you he is merely a friend."

"Yes, which is the same thing you told people about me, and I should think we are more than just friends."

She sighed, picked a leaf from a nearby tree, and flicked it away. "Perhaps that is the problem. Your possessiveness has overreached the reality of our relationship."

"I won't deny that I don't like his hanging about," he continued, "but my main interest is in protecting you."

"Haven't you figured out by now that I'm quite capable of managing myself without a keeper? I don't need your protection. Besides, there is nothing to protect me *from*. He. Hasn't. Proposed."

"He will."

"Are you aware of something I am not? Has he shouted from some rooftop that he intends to ask me?"

"He might as well have. He has dismissed his mistress."

"Yes, he told me he was planning on doing so," she answered with a careless shrug.

Her answer stopped him in his tracks. "He did *what*?"

"He said she'd become a nuisance of late."

"Sabrina, you must see what he's doing. You cannot possibly be so blind!"

"Henry, really. This is—"

"I'll not stand idly by and watch him destroy you."

"Destroy me? He represents everything I desire," she told him.

"Coward." The soft accusation hung in the air between them, a tangible thing.

Her eyes flashed. "I am no coward. If I were, I'd have married Chadwick and been done with this long ago. In fact, I find myself wondering why I did not. He would have been the better choice at the time."

"The safer maybe, but certainly not the better," Henry countered. "You would have been miserable with him, and you know it. You need someone stronger than—"

"You seem to know an awful lot about what I need," she cut in, her temper showing.

"I know that you need to trust your heart. What does it say about Falloure?"

"The heart is a poor judge of character, easily tricked."

"The heart is the *only* trustworthy judge of character," he replied, turning to face her. "But if you trust not your heart, then what of your instincts?" he asked. "What do they tell you? What do they whisper? If you are honest with yourself, you'll find you don't mistrust me—you mistrust yourself."

"I trust my own judgment implicitly and recognize that it is only impaired when I allow passion to interfere with it. Is it so terrible that I would rather make my choice based on logic than emotion? Why may I not do so without being the subject of constant harassment? *If* Percy asks me to marry him, I would have to say that he is the most logical of my current options."

"Why?"

"What do you mean, 'Why?'" she asked. "I like him. I actually enjoy his company. He doesn't constantly harass me, and I'm able to think clearly when I'm with him!" She pressed her fingers to her temples. "You cannot know how upsetting it is to be around someone and be unable to even think."

"I can. I do. Because that is how I am with you. I find myself saying things that I know I shouldn't. I find myself doing things—"

"Then perhaps he will save us both!" she shouted.

He stared, unwilling to believe he'd heard the words. "Did Percy ever tell you that we are friends?" He knew it would ruin his plans to have Percy tell her about Fairford, but that didn't really matter anymore.

She blinked in surprise.

"We served together in the Coldstream Guards many years ago," he went on. "We've been friends since before I left England. Are you not curious to know why a man with his reputation suddenly became interested in you?" He leaned closer. "He did it in order to prove a point to me." It *was* the truth, mostly.

"It hardly matters," she replied, her voice breaking. "Either way, I'll still get what I want. What I have always wanted." But even as she said it, he saw tears form at the edges of her lashes.

Why did she have to be so damned stubborn?

Though it was warm out, Sabrina felt the chill of winter in her heart as Henry stared at her for a moment, and then turned and walked away. The withdrawal of his presence was like the veiling of the sun. She hated herself for hurting him. But it was the only way.

She licked her lips, tasted salt, and realized she was crying. She almost called him back. Almost.

If she married him, she would want him body and soul. She would be what she'd sworn never to become: a jealous, possessive wife. They weren't even wed and just the thought of him touching another woman drove her insane. Could she live with it if he wandered? Her mother had survived it, but she didn't know if she had the fortitude to do so.

Percy inspired no such jealousy. Nor did he inspire passion. And he demanded no part of her heart.

Why did he never mention their friendship? Is he really only pursuing me to make a point?

It didn't matter. If he asked her to marry him, she would accept and she would make sure it happened. She would get what she wanted. She would win.

But is that really what you want? The niggling doubt gnawed at her gut as she started the long walk back to the manor. By the time she arrived, a hundred tiny daggers were poking at her skull from the inside.

Returning to the festivities, she sought out Percy. "You look as though you could use a brandy," he said, shocking a nearby lady and wresting a faint smile from Sabrina's lips.

"It is nothing," she replied, unable to help glancing toward the source of her upset. He was walking with his sister, looking as serene and undisturbed as ever. It was so unfair. She smiled up at Percy. "Let us take a turn about the statuary. I hear Lord Belleford recently acquired a new piece from Athens."

Sabrina agonized over her decision. The strength of her growing attachment to Henry was completely terrifying. The prospect of marrying Fairford was just as unnerving, but in a different way. No matter how genteel his behavior had been since the incident, the memory of that day in the orchard had robbed her of any peace in his presence.

Percy's visits had provided the only solace over the past few weeks. More and more, she had begun to look forward to seeing him, if only to have someone to talk to who did not pose some sort of threat.

If Henry was correct and the man was planning to ask for her hand, she would say yes. Easy to like and companionable, Percy was the perfect companion. He made her laugh. He acknowledged and even admired her intelligence. They enjoyed long discussions on all manner of interesting subjects. He was a wonderful friend.

A friend who never once attempted to take liberties.

Again her glance fell on Henry. She sincerely began to hope his prophecy came to fruition, because she certainly needed someone to rescue her from this mess of her own making.

Chapter Nineteen

ONE WEEK LATER

ABRINA LOOKED OUT THE RAIN-STREAKED WINDOWS AND frowned. Eugenia had sent a note inviting her to visit today, but she rather felt like staying indoors. Just as she turned, movement on the drive caught her eye. It was Falloure's carriage.

She went downstairs immediately.

"Shall I tell him you are not at home, my lady?" asked the butler.

"No. Bring him into the blue salon," she said and went to wait for him there. Mama was out and would no doubt be wroth with her for receiving him, but heaven knew she had little enough opportunity to have a private word with anyone these days.

"Thank you," she told the butler as he showed her guest in. "You may go. If my mother comes, please send her here."

Her unexpected guest bowed. "I apologize for coming unannounced."

"Is everything well?" she asked, growing concerned.

"Quite well. And I hope that it will be even better after you answer my question."

She froze.

"I feel we have become good friends, you and I. We enjoy each other's company, we share a common view on many things, and we understand and accept each other as we are. Such friendships are rare, priceless even. Even more rare is the marriage built upon such a solid foundation. So I will simply ask." He sank to one knee. "Sabrina, I know you are already besieged by offers, but I sincerely hope that you will do me the honor of accepting mine. Will you marry me?"

She hesitated. This was it, the moment she'd planned for and worked toward all Season. It was her moment of triumph. So why did it feel so empty?

Swallowing past the lump in her throat, she answered him. "I will." It didn't even sound like her own voice.

He stood and bent over to kiss her, and she obediently tilted her head upward, hoping to feel something, *anything* other than numbness or revulsion.

"Merciful God!"

Yelping in alarm, Sabrina sprang away.

Her mother stood in the doorway, staring at them in shock.

"Your ladyship, please accept my humblest apology," said Percy. "I meant to speak with you first, but you were not at home. Your daughter has just accepted my proposal."

"Sabrina, a private word. At once," her mother said in a voice like cool steel sliding back into its sheath. "You may wait in the hall," she commanded their guest.

Obediently, Percy stepped out to await the verdict.

Sabrina winced as her mother slammed the door behind him. "Mama, I know you favor Henry, but truly, this is for the best."

"Have you lost your mind entirely?" asked her mother loudly. "You know what kind of man he is!"

"Yes. I do. And he is *my* choice, Mama!" Calming herself, she lowered her voice. "You agreed to let me choose my husband, and I have. He is wealthy, titled, and he genuinely cares for me. Isn't that enough?"

"No! Not if you love someone else. And not if that someone loves you as well. And you know Henry loves you—a blind fool could see it."

"He has never said it," Sabrina countered. But she knew it was true, even if he had not actually spoken the words.

"You do not have to give Falloure an answer today. Let me send for—"

"I still wouldn't consider him. We are not suited."

Her mother stared at her for a long moment before she finally spoke. "I can see there is no point in trying to change your mind." Striding to the door, she paused. "I never thought any of my children would turn out to be cowards, least of all you. God help you both." She jerked it open and summoned Falloure.

Though she'd been cut to the quick, Sabrina pasted on a smile for her husband-to-be.

"You have declared your intent to marry my daughter," said her mother. "I find your proposal acceptable, provided your family is also agreeable to the match."

"My mother will certainly have no objection," assured Percy. "In fact, I believe she'll want us to marry as soon as possible."

Her mother stiffened. "I was going to suggest the beginning of next Season. Is there any particular reason for haste?"

"No, my lady." He flushed at the insinuation. "Other than the most respectful eagerness, I mean."

She relaxed. "Very well," said her mother. "If that is your wish and your parents are amenable, then I also see no point in delay. The end of June shall suffice."

Sabrina was both relieved and pleased. June wasn't that far off. Mama would forgive her as soon as she began producing grandchildren.

Sabrina stood in greeting when Fairford entered. "Good morning, my lord."

Stepping forward, he bowed and held out his hand, but she did not offer him her fingers, as had become her custom. He dropped his arm. "I was pleased to receive your summons and came as soon as possible—to hear good news, I hope."

There was no point in putting off the inevitable. "Lord Falloure has asked for my hand. I have accepted."

Fairford's wary mask fell away, replaced by incredulity. "Why in heaven's name would you marry that, that—"

"He is the logical choice," she cut in, casting a nervous glance toward the door. Mama had deigned to allow her a measure of privacy, but she was not far away.

"Logical? That you would choose him over me is, is incomprehensible! Montgomery I could understand, at least—but Falloure? I have put up with your indecision and Montgomery's insufferable interference in the hope of securing your favor, and now you tell me that this blackguard has charmed his way into your good graces in a matter of weeks?"

"My lord, I—"

"You cannot possibly love him!"

She flinched but did not back down. "We discussed this at length, my lord. I thought you understood I had no interest in a love match."

"I didn't think you actually meant it. Women often say one thing and mean the opposite." He ran a shaky hand through his hair.

"I am truly sorry, my lord," she said, again glancing at the door. "I genuinely regret any pain I may have caused—I assure you such was not my intent."

His normally cool gaze burned with fury, and his hands were clenched into fists. The situation was rapidly deteriorating.

"Please, my lord, you must under—"

"I have nothing more to say to you," he snapped. Turning on his heel, he stalked to the door, yanked it open, and pushed past the startled footman waiting on the other side.

She watched from the window as he stormed out of Aylesford House.

Nervous sweat trickled down between her breasts as her heart finally began to slow. Cold disdain she'd anticipated, but never an emotional outburst like that.

Drained by the encounter, she sat, just as the connecting door opened and her mother peeked through.

"I'd say that went rather well, all things considered."

"Not now, Mama. Please."

"You think that was difficult, just wait," said her mother. "There is still time to change your mind."

"I have made my decision, Mama. Now please, have pity and allow me a moment's peace before he arrives," Sabrina begged.

The door closed, and she sagged into the cushions. Henry would be here soon.

She stared at the ceiling, her thoughts racing. The clock struck the hour, and she looked up in surprise. Where had the time gone? She forced herself not to bolt from the room as the sound of someone being ushered through the front door echoed back down the hall.

Punctual, as always.

Steeling herself, she waited. It had to be done. *Better a little heartache now than complete devastation later*, she reasoned, twitching her skirts straight and taking a deep breath. With a stab of pain, the crack in her heart widened a little further as he entered wearing a happy smile. Her eyes devoured his face, taking in every detail, burning it into her memory.

His smile slowly vanished, replaced by a look of concern. "What's happened? Are you all right?"

She could not bear to look at him, yet could not tear her eyes away. With an iron will, she made her numb lips move. "I've made my decision and accepted an offer of marriage from Lord Falloure. We are to wed at the end of the Season. It's for the best. For both of us. You'll agree with me, one day."

"So fear has won the battle, then."

She did not answer.

Stepping forward, he grasped her shoulders, forcing her to look up at him. He bent, and as his lips moved gently over hers, her body rallied, responding to his touch with enthusiasm for one last time.

Giving back in full measure, she moaned softly, arching into him as his hands roamed down her back to mold her buttocks, pressing her closer.

After only a moment of bliss, however, she broke away, pushing feebly at his chest.

Reaching out, he tucked a stray strand of fiery hair behind a delicate ear. "I will remain in London until the day you wed. Should you change your mind—"

"I cannot." Closing her eyes, desperate to shut out the sight of him before it undid her completely, she waited.

One heartbeat.

Two.

Ten. The door closed with a soft click.

He was gone.

Her lungs felt like they would explode. She waited until his footsteps retreated into silence before quietly following him out. She had no desire to discuss with her mother what had just happened.

Upon reaching her chamber, she flung herself on the bed and sobbed until the light in the windows faded to darkness.

What have I done? her heart wailed.

The only wise thing, her mind answered.

Fairy tales were for children, and she was no child. It was time to grow up. Percy was a fine match, a reasonable match. In a few months' time, she would forget all about Henry and this horrible day. She would be preparing for a new life, a life of peace and domestic contentment.

You will never be able to forget him, her heart whispered, unwilling to be silenced.

Eyes she'd thought incapable of producing any more moisture began to well once more.

Chapter Twenty

ABRINA GAZED AT THE GLITTERING PROMISE ON HER finger. The large sapphire flickered becomingly against her pale skin, its richness set off by the small diamonds encircling it.

A smug gleam crept into Percy's eyes as he made his move.

She'd already made two mistakes this game and was well on the path to losing. A heavy sigh lodged in her throat. The things she'd always enjoyed seemed to have lost their appeal of late. Her next move was an attempt to distract her opponent from her queen's vulnerability.

He wasn't fooled in the least. "Three moves to checkmate."

She conceded.

"I hear Fairford approached Miss Bidewell again, and that she has agreed to give him another chance," he murmured, resetting the pieces for another game.

"Good for her," she replied, attempting to smile. "I hope they will be very happy."

"I hear Chadwick has also found a match."

This time her smile was not forced. "Has he?"

"It seems Miss Chatworth has taken a fancy to him." He warmed to the subject. "Caused quite a stir by accepting his offer. No one expected him to find a wife this Season, but I suppose you changed all that, didn't you, my dear? You seem to have a profound impact on everyone you meet."

He'd said it in admiration, she knew, but his words burned like a hot poker. She'd had an impact, all right. Never for as long as she lived would she forget the look in Henry's eyes when she told him she'd accepted this man's offer. Even now, a week later, when she expected the pain to be fading, it was as sharp as if it had only just happened.

Tears welled, and she ducked her head, busying herself with arranging the chess pieces just so until she regained control. She *had* to stop thinking about him!

"Sabrina?"

The rook in her hand tumbled to the floor as she jerked to attention, a guilty blush stealing up her neck and cheeks.

Percy watched her bend to retrieve the wayward piece. "Is your mother still arguing with you over the details of the ceremony?"

In spite of herself, she nearly laughed aloud, relieved he couldn't read her well enough to know what was *really* wrong with her. Had Henry been sitting there, he would have known exactly where her mind had wandered.

"I'm sorry, Percy. I'm just a bit out of sorts today."

"I've just the cure for your doldrums," he whispered with a wink. He hopped up to reseat himself beside her.

Before she could discern his intent, he kissed her.

A shock ran through her flesh at the contact. It seemed an age since she'd been held this way, and even though it wasn't Henry, her heart and body craved closeness with another human being.

She wriggled impatiently. It wasn't enough. He was being so gentle, so agonizingly slow! All she wanted was the feeling of Henry erased from her flesh, for Percy to ravish her and make her forget! Her fingers sank into the hair at the back of his head, pulling him closer.

Groaning, Percy dipped lower and softly kissed her neck. Exposing her shoulder, he traced a path downward with his lips. Before he reached the neckline of her gown, however, he stopped.

"Look at me."

She pulled at him, demanding that he continue.

"Look at me. Open your eyes."

Obediently, Sabrina cracked them open to find him staring down at her.

For a long moment, they just stared into each other's eyes.

Then, with a regretful sigh, Percy released her. "Sabrina, what is it you want of me?"

Taken aback, she blurted out her ready answer. "To marry you, of course. And to care for our home and our children."

He waved away her words. "I've heard that before. I mean, what do you want of me as a man?"

She shook her head, confused. "I don't under—"

"Do you care for me?"

"I'm extremely fond of you, Percy. You know that. I would not have accepted your proposal otherwise."

"But you do not love me."

Her heart stopped.

"Love is *not* what matters," she snapped. Damn it, she could not lose him now! "Stability and compatibility are the most important elements in a marriage, and you and I are eminently well suited in both areas. Not only that, but I consider you my friend. What better match can one possibly desire?"

"Ah, desire," he said, his eyes lighting briefly. "That's just it, don't you see? You don't desire me."

"I do!" she protested. "Why, just now, in your arms, I wanted you to—"

"Blot out his memory," he finished for her. A faint smile flickered across his lips. "I've comforted enough women in the aftermath of a disappointment to know such when I see it."

"I want to marry you," she insisted. But the look on his face said he didn't believe her. Panic grabbed her and squeezed her in an iron grip. "I cannot marry Henry," she said, her voice shaking.

Resignation crept into the set of his mouth. "You *are* in love with him, then."

"I am not," she insisted. "I will admit to there being some attraction between us, but I refuse to marry him simply because of a physical reaction when I can hardly stand to converse with the man." She placed her hand on his arm. "I would far rather spend a happy life as the wife of a man I genuinely like than chain myself to something as inconstant as passion."

"Sabrina, I would like nothing better than to make you happy, but you don't really want—"

"You *are* what I want!" Technically, it wasn't a lie. She did want him, just not in the same way she wanted Henry. *That* sort of want was madness. This sort of want was reasonable, manageable, safe. "When you proposed, you spoke of building a marriage on the solid foundation of our friendship." She looked up at him, desperate to reestablish that sentiment. "Percy, you are all I have ever desired in a husband. I am not in love with Henry. I wish only to marry you."

A defeated soul looked out from Percy's eyes for a moment before the habitual veil of cynicism fell over them once more. "Then alas for Percival Falloure, the *reformed* Terror of the Ton. If I am truly what you want, then I shall be glad of it and honor my offer."

Relief flooded through her. She was safe!

No, her pragmatic mind corrected. She would not be safe until she was married.

Over the next several weeks, Sabrina carefully maintained the brightest of smiles in public, giving every visible evidence of happy bridal anticipation.

But each night was spent in torment. She tried everything from chamomile tea and warm baths to reading until she could no longer keep her eyes open. Yet each morning, she still awakened with wet cheeks, her body filled with longing.

Each morning, she wondered if the ache in her heart would ever subside.

Henry's gifts she hid away, eschewing anything associated with him. Even so, her mind was constantly filled with remembrances. She found him in the smallest of things: a songbird's call, an elusive scent in the air. The irises in the bloody garden recalled the peculiar color of the man's eyes, for pity's sake!

He was everywhere—and nowhere.

Without Henry harassing her all the time, she felt oddly misplaced, lost. When she caught a glimpse of herself in the mirror these days, it was almost a shock. It felt as though some strange semblance of her was walking, dancing, smiling, and conversing with people. She felt removed from everything except the pain in her heart.

It'll get better with time. Just give it time, she told herself.

Her appetite all but disappeared. Everything tasted like ashes, and nothing, not even her favorite dishes, held any appeal anymore. Her generous curves slowly began to shrink, her cheekbones growing more and more prominent.

When her mother commented on her lack of color and gauntness of cheek, Sabrina panicked. Though it made her feel slightly ill, she forced herself to eat and had her maid begin applying cucumber poultices, creams, and subtle *maquillage* to her face to counter both her pallor and the dark circles beneath her eyes.

Although she detested such subterfuge, it was vital to maintain appearances.

Today, Madame Trillon's models paraded the latest Paris wedding fashions before her, her mother and sisters, and a select group of friends. Every female in the room was in an utter transport of delight—with the exception of herself. Though she tried her best to appear interested, she truly cared not which gown she ended up wearing.

When her mother expressed great admiration for one in particular, she let three more pass and then chose her mother's preference. Measurements were taken amid a flurry of giggles and teasing, and strict orders were given for her not to gain so much as an inch *anywhere*, lest the gown not fit properly on the happy day.

She didn't foresee that being a problem.

Arrangements were moving right along—at a snail's pace, it seemed. It was all she could do not to crawl out of her own skin. Impatience boiled just beneath her serene mask, impatience to be out of this house, out of London. How she yearned for new surroundings, to be in a place with no memories to haunt her! Memories of her father, of happy times with her sisters...of *Henry*.

It was high time to move on, to set aside the past and look to the future. The end of the Season just couldn't arrive soon enough.

Chapter Twenty-One

ENRY STAGGERED OUT OF WHITE'S, LISTING LIKE A rudderless ship, insensate to the chill rain pelting his bent head and bowed shoulders.

His carriage pulled up, and the footman opened the door.

Straightening, Henry advanced with purpose—and banged the top of his head against the doorframe. Clutching his skull, he released a stream of invective and clumsily dragged himself the rest of the way up onto the plush squabs.

"My lord?" the footman inquired, concerned for the trickle of crimson running down his master's forehead.

Having at the moment no tolerance for being fussed over like a wayward child, Henry reached out and grabbed for the door, intending to snatch it shut. In his haste, however, he overreached and tumbled out of the vehicle, headfirst, into the street.

Several passersby laughed outright at the sight of his high and mighty lordship wallowing in the gutter.

Henry groaned, partly due to the pain blossoming in his head, partly due to the smell emanating from the muck now covering the majority of his person, but mostly due to a distant sense of humiliation. This would be all over London by morning.

Carefully bracing himself on the footplate, he stood and removed his soiled cloak, tossing it on the floor of the carriage before clambering in after it. This time, he allowed the footman to assist him and close the door behind him.

His once-shiny boots were now covered in mud, manure, and heaven only knew what else. With great difficulty and much cursing, he removed one and emptied it of the foul liquid it contained, forgetting for the moment that he was *inside* his carriage.

Cursing yet again, he thumped the roof to signal the driver. As the vehicle lurched into motion, he prayed he made it home without adding further to the stink in here—or his own humiliation.

Tonight had been the worst yet. Unable to find rest, he'd ventured down to the club, knowing Percy would not be there, as he was escorting his fiancée to the Yardley ball.

The thought was enough to make his stomach threaten to turn itself inside out—again.

A few rounds of cards, yes. A pleasant distraction. That was what he'd needed. A laugh or two, yes. And a pipe. And a drink.

Perhaps several.

A complete disaster.

He'd done this to himself. He'd brought a cat in to chase off a mouse, and the cat had unwittingly bitten him instead. It wasn't Percy's fault. After all, the man had asked him several times about his feelings for her, and he'd denied any sentiment other than a desire to protect her. He should have told the truth from the beginning and not been such a coward.

He'd lost her.

And now she was marrying his friend. She would get exactly what she'd told him she wanted.

At least she'll be safe from Fairford, he reasoned. And Percy would be good to her. As good as she expected, anyway.

It was small comfort in the face of the misery he was currently experiencing, but at this particular juncture, he would take what comfort he could.

Finally, blessedly, they reached their destination. Two footmen helped Henry out, managing to haul him halfway up the steps before he shook them off. After stumbling and bruising his shins twice, he finally allowed them to help him the rest of the way into the house.

Looking utterly dismayed, his valet took his ruined cloak. His eyes widened as he noticed one of Henry's boots was missing. "M'lord?"

"Not now, Watkins," Henry slurred, batting the man's hands away as he pitched toward the bed.

"But, my lord! You *cannot* go to bed in your present state!"

The note of hysteria in his voice made Henry stop. He looked down at himself. God, he stank! The odor emanating from his fouled garments was absolutely astonishing. They would have to be burned.

Thirty minutes later, he sat in the tub, watching curls of steam roll off the surface of the water. The scent of soap mingled with the strong, acrid smell of coffee as Watkins brought him another cup. Gratefully, he took it.

"M'lord?"

Wearily, Henry turned to face his inquisitor.

"Forgive my presumption, but wouldn't it be better to busy yourself elsewhere for a while?" he suggested delicately. "Paris, perhaps?"

Henry shook his head, wincing at the sharp pain it caused. There was no such thing as a secret in London. Servants always knew. "I shall remain in London until after the wedding."

Even through the lingering fog of inebriation, he knew he'd sulked long enough.

"You look ravishing," said Percy.

She knew he meant it. The deep-lilac silk was a perfect complement to her coloring, as were the amethysts adorning her neck, wrists, and ears. She had worn this gown specifically for him, knowing his love of the color. Her hair was piled high in his favorite style, too, with cascading curls down her back.

"You look rather charming, yourself," she said, inspecting his attire with approval. His jacket was an exquisite confection of violet silk with velvet trim in a deeper shade, picked with gold embroidery and tiny diamonds. Layer upon layer of frothy lace spilled from his neck and cuffs, too.

He looked like a perfect fairy-tale prince—and if ever she had need of one, it was now. Tonight was the dreaded Pembroke ball. She would have to face Henry and his family one last time.

Percy had tried to convince her it was unnecessary to attend, but she insisted on going. She *had* to attend, if only to prove to Henry that she was truly happy.

The affection in Percy's eyes changed to wariness as his gaze shifted above her shoulder. "Good evening, Countess."

Sabrina turned, astonished to see her mother descending the stair. She was dressed in mauve silk, diamonds, and pearls. "I thought you weren't coming?"

Her mother smiled, shaking her head and setting the diamonds at her ears to swinging. "I never said I was not. I wouldn't miss the second most important ball of the Season. Not even under the circumstances."

An hour later, Sabrina strove to exude confidence as they entered Pembroke's grand ballroom. All of London was salivating in anticipation, she knew. Tonight would provide grist for the gossip mill no matter what happened.

Percy was a solid comfort at her elbow as her friends greeted her with undisguised wonderment. Clearly, no one had expected her to show her face here.

Eugenia came at once and appropriated her arm. "Lady Bidewell has just let slip that her daughter will wed Lord Fairford on June twenty-fourth—the day before *your* wedding," she said. "The spiteful cow is deliberately trying to upstage you."

Sabrina could not care less which day Miss Bidewell chose, but for her sister's sake, she made a show of concern. "I wonder how she could have known. We have not yet publicly announced the date. Mama only ordered the invitations last week. Perhaps it was merely chance that made her select that day."

"Ha!" Eugenia said, scoffing. "There are a limited number of calligraphers in London. I'd be willing to wager she made inquiries and bribed the one Mama hired to give her the date. I also heard that she hired the same couturier."

"At Mama's recommendation, no doubt," Sabrina cut in, trying to calm her. "She was helping Lady Bidewell with her daughter's launch, remember?"

Eugenia crossed her arms stubbornly. "Even so, it is unconscionable that she should infringe so upon your plans in this manner." Suddenly, her narrowed eyes grew as round as saucers.

Sabrina's heart began to pound. She turned, and there he was.

"May I have the honor, my lady?" asked Henry, holding out his hand.

Her head dipped in acquiescence before her mouth could decline. She could not refuse the host, in any case, she reasoned. And this would be the last time they ever danced.

She scarcely felt the ground beneath her feet for the insistent drumming in her veins. Everything that had dimmed and dulled into an endless landscape of blurred grey over the past several weeks sprang back into vivid color and clarity. Every nerve in her body was alive and possessed by longing.

"You are unhappy," he said simply.

"I would not be if you would simply leave me alone," she said with heat. "Henry, please. You must understand that I cannot just—"

"Trust in my love?" he supplied. "I do love you, Sabrina. Surely you must know it by now."

All at once, her eyes filled. Love. The one word her heart wanted so badly to believe in, to trust in—and couldn't.

"Marry me, Sabrina," he urged. "Say yes, and I will make you the happiest woman on earth. I swear on my very life that I will never betray you."

His midnight eyes were so earnest, so intense and full of feeling. The thought of them dulling over the years as his love for her turned into resigned tolerance—or worse—was unbearable.

"I cannot," she choked out as the music drew to a close. Disengaging, she turned and forced herself to walk away from him.

She must find Percy and leave. Immediately. The border was only a few days' ride away. It took a while to locate her affianced. She walked into the room, the estate's office of all places, just as he was filling his glass. Her relief on seeing him was like a cool bath. "Thank heaven I finally found you."

Percy downed the liquor and then plunked the empty crystal goblet on the mantelpiece.

Coming right up to him, she placed her hands on his chest, intending to stretch up and kiss him. He staggered backward a little, as though caught off balance. The clumsy motion startled her. Usually he was so controlled and elegant in his movements.

"Percy, I want to get married right away," she said in a rush. "I don't want to wait. If we take your carriage now, we can be in Scotland in less than three days. We'll have a good head start. No one will be leaving here for hours yet."

He stared at her for a moment. "You want to run for Gretna Green?"

"Yes. Right now. This very minute."

"Why?"

"We can purchase a change of clothing at one of the inns along the way when we stop to eat," she pressed on. "It's only for a few days, and then we'll be back in London again. It'll be an adventure!" she added.

"Sabrina, I asked you a question. Why, of a sudden, do you crave an anvil wedding?"

"I simply don't wish to wait any longer," she told him quite truthfully. "We both know what we want, and I think it's pointless to wait any longer to have it."

"Do you think me a complete fool? Sabrina, it's no good. I saw you with Henry."

Her stomach clenched. "A final farewell. I told you, I've made my choice," she said, grasping him by the shoulders.

He pulled back and shook his head slowly from side to side. "Don't. It's not enough, Sabrina."

She blinked, not understanding. "Not enough?"

"I know now that I want what I saw in your eyes when you looked at him. And that's something I can never have from you. You are fond of me, and perhaps in time you might come to feel more, but I would have to be content with only a corner of your heart. I was a bloody fool to think I could ever be satisfied with that as my lot."

"But you and I were agreed regarding what we consider essential to a successful marriage. I thought you understood—"

"I cannot marry you, Sabrina. To do so would only result in misery for us both. And for Henry." His mouth twisted.

"You are breaking our engagement?" The words came out only faintly.

"Go to him, Sabrina, and be happy. Marry Henry. It's him you want, not me. He loves you, you know. He asked me to help him protect you, and I wondered then if he felt more for you than he claimed. He denied it then, but I know now that he is in love with you—just as much as you are in love with him." He looked down, as though unable to meet her gaze any longer. "He is a good man. The very best, in fact. You could not ask for a better husband than he will be to you. Far better than I would have been, despite all of my good intentions."

Shock raced through her, burning down her spine with an unpleasant stinging sensation. Marry Henry? After all she'd done to avoid it? This was a nightmare. Nothing had worked out as she'd planned. *Nothing.*

She backed toward the door, grasping its handle with shaking fingers. "I cannot," she said roughly. "If you will not marry me, then I shall find another, but not him. Never him." She turned the handle and fled.

Chapter Twenty-Two

*D*AWN ARRIVED FAR TOO SOON, ITS RELENTLESS, GOLDEN beams prying Sabrina's swollen eyelids open against their will. Her head ached abominably, her face felt puffy, and her nose was as raw as butcher's beef. Rolling over, she buried her head beneath a pillow. "How on earth am I going to get out of this?" she groaned.

Percy would let her announce the end of their engagement, of course. He would leave it to her and accept whatever excuse she gave out, for he was far too much of a gentleman to tell anyone he'd been the one to call it off.

Would yet another man be willing to brave the notorious woman who'd chewed her way through four suitors in one Season? Hope struggled to stay alive in her. It was possible. It had to be. After all, women who'd suffered far worse events still married, and married well. She rose and, after applying cool cloths to her eyes to reduce the soreness and swelling, dressed. She ate breakfast in silence, taking only toast and weak tea. Truth be told, she hadn't the stomach for much else, in spite of her perfectly healthy constitution.

"I've noted your lack of appetite of late, Sabrina. You are not with child, I hope," her mother murmured quietly after the servants left.

Startled, Sabrina looked up. "Mama, surely you don't think I would do something so foolish? Heaven knows I've better sense than that."

"Heaven may have confidence in your good judgment, daughter, but I've been questioning it for quite some time," her mother said snippily. "Given your fiancé's reputation, I and the rest of London will consider it a miracle if your first child isn't born several months 'early.'"

Fiancé. Sabrina glanced down at the ring on her finger. She'd forgotten to give it back. And that blessed oversight had just saved her from having to make any unpleasant explanations—at least for the time being, provided he didn't immediately demand the token's return. "Then I suppose you'd better prepare to be astonished," she said, lashing back with quiet venom, "for I remain as God intended until I am married."

"Wonders will never cease," her mother said, ignoring her show of temper.

Sabrina rose. "You wrongly malign him, Mama, and I find myself quite dismayed to learn your opinion of me as well. You must excuse me. My head has begun to ache again, and I wish to return to my chambers."

She stayed out of sight until her mother left to fulfill her social obligations. It was midafternoon before she ventured down to the morning room for a change of scenery.

She needed to get around the problem of Percy's defection without her mother or Henry finding out about it. If he did, he'd offer himself up as a replacement, and she'd have no choice but to accept or become a spinster aunt. She grimaced at the idea, but it was better than the convent.

The church! If Augusta had spoken true about her husband's brother having a tender place for her, then perhaps there was still hope. *I wonder if he would actually consider me?*

Squeezing her eyes shut, she shook her head to rid it of ridiculous thoughts. Marrying Saint Peter was not an option.

What am I to do?

She heard a noise behind her and turned, expecting to see one of the servants. It was Fairford. Squealing in alarm, she rose "What are you doing here?"

He held a finger to his lips. "There isn't much time, so I shall come straight to the point. I know Falloure has abandoned you, Sabrina. And I know you think you've no other choice but to accept Montgomery. I've come to offer you an alternative." With no warning, he knelt at her feet and pulled a ring from his coat pocket. "Come away with me, instead. We can flee to Scotland and—"

Her astonishment was complete. "You still want me? Even after—"

"I regret my harsh words," he said. "My only excuse was a bruised heart. I beg you to reconsider."

There was a God in heaven, and He'd just given her the answer to all of her problems.

"I will," she whispered, her head reeling. "I will marry you, my lord."

"I promise you'll never regret it, my darling."

Reaching down, he pulled Falloure's ring from her finger and tossed it into the ashes in the hearth, replacing it with his own. He kissed her then, forcing his tongue deep into her mouth.

When he broke away, she just stood there with her eyes closed, gripping the back of the chair for support. No, she didn't desire him. Just the opposite. And thus she would marry him.

"I'll come for you tonight at the third hour," he said, looking over his shoulder at the door with concern. "Meet me by the east gate, and bring only what you must, for we travel lightly. We'll ride to the edge of the city and meet my carriage there."

He ground his mouth hard against hers one last time before fleeing.

Forcing what she hoped passed for a happy smile, Sabrina waited until the door closed behind him before wiping her lips and giving in to the urge to shudder in disgust.

Pocketing Fairford's ring, she knelt and picked Percy's out of the ashes, looking at it with regret. It would have been far better to marry him. She had at least enjoyed his company. But he'd given her little other choice.

Her course was clear. Wiping the ring clean with a corner of her underskirt, she put it back on her finger. Then she retired to her chambers and rang for her maid to come help her undress.

When her mother returned a few hours later, she came to her chambers. "I believe I understand now the source of your illness last night and this morning," she said gently, coming to sit beside her on the bed. "Lady Brixton told me everything, my dear. I think that perhaps I might have been a bit more harsh with you than you deserved."

Sabrina's gut tightened painfully. Had someone else witnessed her humiliation last night?

"It is obvious to me now that for all of his seeming awkwardness, the man is a practiced seducer, a wolf in sheepskin," continued her mother. "They will have to be married by special license at once, of course. The scandal of it has all but sent Lady Chatworth to her bed in hysterics."

Her mind raced. *Chatworth…*

"And in the library, of all things! No one doubts that it was a deliberate slap at both you and Henry," her mother added with heat.

Sabrina's confusion evaporated, and she breathed again. Good heavens, she'd thought Mama was referring to her having been jilted by Percy. As her fear receded, happiness took its place. Chadwick had compromised Miss Chatworth! She put her head down to hide lips that twitched with the effort it took to keep a smile from forming on them. And, apparently, he'd done it in Henry's library. A laugh tried to escape, but she choked it back.

Clearly mistaking her reaction for a show of grief, her mother looked at her with sympathetic eyes. "I'm so very sorry, my dear. It must have come as a great shock."

"I shall recover in time, I'm sure," Sabrina said, keeping her head down.

"That's the spirit, dear. If it is a disappointment for you, think of poor Miss Chatworth. And her family, of course. Lady Chatworth thought to have the Earl of Scarborough for a son-in-law, for he'd just begun to pay court to Melissa. Now those plans are in ruins, along with her daughter's reputation."

"Yes, of course," Sabrina mumbled. She did not like to think how her own family would react upon discovering her deception. Miss Chatworth's scandal would pale in comparison to the uproar she was about to cause.

"Now then, we must maintain our dignity. A good beginning would be to show support for poor Melissa," said her mother. "It isn't her fault, after all—well, not entirely. She was duped by that trickster." She hesitated, then: "Sabrina, I want you to know that henceforth I shall endeavor to be more civil toward Lord Falloure. Even if he is not my preference, he has at least behaved honorably. For that, at least, we may be grateful."

Inside, Sabrina cringed.

Later that night, she tossed and turned, unable to find a comfortable position in her corset. Tying the blasted thing had been difficult without any help, but she'd succeeded, though only just. A great deal of twisting and wriggling had secured it on her person tightly enough that it wouldn't slide down, at least.

Sleep eluded her, so she arose and lit the lamp, trimming it so that it cast only the dimmest light. A blanket at the bottom of her door and a kerchief stuffed in the keyhole ensured no one passing would suspect she was awake.

Padding over to her writing desk, she sat. Crisp parchment stared back at her, awaiting the stroke of the pen that would transform it into a blade to bury in a man's heart. Henry would never forgive her.

Determined not to cry, she yanked Percy's ring off her finger and set it on the desk. Digging in her pocket, she pulled out Fairford's and crammed it on. The gem sat heavy on her hand, seeming to carry with it the weight of all her guilt and grief. She stared at it with unseeing eyes until the ticking of the clock slowly intruded.

Parchment and ink waited patiently, but time would not.

One hour and several ruined sheets later, she sprinkled sand and passed the blotter over her finished missive. Rolling it up tightly, she slipped the little tube through Percy's ring and left it on her pillow. Then she took up her boots in one hand and stuffed a small bundle beneath her other arm.

With her meager possessions, Sabrina tiptoed down the hall in silence. The servants should all be asleep at this hour, but there was always a chance someone might be up and about, sneaking to the kitchens to pinch a snack or on their way to a tryst.

Her father's estate office was dark but for the thin moonlight pooling beneath the windows. Carefully, she picked her way over to the french doors. It had been so long since they'd been opened that the lock was stiff, and the click sounded like a cannon shot in her ears when it finally gave. After a quick pause to be sure no one had heard, she opened the door, wincing as the hinges protested faintly in their outward swing.

Cool night air fanned her face as she sat and tugged on her boots. Rising, she stepped out onto the path and turned to close the door. Now that it had been opened, however, it refused to shut. Whispering an oath, she propped it closed with a rock and slipped into the night.

"Come," Fairford whispered, stepping from the shadows. He mounted his horse and held out a hand. "We must depart with all haste. The faster we leave London behind, the better."

Nodding, she passed her bundle up and allowed him to pull her into the saddle before him. Through quiet streets they rode, carefully avoiding the watch as well as London's other, less savory denizens. When they at last reached his carriage, he helped her in and then went to speak briefly with the driver and his valet, who was traveling with them. When finished, he climbed in and sat across from her.

She smiled at him, a quick, nervous smile.

"You have no reason to be worried," he told her as the carriage lurched into motion. "I shall see to everything."

"I have complete confidence in your abilities, my lord."

She stared, watching as the light from the setting moon illuminated his face. In this light, his hair appeared white, reminding her suddenly of Miss Bidewell. In her rush to get out of her own predicament, she'd completely forgotten that he was engaged to her. Now, she could not help but wonder how much of his amorous proposal this afternoon was due to a desire to escape marrying her. She said nothing of it, however, and instead closed her eyes.

Poor Miss Bidewell. She doubted very much whether the girl would be as lucky as she was. If her erstwhile rival had disliked her before, she would positively *loathe* her now. She did not look forward to facing the young lady's censure, however well deserved, when she returned to London.

Above all, she did not look forward to seeing Henry again. Perhaps he would be kind and spare her the pain of an ugly confrontation.

Chapter Twenty-Three

*I*T WAS JUST NOW NINE O'CLOCK. WHAT IN HEAVEN'S NAME was taking so long? Henry paced the length and breadth of the salon again, waiting.

When Lady Aylesford at last arrived, consternation was written in the sharp line between her brows. "Henry, I'm afraid Sabrina won't come down. Her door is locked. I've knocked, I've tried talking to her, but she refuses to answer. I don't know what else to d—"

"He has broken off the engagement."

"What?" She sat abruptly, stunned.

"She begged him to elope to Scotland after I danced with her. He refused and withdrew his suit."

"But...she said nothing!"

"If she hasn't told you yet, it's probably because she's hoping he'll change his mind. But he won't. He came to me this morning and told me everything. I've come to ask you for her hand and to request your aid in convincing her to accept my offer. I went this morning and obtained a special license. We can be married today."

"I shall fetch her immediately."

Only a few moments later, he heard her panicked voice calling. He arrived just as she was giving orders to a burly footman to break down her daughter's door. When it lay in ruins, they burst into an empty room.

He saw at once that the bed had been slept in, but where was Sabrina? His eye fell on a curious object resting on the pillow. Coming closer, he saw it was a roll of parchment bound by a sapphire ring. Snatching it up, he tore off the ring and began to read. Halfway down the page, he felt the air leave his lungs. "She's eloped with Fairford."

"Oh my God," she gasped, all the color leaving her face. "Does it say where they've gone?"

"No." Pain blossomed in his chest, but he shoved it away. Pain could be dealt with later. What he needed now was information.

"Have they made for Gretna Green, do you think?" she asked. "Or might he have done the same as you and procured a special license? They might already be married by now."

His face grew grim. "If so, it will not be a long marriage."

"Henry, you know there might not be anything we can—"

"You don't understand," he interrupted. "I had Fairford investigated, and what we uncovered was more than disturbing. The man is a monster, and I cannot allow her to marry him. We must send riders out to check the roads north for their progress."

"What is it?" she exclaimed. "What is so horrible that you look as though you've seen a ghost? Tell me!"

"My lady, Lord Falloure has arrived," a servant interrupted.

"Show him in," Henry commanded him, before the astonished mistress of the house could open her mouth. "If they are no longer engaged, then why is he here?" he asked her.

"To tell Lady Aylesford my news in person and to try and talk some sense into Sabrina," said Percy from the doorway. He pushed past the servant and entered. "Looks like you've beaten me to the mark. Again."

Lady Aylesford snatched the note and thrust it at Percy, along with the ring. "She's gone and run off with Fairford!"

He paled. "How long?"

"My God, do you know something as well? Does everyone know except me?" she asked.

Henry came and grasped her shoulders. "How long, Auntie? It's important."

"I did not go to bed until just after midnight, and I heard movement in her room as I passed. It had to have been sometime between midnight and dawn."

"We must go after them," he said, looking at Percy again.

"What about that Childers woman? Might she know where he's taken her?" asked Percy.

Henry shook his head. "She's his creature...she'll tell us nothing, and even if she did, we can't take the chance of trusting her. She might misdirect our efforts out of loyalty to her benefactor." He paused and then squared his shoulders. "But there is another source we might try. I know where he is keeping the girl he bought from Boucher. We shall go at once."

"And I shall accompany you," said Lady Aylesford, rising.

He shook his head. "This is no task for a gently raised female. Percy and I will deal with this. You stay here and see to sending men to search for her in London and on the roads north."

"You expect me to sit here and wring my hands, waiting for news, worrying myself into a state? I think not! This is *my* daughter, and I am the Countess of Aylesford. I shall go where I bloody well please, and you cannot prevent it."

She rang for service and demanded that her carriage be brought around immediately. While they waited for it, she gave the household staff strict orders regarding the matter of her daughter's disappearance—specifically their silence.

Drawing Henry aside, she lowered her voice. "As for sending out a search party, I have no desire to alert the whole of London to the fact that my daughter has run off with Fairford. If we can find her before anything has happened, I would much rather find a quiet resolution."

He nodded, knowing her intent.

An hour and a half later, the carriage stopped at a plain house, one of a row of similar, nondescript houses on a quiet street. Another carriage full of footmen in Aylesford livery stopped just behind.

"It looks more respectable than I anticipated," stated Lady Aylesford.

"Fairford has no interest in people finding out about his proclivities," Henry muttered, leaping down. "No one would suspect him of keeping a mistress here among the gentry."

The curtains at the window twitched. Someone knew they were here.

Henry walked up and forcefully banged the knocker.

No answer.

"If you do not grant me entrance, I will have the King's Guard grant it for me," he barked, his voice echoing back down the street.

The door cracked open, and a wizened face peered out from the narrow aperture.

"I'm looking for a young Frenchwoman," he told her, not bothering with niceties.

"Ye hae the wrong house, yer lordship. There's naught 'ere but meself and me granddaughter," the old woman croaked in a thick brogue.

"I'll make that determination." He forced his way past her, and the others followed.

A pair of burly men stepped out and blocked the way to the stairs.

Henry drew a pistol and cocked it just as the rest of his group piled in behind. "Is it worth your lives?" he asked softly, leveling the weapon and twitching aside his coat to reveal a second pistol at his waist.

The guards were unprepared for armed intruders and backed off. "His lordship paid us to see the girl didn't escape...he didn't say nothing about staving off nobs with guns," said one, putting up his hands.

"Very wise of you," Henry replied. "See they don't bother us," he commanded those following him.

Four footmen remained behind to see to the task, while the other two accompanied him up the narrow stair. At the top was another door, locked.

"On three," Henry whispered. He and Percy stood side by side and, on the count of three, kicked it down.

Before them lay a bed containing a woman curled up and facing away from them. She gave no indication of having heard them enter.

Lady Aylesford stepped inside, peered into the gloom, and gasped in horror.

Henry couldn't have agreed more. Ugly red weals criss-crossed the woman's back, some of them still raw and oozing, and purpling bruises blossomed across her body. When he came closer, he saw there were many, many scars. Back, ribs, legs, wrists, ankles—all were covered by a fine lacework of pain.

"My God," the countess whispered, tears springing into her eyes. "You poor child!"

Hearing them, the girl tried to turn. She cried out in pain, but it was only the weakest of sounds.

"Don't move," Henry said gently. "We'll come around." What manner of monster could do this to another human being? "Go back down and help the others," he ordered the footmen, strug-gling to maintain a steady voice. "We'll call if we need you."

"Poor, poor child!" she again whispered, kneeling beside the bed to gently brush the girl's hair back, ignoring the dried blood and vomit fouling the tangled mass. "She is so young, no more than sixteen!"

Henry saw that her beautiful face was unmarred, save for the tearstains streaking it. The rest of her, however, had been ravaged. It would have taken months to cause such scarring in her young flesh. Months of what could only be called brutal torture. What he saw up close made the bile rise in his throat. Forcing control to return, he grabbed the coverlet, draping it over her prone form. "Never did I imagine *this*," he muttered softly. "I knew he was a sick bastard, but I never thought—"

"We cannot let this happen to Sabrina!" the countess interjected, looking up at him. "I will kill him myself before I allow it!"

The girl stirred again and struggled to lift her head.

"She's been drugged," Henry announced. He reached out and gently lifted an eyelid. "Laudanum. A lot, from the look of it. It's a wonder she's alive. I imagine vomiting was the only thing that saved her."

"We have to get her out of here," Percy whispered. "We cannot leave her like this! He'll be back, and those men downstairs, they had to have had something to do with it!"

"I would not leave a *dog* in this place!" Henry growled from between clenched teeth, enraged. "Help me move her. Can you see if there are any clothes for her? We'll just wrap her in the sheet for now. Percy, help me take her to the carriage." Once they had her body covered, he bellowed for two footmen. "Grab some clean pillows and blankets, and take them to the carriage," he ordered.

"And these," said Lady Aylesford, shoving an armful of clothing at one of them.

The girl cried out weakly as Henry and Percy tried to maneuver her into a sitting position and wrap the sheet around her more securely.

"I'm so sorry to cause you further pain," Henry murmured at her ear, "but you cannot remain here. We are taking you home with us."

Several hours later, Henry and Percy sat outside the room where the physician attended the girl.

The man came out, shaking his head. "She will live, but she has been severely damaged."

Henry felt ill as the healer cataloged her injuries and left them with medicine for when she awakened. All he could do now was wait and pray.

"She is conscious," called Lady Aylesford a few hours later.

"I am glad to see you awake," he said softly, coming to stand at her bedside.

The girl shrank away from him. "Where am I? Where is my child?" she whispered in French as her gaze darted around the room.

"You are in my house, and you are safe here, my dear," answered Lady Aylesford, switching to the girl's language. "This is Henry, and he will not harm you. He is my friend, and he helped bring you here."

Tears leaked from beneath the girl's lids as she clenched them tightly shut. "I am not in heaven?"

"No, child."

Her eyes opened. "If I am not dead, then he will find me," she whispered.

"Fairford will never touch you again," Henry promised, overwhelmed by pity. She was absolutely terrified.

But his words didn't seem to register, and she began to cry in earnest. "He will know, he will come, and he will kill me. He has said that he will never let me go."

"Shh. He will not come here. You are safe at Aylesford House, my dear," said Lady Aylesford.

The girl sucked in a sharp breath, her eyes growing wide.

"You know the name?" Henry asked as calmly as possible.

"*Oui.* My master spoke often of a Lady Aylesford and her daughter."

"I am Lady Aylesford," said the countess. "Can you tell me where Fairford is right now?"

The girl turned toward Lady Aylesford. "He said last night that he is to marry your daughter today. Do not let him, my lady! He is an evil man."

"He has taken Lady Aylesford's daughter from this house," Henry said to the girl, cutting off the countess's cry of anguish. "Do you know where he has gone?"

"He said he would be away for several days at a place called Gretna Green," the girl answered.

Henry swore softly as he rose from the bedside.

"Let me come with you," said Percy, who'd been listening.

"No. I need you here in case Fairford has played another one of his tricks to throw off a pursuit. If he has, then he's still somewhere in town and will soon learn that we have taken the girl. You must see to her protection and that of Lady Aylesford."

"And what if he has done as you say and Sabrina has married him?"

Henry smiled grimly. "Then the marriage shall be very short-lived." Turning, he made for the stables.

Chapter Twenty-Four

ABRINA STARED OUT THE WINDOW. FAIRFORD WAS QUIET, having said that he preferred to sit in silence rather than attempting to make conversation over the noise of the wheels. Silence suited her just fine. There wasn't much to discuss, anyway. In another day they would be married, and she would have the rest of her life to try and make small talk with him.

They traveled as fast as safety and the endurance of the horses allowed, and the first leg of their journey was long and uneventful. The little market town of Harborough provided a change of team that afternoon while they stopped for a quick meal, and then it was onward once more.

Despite her companion's placid demeanor, Sabrina couldn't shake off a growing sense of unease. It mounted as the day wore into evening, until she felt positively fidgety. Wedding nerves, she supposed. Her heart scoffed at such a shallow excuse, and she smothered any further thoughts along that line. What was done was done; there was no going back now.

The sun was grazing the western horizon, throwing them into deep shadow as they left the rutted road and approached an inn on the southern outskirts of Leeds. It was a decent establishment, one that catered to wealthier clientele than the dilapidated, rather unsavory places they'd passed in the smaller villages along the way.

Scotland was only a day away. They could have ridden through the night on horseback and been there by noon, but Sabrina was just as glad he'd not suggested it. Travel at night was never safe—and truth be told, she was in somewhat less of a hurry than she'd been the day before.

Fairford got out and immediately made a beeline for the inn, not waiting for her to disembark. She took a moment to stretch sore, stiff muscles. Annoyed at having been left behind without any offer of assistance, she entered the inn's dim interior, her eyes adjusting slowly to the hazy glow of firelight and candles.

"A room for myself and my bride," Fairford was saying to the innkeeper, a rotund, bald-pated man of some fifty years.

Stalking over, Sabrina interrupted. "Pardon me, good sir, but we require *two* rooms. We are not yet married."

Fairford turned to her, clearly irritated and trying his best not to show it. "We'll be married by this time tomorrow, my dove. Why bother with the conventions at this late hour?"

"Because no matter how far I've gone beyond the rules of society, I will not defy our Lord's. I will not sleep with a man who is not my husband," she snapped, turning away to hide her fright.

The innkeeper grinned, his moustaches parting to show several gaps between pitted, yellow teeth. "Goin' tae the Green, are ye?" he laughed in his thick brogue. "Yer a good girl y'are, tae make 'im wait 'til the vows is said afore lettin' 'im 'neath yer skirts! Two rooms it is, then." He showed them to her room first. "My finest, an' happy it is I am tae hae the business."

Sabrina looked around with mild apprehension. She'd never stayed at an inn before. She noted the worn shine on the bed's wooden posts, and the faded cloth of the canopy and bed hangings. Immediately, she went and examined the mattress. No evidence of infestation, at least. She'd heard horrifying tales of insects that bit one in the night. The hearth was swept clean, and the floor as well.

"It will suffice," she pronounced.

She listened as Fairford's valet ordered the maids to bring in his master's sheets from the carriage and put them on her bed. He then demanded of the innkeeper that the guests in the neighboring room be moved so that his master could take up residence next to his bride—for her protection.

After a quick toilette, Sabrina came down to join her affianced for dinner in the common room. The inn's other guests sat in the dim corners, covertly eyeing their finery. At one point, she saw Fairford lay a hand on the hilt of the sword hanging at his side and look each man in the eye. There would be no trouble here.

The fare was nothing fancy, despite the owner's boasts. Roasted capon, new potatoes, and carrots swam in a thin, distinctly unimpressive sauce. Cotters' food. Still, it was hot, plentiful, and welcome after the long journey. Sabrina finished hers as quickly as manners allowed and then rose. "I am most weary from our travels, my lord. I bid you good night." She dipped a polite curtsey.

Rising, Fairford bowed. "Are you certain you do not wish me to accompany you?"

Sabrina shook her head. "Thank you, my lord, but you need not trouble yourself. I well remember the way." It came out rather more sharply than she'd intended.

Stiffly, he bowed acquiescence.

Sabrina fled to her chamber and immediately barred the door behind her, sliding a heavy trunk across the floor to brace against it, for good measure.

A tub of hot water had been brought up while she'd dined, and she availed herself of it with gratitude. An hour and a half later, as she was drying her hair by the fire, the sound of someone entering the room next door made her wonder just how thick the walls were. She recognized Fairford's voice, along with that of his valet. Their conversation came through with crystal clarity.

"Victory is mine, Grimsby," said Fairford. "Impertinent chit. She'll be a pleasure to break, I tell you. By this time tomorrow night, the wench will properly respect her lord and master."

"Yes, m'lord," said another voice—Grimsby's.

Sabrina wrapped a blanket around her and padded cautiously over to the wall, not daring to sit on the bed for fear of making some noise that might be heard on the other side.

"I'll stick her 'til she begs for mercy," Fairford boasted, slurring a little. "And when her belly's full, I'll find another little sparrow to tickle. Once the babe is born, so long as it's male, I'll no longer have need of her."

"And if it's a girl?" asked Grimsby.

"Well, I'll simply have to keep plowing the field until I get a *proper* result, won't I?" laughed Fairford.

Though disgusted by his vulgarity, Sabrina reasoned that it was only what she'd expected—wanted, even. He would get her with child and then send her away to live in peace. The delicate clinking of crystal carried through the thin barrier. He must be pouring another drink.

"You should get some rest, m'lord," said Grimsby. "You've not slept since yesterday."

"Yes, yes, I know! Stop your fussing! You're worse than an old woman," Fairford grumbled. "I shan't disappoint the bride, I assure you. I promise you'll hear my little redbird sing out tomorrow night when I prick her."

A loud thump, as of a boot dropping to the floor, sounded, followed by another, and then the sound of creaking wood.

"By the by, speaking of birds, I think my little French nightingale has outlived her usefulness. Her singing is no longer to my taste. Pity. I was going to wait a bit longer, but I'd rather not take any risks just now. See she's taken care of, Grimsby."

"Same as the others, m'lord?" Grimsby's voice had lowered but was still discernible.

The *"others"*...? Sabrina shifted a bit closer, wondering what Fairford had meant by "taken care of."

"No," said Fairford. "The river is off-limits. The last one surfaced after only a few days and sent the whole of London into a bloody panic. People are still talking about it, and the banks are probably being watched more closely now. Even if they aren't, if another body turns up, there might be an investigation. We wouldn't want that, now, would we?"

Sabrina stood rooted to the spot, hardly able to believe her ears.

"I shall find another means of disposal, m'lord."

"See that you do. Just to be sure you don't get careless, I'm only giving you half the money up front. You'll receive the rest after six weeks have passed without discovery."

"And what of the Childers woman?" asked Grimsby. "Two might be difficult to get rid of at the same t—"

"Not her," interrupted Fairford. "She owes me everything, including her life, and will remain true to me in all things. In fact, once my lady wife has borne my heir and met a tragic end, I believe I shall marry *Mrs.* Childers."

"Surely not, m'lord!" exclaimed Grimsby. "The woman is naught but a common actress."

Silence.

Then, meekly: "Sorry. Very sorry, m'lord. I only meant that a man of your stature deserves—"

"Mrs. Childers may very well be Lady Childers in the near future," his master snapped coldly. "I advise you to remember your place when you speak of her."

"Yes, m'lord."

"Think of it, Grimsby!" chuckled Fairford, cheerful again. "Once my bloodline has been secured, I'll finally be free to do as I please. And having her play stepmother to the brat will be the ultimate revenge on the redheaded bitch, don't you think?"

Sabrina's hands flew to her mouth, preventing the escape of anything other than a slow, silent exhalation of dismay. Beneath her quiet terror, she felt a dangerous stirring of indignant rage.

"Of course, m'lord," she heard Grimsby say. "Good night, m'lord. I shall awaken you an hour before dawn."

"By George, it just isn't right for a gentleman to have to be up before the sun," whined Fairford. "When this is over, I shall be sure it never happens again. Now, get out. And sleep with the carriage tonight. I expect everyone in the vicinity has learned of our presence, and I want no thievery to get in the way of my plans tomorrow."

A rhythmic creak of strained wood moved away from the wall. A door opened and then shut. Sabrina dared not even breathe as footsteps paused in front of her door. After a long, tense moment, however, they progressed onward. Quietly, she released the air from her lungs.

The man she'd set out to marry was a murderer! It didn't matter that someone else had committed the actual killings; he'd ordered those deaths with the same sort of nonchalance as one orders a new suit of clothes. There was blood on his hands.

She had to escape. Her terrible error in judgment would be a fatal one if she didn't manage to find a way out before it was too late. But how? There was no way Fairford would just turn around and take her home, and they were a great many miles away from London, in the middle of nowhere.

Fear and hopelessness fought for supremacy in her breast.
Henry.

His face flashed before her—his sparkling violet eyes and warm smile. Her head lifted, and she swiped at her eyes before the flood of tears could begin and alert the monster next door. If she could just get to Henry and explain, perhaps he would forgive her for being such a fool and help her.

But would he still want her?

It didn't matter. The only thing that mattered was getting out of here. Now that she had an escape to plan, however, her legs refused all commands. Fear of treading on a noisy floorboard paralyzed her, so there she remained, motionless, until a log shifted in the hearth behind her, causing her to flinch.

A distinct rumble intruded upon her consciousness a moment later. It was the sound of snoring. Fairford was asleep. Deeply so, from the sound of it.

This knowledge freed her from terror's spell, and she tiptoed over to the satchel she'd brought up with her. Quickly, she pawed through it, finding clean stockings, a spare cloak, a hairbrush, and a pair of combs. There was a small amount of money, too: a little over ten pounds tied in a kerchief.

She grimaced with disappointment, mentally kicking herself for not bringing more. It would have to be enough. A small bottle of wine and an apple joined the contents of the bag. Other provisions would have to be bought along the way in one of the many little villages along the road back to London, for she dared not send to the kitchen here for food.

He'd be sure to follow her as soon as he learned she was gone, but if she had a good head start...

All she needed was a horse.

Her only other gown had been hung to let the wrinkles out. Her shaking fingers smoothed over mint brocade and creamy lace; how odd to think she'd come so near to being married in this. A clean change of clothes might be needed, so she took it down and refolded it, stowing it with the other items. The outfit she'd worn today was dark blue and would better serve for an escape in the dark.

Looking to the door and the heavy trunk she'd put in front of it, she frowned, again berating herself. The whole bloody place would stir if she tried to move it. The window looked as if it hadn't been opened in an age, but it was her only other option. She had to try. Maybe he'd downed enough liquor to keep him unconscious.

Biting her lip, she tried the latch. Surprisingly, it released with only a small complaint. Easing it open, she looked out. There were no trees to climb down, but there was a narrow ledge she could follow until she reached the long, low slope above the entryway.

Motion below made her hastily draw back from the casement. She peeked out to see Grimsby walking out into the courtyard toward the stables.

She would have to wait until later in the night, and she'd have to find a horse someplace else. The nearest village was only a short distance away, just to the west, the innkeeper had said. The moon should be bright enough to guide her.

Quietly, she dressed, struggling once more to tighten the stays of her corset unaided. No wonder women never traveled alone! She managed to get it secure and donned the blue gown.

Drawing her cloak over her shoulders to ward off the encroaching chill, she planted herself on a little stool before the fire and waited, unwilling to lie on the bed for fear of making a noise—or of sleep overtaking her. Despite her fright, she felt exhausted enough to nod off.

All around her, the inn quieted. The fire died down until all that was left were the dim embers at its very heart. When she felt she could stay awake no longer, she rose, shook off her drowsiness, stretched, and padded over to the window once more.

The courtyard was dark and empty. The dim light from the windows only reached out a short distance before being swallowed by total blackness. Sabrina gazed up in dismay. The moon would provide little, if any, light through the thick clouds that had moved in over the past few hours.

Under her breath, Sabrina let out a stream of invective. There was nothing for it. If she did not get out now, she'd have to try and pretend ignorance until another opportunity presented itself, if indeed one did. Could she manage to hide her terror well enough?

Then, too, there was the danger that Fairford or Grimsby might hear her moving about through the wall in the morning and wonder if she'd heard anything she oughtn't the night before. Even if she managed to fool them both, escape would be impossible once the vows were spoken.

It was now or never.

Stuffing her boots and cloak into the satchel, she tossed it out the window as far as possible, praying no one heard it land. After a moment of reassuring silence, she hiked up her cloak and gown and eased a leg over the sill.

Chapter Twenty-Five

*H*ENRY GRIMACED AS HE MADE HIS WAY TOWARD THE INN, its dim windows a blaze of brightness against the pitch backdrop of a moonless night.

For a little over three years, there had been whispers about town, rumors of girls going missing from Covent Garden. And bodies had been washing up along the banks of the river every six or seven months, bodies so horribly mutilated as to be unidentifiable, save for the fact that they were female. No one had so much as an inkling who the murderer might be.

Until now.

Fairford had moved to London a little over three years ago. Coupled with what he'd learned through his investigation of the man, Henry had little doubt he'd discovered the killer's identity. And Sabrina was with him.

He'd ridden all day and all night, stopping at this or that village to verify whether Fairford's carriage had passed through. Thankfully, the man's desire for haste had driven him to take the most direct route from London.

He had also used his own carriage rather than a hired affair.

If the bastard wished to announce his presence to the whole English countryside, so much the better.

He walked his horse as near as he dared before loosely tying the reins to a branch and creeping up behind the stables.

There it is. Adrenaline rushed through his veins at the sight of Fairford's coat of arms emblazoned upon the door of a carriage in the courtyard.

She was here. Somewhere in this shabby building, Sabrina lay sleeping—alone, God willing. He prayed she had made Fairford wait for the ceremony.

The front door was locked. He moved around the sides, looking for another means of entry. The door to the kitchen was propped open, allowing for some relief from the heat within.

Drawing his pistol and loosening the hilt of his sword, he made his way to the innkeeper's quarters.

A floorboard creaked softly outside her door, and Sabrina froze, one leg out on the ledge outside her window, the other still inside the room. Grimsby must have come to check on her!

The latch rattled once, and then there was quiet.

She breathed again, just as the door shuddered from a heavy impact. A muffled outcry of discontent came through the wall from Fairford's room, even as her door banged against the trunk. Whoever it was trying to get in, it was not her fiancé! Panicking, she made haste to pull herself the rest of the way out.

With a muffled grunt, her uninvited guest shoved the offending obstacle out of his way and leaped into the room. "Sabrina?"

She nearly lost her grip on the sill, so startled was she to hear that voice. "Henry?" she called back, unbelieving.

He rushed in and plucked her from the opening.

"*Henry!*" Never in all her life had she been so glad to see another human being! Hysterical sobs erupted as she clung to him with all her might. Now that he was here, the full terror of this night held her in its grip.

"Has he hurt you?" he inquired, prying her loose to examine her face in the hearth's glow.

"No, he has not touched me." She was shaking so hard she thought her bones must be rattling against one another. "I refused him my bed until after the wedding."

Doors had begun opening down the hall, and angry voices could be heard inquiring about the hubbub.

"I say! What is all this commotion?" Fairford's voice bellowed out into the hall. "What sort of an establishment is this? Where is the owner? I demand an answer this inst—"

His voice suddenly fell silent. A moment later, he appeared at Sabrina's demolished door, which was now dangling by one hinge at a crazy angle. "Bloody hell!" he exclaimed. "Sabrina?"

Henry's arm whipped up. In it was a pistol. "If you so much as twitch a finger, I will pull this trigger and rid the world of your worthless hide."

"Montgomery? What the hell do you mean coming here in the middle of the night and accosting *my* fiancée?" barked Fairford.

"I mean to take her back home, you son of the devil!" he replied. "And if you follow us, if I so much as see a hair of your head on the horizon, I will kill you."

She knew Henry meant it. And, as he was the one holding the weapon at the moment, there was nothing Fairford could do but concede.

"I would not dream of it," said he. "Only have the simple manners to allow the lady to make her own decision regarding whether to go with you or to remain here with me." He turned to her, holding out a hand. "Sabrina?"

"I will go with Lord Montgomery," she answered, drawing closer to Henry.

Fairford's brows drew together. "With this...this *madman*? But why? I thought you wished to marry me?"

"Be—"

"Because there are no fitting words to describe the sort of twisted, cowardly animal you are," interjected Henry.

"Cowardly? Who is the one pointing the gun at an unarmed man?" shouted Fairford, plainly hoping to garner the sympathies of those gathering behind him in the hall. "Sabrina, don't listen to this raving lunatic. Come with me and let us have done with this nonsense!"

"I know about the girl," snarled Henry.

Fairford paused for a moment, then: "Girl? What girl?"

"The French girl you bought from Madam Boucher."

She watched the other man freeze into damning stillness.

"If you come after us," said Henry, "if you give us any sort of trouble at all, I will publicly expose you for what you really are, right before I personally relocate your vitals."

Swallowing nervously, the other man nodded.

"Now, move back," commanded Henry, keeping the gun leveled at his enemy's gut.

Fairford did as ordered, backing up until he was completely out of the room.

The moment the people in the hall saw the gun, they wisely chose to disappear back into their rooms.

Henry thrust her behind him when they reached the stair. "Go outside and wait for me. I'll be right there. I really wouldn't advise coming after us," he said, again addressing Fairford. "Not unless you like the idea of a hole in your belly."

When she reached the bottom, she stopped and watched as Henry slowly backed down, keeping the gun trained on his target. As he joined her, she whispered a quick warning about the valet in the stables.

"Then I'm afraid we'll have to ride double for a while," he replied.

They moved quickly across the dark yard, avoiding the stables. Just as they reached the middle, however, a shout sounded from the inn, and Sabrina turned to see a shadow at her window, which was still open.

A heartbeat later, she saw a flash and heard a shot ring out. She screamed over the neighing of the horses in the stables as Henry lifted his weapon and returned fire. "Go!" he shouted, hurrying her toward the woods.

He found his horse, and they quickly mounted and fled.

"Wait!" she cried, thinking of the bundle she'd thrown in the yard. "Go back! My things—I've money and clothing, and my boots! I threw them down before you came in and—"

"Leave it!" yelled Henry over the wind.

"But I'm barefoot!"

"It's not worth getting shot over. We'll be back in London by midmorning, and you can worry about shoes then. Now be quiet so I can listen for pursuit."

His anger was deserved, every bit of it and more.

Her tired mind simply couldn't push beyond the moment, and her heart was reluctant to even try now that Henry was here. Instead, she leaned into him, savoring the solid warmth of his broad chest against her back.

Though it was early May, her bare feet were like ice. But she didn't care. All that mattered was that he was here, and that the distance between her and hell grew with every second that passed.

The moon rode high between racks of clouds, peeking down at the fugitives every few minutes, along with the occasional glimmering star. Utterly drained, she drifted into a state on the very edge of slumber. Reality seemed very far away as they galloped along the dull ribbon of the road winding between the hills.

Chapter Twenty-Six

As soon as he was certain she was asleep, Henry gradually turned his horse in a long, smooth arc until they were headed back northwest. Giving Leeds a wide berth, he passed through Armley, crossed the river at the shallows of Kirkstall Ford, and headed for the Dales.

He would like to have shot Fairford and ended matters there, but the blackguard had been unarmed and there were too many witnesses. It wouldn't serve him to rescue Sabrina only to hang for murdering a murderer.

Scotland was the only viable solution. There would be a pursuit, of that he had no doubt. With any luck, his enemy would assume they'd headed straight back to London and try to catch them on the southerly road. With his man at his side, the odds were in Fairford's favor, should they be caught.

Dawn tinged the east with deepest cobalt. Slowly, it spread and lightened until a streak of deepest rose broke through at the horizon.

He sniffed the air. The clouds scudding across the sky had a look of rain about them. He prayed it would hold off for a little longer. As they neared Hawes, he let his tired horse slow to a walk.

The change of pace along with the encroaching light awakened Sabrina. "Where are we?" she mumbled roughly, blinking up at the turbulent sky.

"We're going to have to change horses here. You'd best get down and have a stretch of the legs while you can when we stop."

"I can't," she grumbled. "I have no shoes, remember?"

"I'll try to purchase some in the village," he promised. "For the right price, I'm sure someone will have something suitable."

Cresting a low hill, they paused briefly to gaze down at the little hamlet spread out below. All was quiet and still as its denizens slept in the predawn silence before the cock's crow.

They picked their way down, and he stopped them in front of an inn, dismounted, and helped her down, spreading his cloak over the grass to keep the dust from her feet. "I'll speak with the proprietor and see where we might be able to purchase some shoes, as well as arrange for a new mount. Wait here for me."

Sabrina stretched and winced, longing for a soft bed, not to mention something to silence the rumbling in her middle. Where on earth were they? Wherever they were, it certainly didn't look like any place she'd passed yesterday. Dark, forbidding clouds hung low, diffusing the light so that she couldn't even tell where the sun was.

Turning, she saw a skinny, blond girl carrying an enormous bundle of what looked like wool. The threadbare rags she wore barely covered her, and she looked half-starved. "Pardon me, but could you tell me where I am?"

The waif cracked a knowing grin. "Stole ye away, then, did 'e?"

"I came of my own free will."

Freckles elongated as the girl's mischievous smile broadened. "'E must be a catch indeed fer yer ladyship t' come a'runnin' t' the anvil wi' bare feet!"

"Are you going to tell me where I am or not?" Sabrina repeated a little crossly, her patience wearing thin.

The girl chortled, obviously in no hurry to oblige. "Yer in Hawes," she finally said.

Sabrina frowned. "And where is that?"

With a sigh, the girl set her bundle down and scratched her nose. "Ye really don't know, do ye? Yer in the Dales."

"What? But that's the wrong way, that's—" *Halfway to Scotland.* North. They were headed north.

"Now ye see it!" the little ragamuffin said with a smirk, shouldering her load again and ambling off.

Henry came out of the inn, a pair of boots in one hand, some stockings, garters, and a worn cloak in the other. "Here. They might be a bit bigger than you want, but they'll keep your feet dry. Damn things cost almost as much as a new pair in London," he grumbled, presenting the footwear. "The innkeeper's wife refused to part with them for less than a small fortune."

Sabrina looked at the offering. The boots were not pretty, but they were in decent condition. Snatching them and the other items, she immediately sat to don them, not caring if the entire world saw her calves and ankles as she pulled on the stockings. She tied the knee garters quickly and slid on the still-warm boots; he must've bought them right off the woman's feet. It was an odd sensation, wearing someone else's shoes. But it was that or do without.

Feeling less vulnerable now that she was no longer restricted to a square of cloth, she faced her kidnapper. "Why are we traveling north?"

Henry's eyes twinkled as he gave her a lopsided smile. "Because Fairford will expect us to run for London, and I don't fancy the idea of him and his man catching us out on the open road. Two armed men against one is not what I'd call favorable odds. We'll go to Scotland and return home by a different route."

A flush crept into her cheeks. "And when I return after being gone so long?"

"Other than me, your mother and Percy are the only ones who know."

"Oh."

"Sabrina, why were you climbing out of your window in the middle of the night with no shoes on?"

She lowered her voice, even though no one was around. "I overheard him talking to his valet. He planned to marry me, get an heir, and then have Grimsby kill me so that he could marry that Childers woman, if that is even her real name."

"Grimsby?"

"Yes. He's paid him to kill women for him before—many times, from what I overheard last night. And he's planning to do it again sometime very soon. He spoke of another woman he's been keeping. He called her his 'French nightingale.'"

"She's safe at Aylesford. He'll never hurt her again."

Her eyes widened at the implication. "You knew about him?"

"Not until recently. Or not entirely, at least. We should have told you about him after we discovered what he'd been up to at Boucher's, but we didn't think you'd listen."

"We? Wait. Who is *we*?"

After a guilty hesitation, he answered. "I suspected something wasn't right with Fairford after he confronted me at Rebecca's party, so I asked Percy's help to have him watched."

"He never said a word," she breathed, bewildered.

"He saw no reason to enlighten you. The moment you accepted his offer, Fairford ceased to be a threat."

"I see," she said, her temper flaring. "I've been played for a fool in every possible way, haven't I? His interest in me was solely at your direction, wasn't it?" she said, accusingly. "Tell me, did this 'help' you mentioned extend to him asking me to marry him?"

"God, no!" he exclaimed. "I only asked him to provide a distraction to help keep Fairford at bay. Asking you to marry him was his own decision entirely, and an enormous damned surprise to me."

"Then, he really *did* want to marry me?"

"He did," he said bitterly. "And I wanted to kill him for it."

"If he is your friend, then how could he do such a thing, knowing that you—"

"I didn't tell him how I felt about you. I let him believe that I was only interested in you as far as to keep you safe."

She blinked back sudden tears. "Why did he not come with you? Surely it would have been safer with two."

"He stayed behind to watch over your mother and the girl, as well as to be sure Fairford had not sent us all on a wild-goose chase."

"How did you know where to find me? The girl?"

He nodded. "Percy came to me the morning after the ball and told me what had happened. I went at once to Aylesford, and that was when your mother found your note. We didn't know if Fairford intended to marry you over the border or by special license in London, so we decided to pay his leman a visit before haring off. That's how I knew where to look."

Her mouth formed a little *O* of comprehension.

He took her into the inn and had them bring whatever hot food was available, while he finished making arrangements for two fresh mounts. They ate the leftover stew and bread hurriedly, not wishing to waste any time. As they were finishing, the innkeeper's wife brought them a basket filled with some loaves, a bottle of wine, and several small wheels of Wensleydale cheese.

Guiltily, she peeked down at her hostess's bare feet. When she looked up, however, the owner of those naked toes wore a delighted grin between her dimpled cheeks.

"Be not troubled, luv. 'Tis proud I am to 'ave made sich a bargain," the plump goodwife whispered with a smug wink. "I'll 'ave me two new pair an' a luvly gown, too, fer what ye're wearin'!"

Sabrina ducked her head and laughed quietly. Henry really *had* been rooked!

"I'd planned to stop and rest here for a few hours, but I think we should ride on, instead," said Henry, frowning at his pocket watch. "The less people see of us, the better," he explained. "Fairford will probably inquire as to our passage on his way south, the same as I did on my way to find you. If he catches on to us quickly enough, he might decide to turn around and give chase."

Less than half an hour later, they were again riding out across the wold, skirting the edges of the now-bustling little market town.

The sun was high in the dome overhead when they stopped just north of Penrith to water the horses. Henry had opted to avoid being seen in the town.

She slid off her mount with a groan. She'd ridden astride for the sake of speed, and now her thighs ached abominably.

Henry walked the horses over and let them drink from the little stream.

"You don't have to marry me," she blurted, the sound of her own voice startling after so many hours of silence. "Mama will likely demand it, circumstances being what they are, but I will not hold you under obligation. You can take me home, and we can simply pretend none of this ever happened. I'll let Percy go his way, if he truly has changed his mind, and I'll threaten Fairford with what I know if he tries to force my hand."

In two strides Henry was before her. "I didn't ride all day and night to return without a bride."

Her heart pounded. "But how can you still want me, after—"

"You little fool." He took her quivering chin between gentle fingers, lifted her face, and kissed her tenderly. "Because I love you. And I'm not letting you out of my sight ever again."

Tears coursing down her cheeks, she looked away in shame. "I am afraid to love you," she admitted. "But I cannot help it, even if it brings me to misery."

"I told you once that I am not the sort of man to keep a mistress or take lovers, Sabrina. I love you, and I have no desire for any other woman."

"My father probably told my mother the same thing," she said bitterly. "He was a good man, a wonderful father, and I loved him, but he broke my mother's heart. I do not want—"

"For the last time, I am *not* your father, and I won't be punished for his poor judgment."

"And if the physician tells me to have no more children at the risk of dying? What then? Will you become a monk?"

Sunlight flashed in his wicked, violet eyes as he slowly grinned. "There are *many* ways of pleasuring that do not involve the final 'act,' my love. I've already shown you some of my knowledge. Do you require further demonstration?"

Alarmed, she took a hasty step back. "I am well aware of your...intimate knowledge," she stammered. "But will it be enough for you to pleasure me without finding equal satisfaction yourself?"

His grin broadened as he deliberately narrowed the gap between them.

Chapter Twenty-Seven

THE HEAT OF HIS GAZE SANK INTO HER BONES, AWAKENing a painful yearning in her flesh.

"There are as many ways for a woman to satisfy a man as there are techniques to pleasure a woman," he said. "I will teach them all to you."

Cheeks burning, her mind flashed back to some of the illustrations in the book he'd given her. Something of her thoughts must have shown on her face, for Henry's laughter rang out. She opened her mouth to protest, and he claimed it, breathing in her gasp of surprise as he moved to caress the sides of her breasts, thumbing the nipples briefly before skimming down to reach back and cup her derriere.

Familiar fire spread throughout her body, the backs of her legs tightening with each stroke of his tongue as it delved into the dark, velvet recesses of her mouth to play touch and seek. Shudders of pleasure rippled through her, and unable to help herself, she moaned aloud with want.

Sweeping her up, Henry carried her to a grassy copse down by the stream. The horses turned their curious, liquid brown eyes to watch the two humans briefly before returning to the more interesting grass before them.

Quickly, he divested her of her cloak and spread it out on the soft, green turf. Laying her on the makeshift bed, he kissed her until the earth beneath her melted away. Her skirt and petticoats he pushed up, slowly massaging her thighs, soothing muscles that ached from riding. With lips and hands, he wooed her body, planting kiss after gentle kiss on her sensitive skin until she writhed and pulled at him. Finally, he parted her knees to sample the delicate flesh between.

Her breathy exclamation of pleasure made the horses' ears perk, and they nickered in answer. Their encouragement went unheard, however, as the tide rose within Sabrina, gathering strength. Just as she was about to cross the threshold, Henry rose to his knees, freed himself from his breeches, and sank back atop her.

His hot, heavy manhood prodded between her thighs, but to her frustration he did not immediately seek entrance. Instead, he chose to tease, rubbing his hard length against her dewy heat.

She thought she might go mad with desire.

"If you say the word now, I will stop," he told her. "As I said, I can bring you to your pleasure without completing the act."

She stilled beneath him. "Do you not want me?"

He answered her meek inquiry with a gasp of laughing disbelief. "Sweetheart, I would like nothing more, but I thought you'd want to wait until we are wed bef—"

The words were silenced as she pulled him down to kiss him again. The tingling between her legs mounted as she felt the blunt tip of his shaft graze her entrance. She wriggled, seating him more firmly against herself.

With a groan of surrender, he at last thrust, fully sinking his thick shaft deep into her slick, tight passage.

Her squeak of momentary displeasure was quickly transformed into a sigh of contentment as the empty place within her was filled by his heat and hardness. Every throbbing inch of him was buried inside her, and it was the most fulfilling sensation she'd ever experienced. Holding him there, she savored a sudden feeling of fierce ownership.

He was hers. All of her fears were meaningless while she held him thus. If she was doomed to suffer heartbreak in the years to come, she would at least have this moment.

And there would be the children and their home to care for. Mama had done it. She had survived.

So will I…

When he moved again, such thoughts were lost as the friction sent little ripples of mild pain mingled with intense pleasure radiating outward from her core. Slowly, he pulled back, and she felt the tide withdraw. As he sank into her once more, pleasure again flooded over her like an ocean wave, and she cried out as the delicious fullness returned.

Such tight, wet heat! Henry sweated with the effort to restrain himself, to stave off the inevitable explosion as he sank into her depths again and again. Her pleasure was like a drug, increasing his own enjoyment beyond anything he'd ever known. He forced himself to hold back, waiting.

At last she shuddered, her head rocking back, lashes fluttering, lips parting in a soundless cry as her sheath tightened around him in a series of sweet, powerful spasms.

With a strangled shout, he withdrew almost fully, and then sank back into her heat, gripped by shockwaves of ecstasy as his seed rushed into her welcoming embrace. Afraid of hurting her, he sought to withdraw almost immediately, but Sabrina, still in the throes of her pleasure, would have none of it.

Slipping his hand between them, he gently stroked the place where their flesh was joined, prolonging her bliss. She cried out hoarsely as her passage convulsed around him once more. To his great astonishment, he felt another corresponding pull deep within his loins an instant before the unmitigated joy of release took him once more.

Breathless, vision blurring and arms trembling, he rolled over and lay back, pulling her atop him.

The sun was a good deal lower in the sky when he awoke.

Bloody hell. They had less than three hours before nightfall. Looking down at the woman nestled at his side, fast asleep, he knew it had been worth the delay.

Gently, he shook her, caressing the strands of fiery hair away from her beloved face. Faint violet crescents lay beneath her eyes; she must be exhausted. "Come, we must hurry," he whispered as she stirred. "With any luck, we can cross the border before midnight. Once we're married, we'll ride to Brampton and stay there until dawn."

"Why not just stay at Gretna Green?" she asked wearily, eyeing her horse with ambivalence as she sat up.

Guilt pricked him, along with sympathy. He was sick of riding, too. The beasts had no ill intent toward their aching backsides and bruised thighs, but knowing this didn't make the thought of remounting the animals any more appealing. "We dare not. Once Fairford discovers my little deception, he might ride through the night to try and overtake us. I know you're tired, but we have to get there quickly, marry, and then immediately head east."

"But why run after we're married?" she asked. "It isn't as if he can protest. We've already—" She blushed furiously and looked at her toes. "There's nothing for him to pursue now."

"Except revenge," he muttered. "His pride has been sorely pricked, Sabrina. And if he is capable of murder, then there is no knowing what he might do should he catch us out here. It's too big a risk. Once we're in London, he'll think twice before making any foolish attempts."

Rummaging around in the saddlebag, he passed her a hunk of bread and broke off a piece of cheese to follow it. "Here, have a bite. I'll open the wine. Water is good for quenching thirst, but this might make the ache in your muscles easier to forget."

"I cannot wait to get back to London," she said, making a sour face as she took a bite of bread, chasing it with a swallow of warm wine.

"What happened to your sense of adventure?" he chuckled. "Where is the woman who ran off in the night, not once but *twice*? Come! You can rest all you like on the journey to Brighton. There's not much to do on a boat except dream, feel the wind, and watch the waves."

Grumbling under her breath, she finished the light repast and, with his help, again mounted the horse.

Chapter Twenty-Eight

*O*VER THE LOW HILLS THEY TRAVELED, ALTERNATING between a canter and a trot, crossing the occasional stream, passing the greater town of Carlisle, and avoiding the tiny settlements nestled in the sheltered areas beyond it. When they entered the Eden's floodplain, the ground grew flat, enabling them to quicken their pace.

The wind picked up, and Sabrina caught a hint of salt tang on the breeze.

"Not far now," Henry told her, coming alongside. "See those lights there in the distance? That's the main village. When we arrive, let me do the talking."

In spite of her exhaustion, her tired body experienced a peculiar jolt of nervous energy. In approximately an hour, she would be Lady Montgomery.

As much as she'd fought against this, she could not help feeling joy at the sight of the village ahead.

Gretna was an average village, looking no different than the ones they'd passed along the way. Henry led them past houses, entering the tiny marketplace. An elderly man outside a tavern pointed with a knobbly finger when asked for directions to the nearest kirk. As they trotted away, he called out: "Guid luck, laddie! You'll need it, wi' tha' red hair o' hers!"

Finally, they drew near the church and dismounted. Warm, welcoming light shone from its windows.

Henry held her hand tight, warming her cold fingers as he led her to the gate and up the steps to the heavy wooden door. Taking out his purse, he knocked.

In a few moments the door opened to reveal a friendly, curious face. The clergyman took them in at a glance, and a smile creased his lips. "Coom tae marry, hae ye? Ma apologies if ye've coom a long way, but it'll hae tae wait 'til mornin'." He made to close the door.

"And if I were to make a generous donation in addition to the usual fee?" Henry quickly asked, jingling his purse for emphasis. "It is imperative that we marry immediately, and I want a legitimate ceremony before God, not a handfasting."

The clergyman paused at the jingling noise of the coins in the pouch. Flinging the door wide, he bade them enter, taking the proffered payment as they crossed the threshold. "There be hungry mouths tae feed in this parish. Far be it from this lowly servant of God tae deny His divine providence. Wait here. I'll need tae gather witnesses."

"Is there a place where I may change my clothes?" Sabrina requested timidly. Henry had managed to procure a comb and a serviceable gown along the way for her to wear at their upcoming nuptials. It wasn't a Madame de Salle creation, but it was clean and had looked as if it would fit well enough.

Flushing beet red, the little man turned and pointed at a door to the side of the vestibule before scurrying away.

Ducking into the tiny little antechamber, she quickly removed her travel-stained clothing. Smoothing the wrinkles out of the gown, she donned it, struggling to tie the ribbons on the bodice with shaking fingers. When the last was finally secure, she stood. A bit snug in the bosom and a bit loose in the waist, but it was at least clean.

There was no mirror in which to check her appearance, but if the long, ragged braid hanging over her shoulder was any indication, she must look a complete fright. Trying in vain to smooth down the loose wisps at her temples, she jumped in alarm at the gentle tap on the door.

"M'lady? May I coom in?"

Settling her frayed nerves, Sabrina opened it. A sweet-faced woman of some fifty years greeted her with a kind smile.

"I'm Eleanor," she whispered. "I'm told ye're tae be married?"

"Yes. But I'm afraid I don't look very much like a bride," Sabrina laughed, trying again to smooth down her wayward hair. "We've been riding for days."

"Here, let me help." Stepping inside, the woman reached into an apron pocket, withdrew a brush and comb, and set to work combing and plaiting Sabrina's tresses.

Tears sprang into Sabrina's eyes. "Thank you," she murmured thickly.

"Now, now, lass. No tears! I hope 'tis happiness tha' brings ye tae Gretna?"

"Yes. Yes, it is," Sabrina affirmed, mopping at her eyes.

"Ye're in love, then?" said Eleanor as she wound the long braid into a small coronet, leaving the remainder to hang down her back.

"I am," she finally admitted, smiling damply. It felt good to say it, even to a complete stranger. Peace settled over her heart and her nerves calmed. She would no longer deny her feelings for Henry. Mama had been right. Her heart had been in his possession for a long time, and she had not even realized it.

Whipping out a slender length of pale-blue ribbon, Eleanor tied off the braid. "Somethin' blue," she whispered with a wink. Another foray into her apron pocket brought forth a small cluster of tiny white flowers. Carefully, she tucked them into the coronet. "There! Ye're as bonny as any princess! Are ye ready?"

Nodding happily, Sabrina rose. On impulse, she turned and hugged Eleanor. "Thank you again for your kindness."

Eleanor blushed. "'Twas my pleasure, an' I wish ye joy."

Together they walked to the front of the church, where Henry stood waiting with the minister and another man who'd obviously just been pulled from his bed.

Chapter Twenty-Nine

THE BREATH IN HENRY'S LUNGS STILLED WHEN HE SAW Sabrina's face. Gone was the pale, tired, pinched look, replaced by a soft radiance. Her bright eyes held his gaze steadily, and her blushing smile struck him with the light of a thousand sunrises.

No silk wedding gown covered in pearls and lace. No glitter of gold and jewels. No bishop, no choir, no illustrious company of guests lining the aisle. His bride wore the humble dress of a villager, right down to the worn boots, yet no expensive finery could have made her more beautiful. He held out his hand, distantly noting how it trembled in time with the thundering in his chest as the ceremony began.

A few minutes later, Henry gently kissed his bride. The witnesses signed the testimony, the officiating clergyman put his seal upon the parchment, and it was done. Sabrina was now his in every respect.

They did not tarry to celebrate, but immediately set out south toward the docks of Solway Firth. When the lamps and windows of the village were no more than dim pinpricks of light in the distance, Henry turned them in a long, slow arc north, back toward English soil.

Crossing the River Esk to the southeast of tiny, slumbering Longtown, they made for Brampton. For two and a half hours they rode in silence, carefully avoiding settlements along the way, until at long last they reached their destination.

Though he'd seen nothing, every instinct told him they were being pursued. He hated the idea of stopping, but they could not continue on. Sabrina looked half ready to fall off her horse, though she had not uttered a single word of complaint.

He could put her on his horse and they could ride double for a few more hours, but he was just as weary. He prayed his ruse had fooled Fairford.

Bathed in the light of the setting moon, he led them quietly down to the inn, if it could even be called such—it was really only a large house. The windows appeared dark at first, but as they approached, a faint, red glow crept from between the shutters. He hoped there was room for them here. If not, they would have no choice but to continue to the next village or beg lodging at one of the nearby cottages, a dim prospect at this hour.

Rather than knock and risk waking everyone sleeping inside, he eased the door open and peered into the gloom. A man sat near the hearth, feet propped up, head on his chest, snoring gently.

Henry cleared his throat softly, and the man awakened with a startled grunt, quickly reaching down to grasp the wooden club lying across his lap.

"Peace, friend. My wife and I only wish to stay the night," Henry said quietly, drawing Sabrina into the room.

The man squinted in the dim light, relaxing a little when he saw her. "You have money?"

"Enough to buy a night's rest and some food, yes."

"I've one room left. You have horses?"

"Yes, tied just outside."

"I'll show you to your room and then care for your beasts. It's late, but there should still be food enough for both you and them. I'll just have the payment now, if you please." He held out one hand expectantly, while his other tightened on the cudgel.

Henry eased back his cloak to reach his purse, purposely revealing the gold buttons and costly trim of his rumpled, but still elegant, jacket. The innkeeper's eyes widened farther as the jeweled hilt of his sword glinted in the firelight.

The cudgel lowered.

"Londoners," said the man a bit more amiably as he received the coins. His eye fell again on Sabrina and he chuckled. "Fresh from the Green, is it?" Then his brows puckered in confusion. "We don't get many of you lot through here. Begging your pardon, m'lord, but shouldn't you be heading south instead of east? Are you lost, then?"

Henry remained silent and held up an additional coin.

The proprietor took the money and turned. "This way, m'lord."

"I expect my additional fee to include your *continued* silence, as well as that of your staff, should anyone come asking questions," Henry said softly, allowing just a slight touch of menace to enter his tone.

"Of course, my lord. I'll send someone up straightaway to light the fire and bring bedding and whatever food I can find."

"And hot water, enough for us both to wash," Sabrina chimed in softly. "With soap, if you have it, and some drying sheets."

"Of course, m'lady. At once." The innkeeper bobbed and went to do his bidding.

The fact that it was the middle of the night mattered not, Henry knew. They could have asked for the moon and the man would gladly try to reach it, for he'd just likely paid him more than he earned in a solid month with no vacancies.

It felt so good to be without a horse beneath her rump! The remains of their makeshift dinner had just been removed, and a small tub of hot water stood near the hearth, which now blazed merrily.

Sabrina unabashedly stripped off her borrowed clothes and washed from the neck down, blushing furiously when she realized Henry was intently watching her every move.

"I've seen all of you already, you know," her new husband murmured.

Her cheeks heated further as she wrapped the sheet around her. "Yes, but things are…different now."

"I don't see how they could be," he said, grinning as he came to take his turn. "Did you really think things would change between us the instant the vows were spoken?"

That was exactly what she'd thought. "I thought they might after…after…"

"Such preposterous ideas, Pest," he chuckled. "When will you understand that I meant every word I said when I promised to love you forever?" When she did not answer, he bent and kissed her gently. "I will teach you to trust in my love even if it takes the rest of my life." With that, he gave her his back, peeled off his clothes, and stepped into the shallow wooden tub to begin washing himself.

Even as his words stirred up a tender clamor in her heart, a pang of desire stabbed deep into her vitals at the sight of his unclothed form. He was, for lack of a better word, beautiful. Firelight flickered across his taut skin, painting it red-gold, spangling it with bright amber droplets as the water trickled down his muscled back. Her fingers itched to feel the rippling bunch and pull of the sinew beneath.

The instant she touched him, he stilled.

She flinched in panic, pulling back as if burned. Brazen behavior might be expected from a lover, but it was surely unacceptable in a wife. She needed a legitimate reason for having touched him. Spying the washing cloth, she grabbed it and began scrubbing between his shoulder blades.

"I've a bit of the road on me, but I'm not a dirty pot to be scoured," he said after a moment.

Though too embarrassed to speak, she answered by gentling her touch. Gradually, her inhibitions drained away. Soon, the cloth was forgotten, and her bare palms slid once more over his broad shoulders and trailed down his long spine.

Slowly, he turned to face her.

Sabrina paused in her ministrations, staring at his broad chest. His was the body of a laborer or a warrior, not a soft aristocrat. She marveled at the clearly defined muscles, the hard, ridged stomach. A few old scars marred his flesh, mostly fencing nicks, but there was one long, faded weal across his ribs that looked a bit more serious.

Briefly, she wondered how he'd earned such a ghastly memento. Before she could think to ask, however, her eyes were drawn to the trail of dark curls beginning just below his navel. Curiosity led her gaze downward to the dark thicket from which proudly sprang his manhood.

A mighty weapon, to be sure.

Had she not already known the bliss it could bring, fear might have overcome her, but the memory of that afternoon's pleasure allowed no such trepidation. With a single, tentative finger, she gently circled its soft, plum-colored rim. His member leaped at her touch, seeming to have a life of its own. A giggle escaped before she could stop it, and she looked up sheepishly.

"I am finding it incredibly difficult to remember you were a virgin earlier this day," he said, his violet eyes filled with mischievous warning.

Still, he allowed her to explore, and she took her time, well aware that she was tormenting him. The smile that crept over her lips as all of his muscles tightened, as his breath caught, was irrepressible. Dipping into the clean water bucket, she doused him from the neck down, rinsing away the soap. Stepping back, she unfolded a drying sheet and shook it.

Obediently, he stepped from the tub and held out his arms, inviting her to continue her ministrations.

She dried him as slowly as possible.

When she straightened from toweling off her husband's taut buttocks and legs, she was again confronted by his broad chest. An outrageously naughty idea popped into her head.

A strangled gasp erupted from her husband as her mouth closed over his nipple, and his hands flew to bury themselves in her hair. He groaned as she circled and flicked, gently drawing on him in a mimicry of what he'd done to her breasts earlier.

She took it as a signal to switch to the other side.

That lasted about ten seconds.

With strong arms, her husband scooped her up and carried her to the bed.

Heated skin met cool linen, raising gooseflesh all over her body. He kissed it away, slowly, meticulously. His mouth closed over one puckered, aching nipple, teasing until she gasped, crying out wordlessly. Helpless against the invisible, inexorable chains of desire binding her, her hips bucked, silently pleading.

Smiling, he shook his head and turned his attentions to the other breast, paying it equal, loving homage.

The limit of her tolerance rapidly approaching, she clutched him fiercely, demanding that he move beyond such torments.

He grinned and sank to his knees before her.

With a shiver of anticipation, she let her knees fall apart for him, presenting herself for his delectation. Liquid fire spilled into her limbs, saturating her, tightening the backs of her quivering thighs as his tongue worked fiery magic on her swollen flesh.

The pleasure was almost unbearable. Her every nerve was alive, her straining body singing in rhythm to the drumming of her heart, wracked with uncontrollable shivers as he propelled her closer and closer to, but never over, the chasm's edge.

When she could take no more, she drew him up, meeting his lips with her own. The taste of herself on his mouth nearly drove her mad. "Please, Henry—*please!*" she heard herself whisper raggedly.

Chapter Thirty

TASTING A FRESH BURST OF HONEYED SWEETNESS, HENRY chuckled with satisfaction and withdrew. His already throbbing cock strained forward, becoming granite. He'd never been so hard in all his life. In an agony of need, he rose from his knees and stared down at her. Her glistening, pink lips were parted in a purely wanton expression, and wild desire blazed in her smoky, lust-glazed eyes.

Laughter rumbled deep in his chest. How she could *ever* imagine him wanting any other woman was unfathomable. Bending swiftly, he reclaimed her lips, reveling in their softness, nipping, tasting.

Poising himself above her, he hesitated. He wanted—*needed* to be gentle, since it was only her second time; but the way she writhed beneath him, pulling at his shoulders, suggested that gentle might not be enough. For either of them.

Luminous hazel eyes flew open, plainly demanding to know why he was not yet inside her, and he at last surrendered. With one long, satisfying thrust he impaled her, burying himself in her tight, moist heat.

For one instant, he worried he might climax then and there.

He stilled, feeling the sweat form on his brow, the breath rasping in his lungs as he fought for control, fought to climb back from the brink. The moment slowly passed, and he began to move once more, withdrawing almost completely before slowly sinking back into her depths.

Her hips bucked, demanding more.

Restraint vanished, and he grasped her hips. With a growl of satisfaction, he thrust again and again, her little cries of encouragement fueling his excitement to fever pitch. Her sheath tightened, and he braced himself. Again and again she gripped him, crying out softly with each spasm.

His own release was a breath away—but he was not done, not quite yet.

Withdrawing, he flipped her over and hauled her up onto her knees. Running his hands up her back and down again, he molded the curve of her pert, rosy rump with his palms, giving the firm flesh a playful smack before reaching down to gently stroke between the plump petals peeking out below.

With a low moan, she arched her back, pushing out her bottom.

Sending a silent prayer of thanks heavenward, he once more guided his aching cock to her honeyed entrance. Slowly, he penetrated the hot, tender flesh, sinking into her inch by delicious inch until he felt himself touch her very core.

Her shuddering cry and the sight of her fists gripping the sheets sent him over the edge. Again, he thrust home. And again. Her passage was so hot, so tight! Her muscles once more gripped his shaft as she climaxed, and Henry shouted with pleasure as his own release burst forth.

As they lay spooned together on their sides, still joined, he whispered at her ear: "I will *never* stop loving you, Sabrina. This I swear. All that I am, all that I ever will be, is yours for the keeping. I will never love another."

Through the dark-red haze of desire, he felt her begin to shake and heard her sobbing cry, heard at last the words he'd so long awaited.

She loved him.

He awakened in the predawn silence to find his wife's naked form curled beside him in the bed. Lovingly, he stroked her hair back from her face. Then his hand wandered, tracing the line of her neck and shoulder, moving across the silky warmth of her skin. When it progressed to the curve of her waist, she rolled over to face him, wide awake.

What started with tender affection soon culminated in fevered lovemaking. Now he sat across from her, pulling on his boots.

"Must we leave so soon?" she asked, finishing the last bite of breakfast.

"If we wish to make Newcastle in time to catch tonight's tide, yes," he answered, her disheveled loveliness eliciting another pang of desire. He quashed it. There would be plenty more such delightfully mussed mornings once they reached London.

Leaving the little inn, he turned them east into the rising sun and kept a steady, but gentle, pace. Four and a half hours and only one brief rest later, Broomhaugh lay within sight, the river Tyne wending its way just beyond.

When they finally stopped, he marked that Sabrina did not immediately dismount. "Are you unwell?"

Her face was pinched with discomfort. "My legs simply refuse to move," she said in a hushed voice, flushing. "I'm afraid I shall require assistance."

Cursing silently, he helped her down and supported her as they made their slow way to the nearest public house. Though her stiff movements clearly told him she was in agony, she made no complaint. "I'm so sorry, but you must move your legs in order to keep the stiffness from worsening."

She kept her head down, but nodded understanding.

The idea of forcing her to climb back into a saddle made Henry sick with guilt. While she ate and rested, he inquired into an alternate means of transport, but unfortunately, there were no carriages to be had in the tiny village.

Half an hour later, he escorted her to the stables. When they rounded the corner, however, it was not the dreaded pair of beasts waiting for them, but a small wagon hitched to a single, enormous dray. In the back was a straw pallet covered with a worn quilt.

Without a word, his wife wrapped her arms around his neck and buried her face in his shoulder.

"Once we are safely home, you shall never have to ride again if you do not wish it," he promised.

The going was much slower than before, but it was a pleasant enough journey. Henry tried not to let her know how nervous he was, but every so often he could not help turning to check behind them. They reached Newcastle without event just before tea.

"I'll ask after a ship while you order dinner for us," he told Sabrina, stopping the cart before one of the quieter dockside inns. "We've plenty of time before the evening tide, and no knowing what fare will be available aboard."

The captain of the *Dove*, a small ship transporting flint glass, was unwilling to have a woman set foot aboard his ship under any circumstances, but the captain of the *White Crest*, a collier sailing that night with a shipment of coal, was glad enough to take a couple of passengers to London—for a price.

Henry counted out the fee with pleasure, including a bit extra for the use of the captain's quarters, and invited the delighted captain to share their dinner.

An hour later, the newlyweds sat on deck and watched as the banks slid by. Sunset splayed its colors behind them as they approached Tynemouth. Not long afterward, a dim glow on the eastern horizon appeared, signaling the outgoing tide.

Sabrina leaned into him as they swept out to sea, while the captain pointed out the stars and gave their names. "I'm sorry I put you through all of this," she said softly. "If I hadn't been so stubborn and mistrustful, none of this would have—"

"Shh. That was no fault of yours," he told her, giving her a light squeeze. "Your father made some very foolish choices, Sabrina. He hurt your mother deeply and he knew it. I'm certain he never intended to hurt you. If he had known, I'm sure he would have reconsidered his actions. But that's over now, and as I said, I will spend the rest of my life proving to you that not all men are like him."

Turning in his arms, she buried her head against his chest. Gently, Henry stroked her hair and held her as she cried. He held her until her breathing evened out and her body went limp and heavy.

Now he knew all would be well between them. Looking back at the dwindling coastline with satisfaction, he at last relaxed.

They had a couple of days before facing whatever awaited them in London.

Fairford would certainly retaliate. The only question was when and in what manner. Looking down at his wife's peaceful face, Henry sincerely hoped their enemy had indeed pursued them all the way to Scotland; it would give them a chance to beat him back to London and maybe allow for some preemptive measures.

If the twisted bastard had given up and turned back before reaching Scotland, however...

An unpleasant shiver ran down his spine, a fluttering trail of ice that touched each of his vertebrae like ghostly fingers.

Chapter Thirty-One

TWO DAYS LATER

ABRINA WATCHED WITH RELIEF AS LONDON SLIPPED PAST her window. *Home.* How she longed for it, for the sight of her mother's face. Then it occurred to Sabrina that Aylesford House was no longer her home. She was Lady Montgomery now, and home would be Pembroke.

As they approached Charing Cross, her husband rapped on the roof and instructed the driver to turn.

"Are we not going to Pembroke?"

"Our homes are likely being watched," he replied. "I doubt Fairford would be so bold as to attempt anything so soon, but I dare not risk it. We already know he has men in his pay to take care of any inconveniences, and I'm certain we qualify as such. No, we must go where he'll least expect us to, and get some help before he learns of our return."

"I agree, but from whom?"

"Percy."

She sucked in a breath. "Do you truly believe he will help us after everything that has passed?"

"He has already offered."

"I am glad your friendship withstood my assault," she replied. Shame filled her. "I admit I am not eager to see him again."

"He holds no ill will toward you," he told her. "And rest assured, he will do all he can to help us against Fairford."

Not long after, she sat in Percy's elegantly appointed parlor, embarrassed right down to the soles of her borrowed boots. "I look a mess," she whispered.

Henry smiled and kissed the back of her hand. "You look lovely."

"Thank God you're alive!" exclaimed Percy upon entering the room. "Lady Aylesford is beside herself. Fairford returned to London yesterday afternoon and hasn't shown his face since. We were beginning to wonder when—*if* you'd ever return. Lady Aylesford was going to begin a formal inquiry into the matter if you hadn't appeared by tomorrow. I suppose you sent the old dog home with his tail properly tucked between his legs?"

"Not quite," Henry told him. "We need your help."

"You needn't even ask," said Percy. "I'm assuming you wish to go to Pembroke?"

"Yes, but we dare not go unprepared. If he returned yesterday, he's had time to put plans into action. I fear an ambush or some other foul play on his part."

"You'll use my carriage and take a contingent of footmen along."

"Will you convey the news to Sabrina's mother?"

"I shall, as soon as I'm certain you're safe."

Henry's shoulders sagged with relief. "Thank you. You're truly a decent fellow."

"I am, aren't I?" said Percy, laughing. "You look the very devil, the both of you," he said, wrinkling his nose at her. "What *is* that you're wearing?"

She flushed. "I had to leave all of my own clothes behind when we made our escape."

"Ah, I see." Percy's eyes glimmered with amusement as they flicked between them.

"It wasn't like that!" she laughed, forgetting her embarrassment.

"Indeed, I'm sure it was quite harrowing. How did you manage to get away?"

The rest of the tale came pouring out. As she spoke, she watched Percy's face darken.

"Murdering bastard!" he spat. "Hanging is too quick and merciful for the likes of him—he ought to be burned at the stake so that his suffering might be prolonged before he goes to the devil! Thank God I brought Raquel here yesterday. At least here, I know she'll be safe."

"How is she?" asked Henry.

"Her wounds are healing, but it'll be several weeks before she's fit for any real travel. I intend to take her back to her family in France as soon as possible and make arrangements for her care."

"You're going with her?" Sabrina asked at the same time as Henry.

"She's only a child, and she needs a guardian to look after her," he snapped, as though daring them to contradict him. "She's had enough of pain and tragedy in her short life. I'm going to purchase a house and pay for her education so that she will be able to earn a living without—" His eyes darted to her face and he stopped short.

"You needn't say more," she told him softly. He truly was a gentleman and would make an excellent husband someday—for someone else. "If I can be of any help, you must tell me."

"Thank you," he said, clearly flustered. "Now, you both require a bath and something...else to wear before traveling to Pembroke," he continued, again looking at their clothes with frank distaste. "Mrs. Latham will find something suitable for you, I'm sure. I doubt anything of mine will fit you, Henry, but we may still have something of my father's."

"Thank you," replied Henry.

Two hours later, Sabrina descended the stair and was shown to a parlor where the gentlemen awaited. Her borrowed gown was a bit short and fit a trifle snugly in a few places, but not so much as to be uncomfortable. It felt delicious to be back in lawn and silks again.

"We were discussing how to deal with Fairford," Henry informed her. "I could call him out, but if he dies, there'll be hell to pay with the king."

"I'll call him out," said Percy, his voice chill.

"You can't," said Henry. "You don't have just cause."

"No one knows I broke off the engagement," Percy replied, looking at Sabrina. "I can always say he abducted my fiancée. That is cause enough."

"And how do you propose to explain the fact that *I* went after her and came back married, while you stayed here?" asked Henry. "You'd have to call me out, too, in order to make it plausible."

Here, Sabrina spoke up. "Not if you say you married me in order to prevent my ruination. Percy could say he thought I'd been taken somewhere in London, and so stayed here to look for me, while you were sent north at my mother's bidding. Everyone would think it was just the luck of the draw that you were the one to find me."

Henry shook his head. "No. I'd rather not have anyone know what really happened. Married or not, you would be ruined if anyone found out about you running off with Fairford in the first place. Percy told me your mother has been saying you've been ill these last several days, in order to prevent any awkward questions."

"How do we explain our marriage, then?" she asked. "As you said, according to London, I'm still engaged to Percy."

Henry looked at Percy apologetically. "I'm afraid you'll have to throw him over and marry me. Again. Publicly. I obtained a special license before coming to see you the day you fled. Your mother kept it for me when I came after you. We can have a quiet ceremony as soon as arrangements can be made. No one need ever know about Scotland."

"You'd let him get away with it?" asked Percy angrily.

Henry shook his head, his smile turning vicious. "Once he realizes we've not told anyone of his perfidy—and we *won't*—I've no doubt he'll attempt some treachery. If and when he forces a confrontation, people will think he's lost his senses in a fit of jealous rage. I'll let him publicly provoke me so that when I kill him, his death will be on his own head."

"And what of the servants?" she interjected. "I'm sure half of London already knows we're—"

Percy held up a hand. "My entire household is sworn to secrecy regarding all matters occurring beneath this roof, on pain of being dismissed without wages and turned out into the street. Lady Aylesford has recently taken similar measures regarding your 'illness.'"

"A message has been sent asking her to come here, incidentally," added Henry. "You shall return to Aylesford with her in the guise of a servant. If anyone asks her about coming here today, she will say she came to deliver the news of your decision to marry me. I shall arrive at Aylesford shortly afterward to renew my suit."

"Is it safe for her to venture out like that, with Fairford back in town?" she asked, too worried to acknowledge the twinkle in his eye.

"I warned her to come prepared," said Henry.

Chapter Thirty-Two

THREE WEEKS LATER

*T*HE TIME SINCE HER RETURN HAD BEEN SPENT IN A whirlwind of chaotic activity, punctuated by moments of quiet bliss and contentment. Now the day had finally arrived, and Sabrina stood before her glass and fussed over her reflection.

Her pale pink manteau was cut in the latest fashion, with pleats that fell loosely from the shoulders to gather in graceful folds down the back of her wide skirts. Turning to the side, she scrutinized her profile with a critical eye. Her bosom had grown significantly, and there was no masking it, not even with a fichu and lace.

Damn.

Amid the hubbub of preparations, she'd come to realize that the time for her menses had passed unmarked. Henry, of course, had been elated at the news. But like her, he feared Fairford's reaction. They had agreed to keep it a secret from everyone save her mother for as long as possible.

Her hand moved to rest protectively on her abdomen, which had not yet begun to swell, and noise behind her made her turn.

In the doorway stood her mother. "May this be the first of many such happy events," she said, smiling softly. "I am absolutely ecstatic, my dear, but I must say that I am also extremely concerned."

"There is no need for worry, Mama. The house and grounds are bristling with armed men. The queen herself is more vulnerable," Sabrina assured her. "I'm sure the matter will be resolved quickly. Henry has sworn to beard Fairford in his den if he does not show himself soon."

"Nevertheless, I shall come and stay with you until things are sorted out once and for all," her mother replied, her light tone contradicted by her gimlet stare. "You'll need help with the arrangements for your lying in, and there are a thousand things that must be done before the babe arrives. The nursery must be looked at, nurses must be interviewed, clothing must be made for the little darling…"

Even though the blessed event was not due to happen for another eight months, Sabrina nodded agreement. It was pointless to argue. "Yes, of course, Mama."

"Good girl. Now, Sheffield is waiting for you downstairs. Are you ready?"

"I am."

As she spoke her vows for the second time before witnesses, Sabrina was touched by the sight of familiar faces. Several of her sisters were present with their husbands and children, and her friend Lavinia was here. Several members of Henry's family were present as well.

All seemed pleased, with the exception of Lady Bidewell and her daughter. Lady Bidewell stared at her with undisguised rancor, and her daughter's look was equally sour.

Miss Bidewell's smile was particularly nasty as she congratulated them, yet still Sabrina's conscience pricked her. No matter how unpleasant the girl was, she could not allow her to marry a murderer without giving her some form of warning.

Henry must have seen something of her thoughts in her face, because he quickly drew her aside. "You cannot!" he breathed in her ear. "Have no fear. She shall never marry him, I promise."

Percy was there as well. Everyone had been quite shocked when he had arrived only moments before the ceremony, laughing and praising "the happy mistake that freed me from the incarceration of marriage." She and Henry had made it a point to greet him with warmth, assuring everyone that they were on the best of terms.

Sabrina noticed the quiet and very pretty young woman on his arm and wondered who she was. Before she could think any more about it, however, another guest came forward to wish them well.

Taking Percy aside during a quiet moment, Henry ushered him into a salon and closed the door.

"Before you begin berating me for bringing a whore into your house, allow me to explain," Percy began in a low, tight voice, walking directly over to the decanter and measuring out two glasses of brandy. "Fairford visited the Childers woman last night and left with her this morning."

"And?"

"He must have been aware he was being watched, because he gave us the slip."

Henry's fingers tightened on the stem of the glass Percy had thrust at him. "How?"

"They visited several merchants, made a lot of purchases, and then, at the last one, he simply didn't return to the carriage with her. When my man went into the establishment to investigate, Fairford was nowhere to be found. The proprietor claimed ignorance until pressed, and then he said Fairford had paid up and asked to be let out through the back. Another conveyance must have been there waiting for him."

"And you've no idea where he is now?" Henry's heart sank as the other man shook his head.

"You don't think he'd actually come here, do you?" asked Percy. "It'd be tantamount to suicide."

"All the same, if he does show, we'll be ready," Henry muttered. "I doubt he'd make any open attempt, but that doesn't mean he might not try something. I'd better warn Sabrina. I'll assign a couple of men to look after Raquel, too, while she's here."

"I thank you," Percy replied quietly. "Your willingness to help me protect her is quite appreciated, especially under the circumstances."

Something in his eyes, in his tone, gave Henry pause. "Percy, you're not…"

"In love with her? No. She's naught but a child, and a broken one at that." The grim fury in his brown eyes deepened. "She needs looking after, however, and I intend to see to it. No one shall ever harm her again."

All Henry could do was nod in surprised agreement as his friend knocked back the remainder of the amber liquid in his glass. "Do you still plan to take her to France?"

"As soon as this business with Fairford is finished, yes. She wants to open a charity school for girls. I've agreed to provide the funds."

"Damn me, you're practically turning into a saint," Henry said, chuckling.

Percy's smile turned wicked. "Don't start placing any bets at White's, old boy. I've not changed so much that I'll turn down a bit of pleasure when it's offered. But only where it's safe. I want no complications."

"You mean to return to seducing other men's wives," Henry translated.

"Precisely," agreed Percy, setting his now-empty glass on the table. "However, you may rest assured that I shall leave *your* lady wife unmolested. I have been well and truly cured of my fascination with her."

Henry relaxed. "I can't say I'm sorry for it. I hope you find happiness in your new direction. Do you think you'll ever marry?"

"Perhaps one day I shall meet a female strong enough to withstand my blackened past in all its dubious glory," mused Percy. "In the meantime, when were you planning to share the news?"

"What news?"

A wry brow lifted. "Oh, come now, Henry. I've seen enough women's bosoms to know when a lady is expecting."

"Damn. Is it that obvious?"

"As the nose on George's face," said Percy with a droll smile.

"Wait…what were you doing admiring my wife's bosom?"

"I very nearly married the lady. Do you think I would not know every detail of my once-prospective bride's appearance?"

Henry glared. "In the future, I shall thank you to keep your eyes above her neckline."

Chapter Thirty-Three

"WOULD YOU LIKE SOME REFRESHMENT?" OFFERED Sabrina, having at last made her way over to the young woman she now knew as Raquel.

"*Oui*—thank you."

Sabrina signaled a servant and watched as Raquel took a glass of punch from his tray. It was a bit disconcerting to think of the wounds hiding beneath the silk of the young woman's gown. Her mother's descriptions had been chilling, to say the least. *He might have done the same to me...*

"I know you must be displeased to see me here, but Per—Lord Falloure insisted on my coming," the girl said after a sip.

"I am honored to have you as my guest," Sabrina insisted. "You need fear nothing while you are here," she added quietly. "There are armed men everywhere. You're safe."

The girl's shoulders relaxed a bit. "I wish I had been able to prevent what happened to you."

"It makes no difference now," Sabrina assured her. "We are both safe here. He cannot harm us anymore."

The girl nodded, but Sabrina got the distinct impression she didn't believe her. "I hope you enjoy the evening," she added. "If there is anything you desire, you have but to ask, and it shall be done."

Just then, Henry and Percy emerged from their conference and came to join them.

As Sabrina danced with her husband, he filled her in on the discussion.

"Fairford has come out at last, but he seems to be lying low for the time being," he informed her.

"Do you think he might simply let the matter drop entirely without raising a scandal?" she asked, full of hope. The look on Henry's face spoke for itself, and her heart sank. "It is probably very foolish of me, but I almost wish he would show himself now and try to cause trouble. I feel that the longer he waits, the worse it will be," she said, with a meaningful glance down at her belly.

"You've nothing to worry about," Henry assured her. "You will be safe as long as you are with me."

"And what of Raquel?"

"Everything has been arranged for her to leave England," he said. "As far as anyone need know, she is Percy's distant cousin from France, recently orphaned and become his ward. She will claim a disagreement with the climate here, and he will take her back to France as soon as it is safe. Once she is settled, he will return."

Though his words comforted her, something in her gut just would not rest tonight. Her gaze struck out again, as it had countless times this evening—only this time it met with a pair of ice-blue eyes. Her step faltered, and a couple passed by, blocking her view for an instant. When they'd passed, the eyes were gone.

"What is it?" asked Henry.

"Nothing, I just thought I saw…"

Stopping, he turned to follow her gaze, his face hardening.

"No, I—I must have imagined it," she assured him nervously, taking his arm again and allowing him to lead her over to a chair. Her heart pounded, and her palms were damp. "The waiting is getting to me, I suppose," she said with a weak laugh.

"I have men everywhere watching for him, darling. Rest here for a moment," he commanded. "I'll get you something to drink."

Fanning herself as he moved off, she told herself over and over again that she was being silly. Of course Fairford would never show his face here! He'd never even get past the door. Tilting her head back against the column, she let her lids drift shut and breathed deeply to restore her calm.

"Congratulations," a soft voice murmured. "A shame this isn't *our* wedding celebration."

A shriek clawed its way up and out of her throat as her eyes snapped open to see Fairford standing before her—wearing a grey wig. All around her, people turned to see what the commotion was about. Before she could even rise, Henry was there.

"Much as it would delight me to do so, I can't run you through where you stand without causing an uproar," he growled. "But I guess you knew as much when you decided to come here tonight, didn't you?"

A slow smile broke out across Fairford's features. "Come now, Montgomery, let us be civil, here among all of our friends. We both know she's not worth it, old boy. None of them are. Calm yourself. I merely came to offer my condolences to the newlyweds, and then I'll be off."

"You've just done so. Now begone," said Henry with death in his eyes. "You are not welcome here."

But Fairford did not budge. "Tell me, are you well pleased with your stolen bride?"

"You have offered your felicitations," replied Henry. "Now I will ask you again to leave, or I shall have you thrown out."

She watched as her husband's hand strayed toward the folds of his jacket skirts.

"No need for any ugliness," said Fairford, his gaze dropping to Henry's hand as well. "I didn't come to fight. At least not here." His attention shifted to where Raquel stood peeking out from behind Percy. "I would, however, very much like to reclaim at least part of my stolen property before I depart. Come with me, Raquel. Quietly."

"You'll never touch her again, you miserable piece of offal!" spat Percy, stepping forward to face Fairford.

Fairford smiled and dropped his voice. "Unless you wish to see your erstwhile fiancée utterly humiliated, I suggest you return my misplaced goods to my possession immediately. You've no claim to the little baggage. She is mine. I bought her outright."

"My wife's reputation is my concern, Fairford," replied Henry loudly enough for those around them to hear. "If you've an issue pertaining to her honor, you may take it up with me."

Everyone nearby gasped, and Sabrina heard the whispers begin to spread.

"So be it," murmured Fairford, his lips stretching in a crafty grin. "I challenge you," he said more loudly, "on the grounds that you stole *my* fiancée. Lady Sabrina had agreed to marry me after Falloure abandoned her at the Pembroke ball, but you abducted her before we could make the announcement. I gave chase and tried to rescue her—as witnesses can confirm—but by the time I reached Scotland, it was too late!"

Several nearby ladies let out squeals of dismay. Sabrina caught a glimpse of Regina Cunningham, whose gleeful smile said she was enjoying this immensely. Fury filled her. Her husband, the father of her child, was about to risk his life, and the little wretch thought it entertaining!

"Yes. I rescued her from you, and we said our vows in Scotland," replied Henry in a strong, clear voice. "I wasn't about to let the woman I love marry a bastard like you."

"You see?" shouted Fairford, turning to the crowd and spreading his arms wide. "He admits it! Tothill Fields at dawn, then. May the better man win—and trust that this time, luck will *not* be on your side," he added through his teeth.

She watched him go, shaking so hard that her teeth rattled against one another as though she'd taken fever.

That night, she slept in her husband's chamber—not for safety's sake, for the house was secure, but for comfort.

"How can you be sure he won't employ some foul trickery? Raquel says—"

"I'm well aware, my darling," he said, stroking her hair. "Knowing that we possess intimate knowledge of his doings, he wouldn't have challenged me unless he'd arranged for it to come out in his favor. I fully expect him to act in an underhanded manner. Percy shall second me and ensure the confrontation is agreeably finished. Sheffield and your mother will remain here with you, along with a large contingent of men, to ensure the blackguard doesn't send someone to harm you while I'm otherwise occupied."

"I suppose there's nothing I can do to help you, then. This is all my fault," she sniffled, fresh tears brimming from her already puffy, sore eyes. "I should *never* have—"

He took her face between his hands. "You couldn't have known. As for helping me, you can do so by remaining safe and bearing us a healthy son or daughter. As long as I know you and our child are safe, I can do what must be done."

She did her best not to cry as she bid Henry a heartfelt safe return the next morning. In spite of the danger, she wanted terribly to go with him. Had it not been for the babe she carried beneath her heart, she would have rebelled and done so; but for the sake of their child, she remained behind to anxiously await the news. Percy would ride straight to Pembroke with all swiftness the instant the outcome was clear.

Grim-faced, the men departed, the physician Henry had hired to accompany them grumbling about the idiocies of dueling, despite the fact that this morning's confrontation was handsomely lining his pockets.

As the carriages rolled away, her mother put an arm around her shaking shoulders. "God bless them. May His swift hand deliver justice to those that deserve it, and likewise deal mercifully with those on the side of good." She led her away from the window. "Come. Let us have breakfast."

"I couldn't eat anything, Mama," Sabrina protested, feeling green about the gills at the very idea.

"You must, for the child's sake," admonished her mother. "Come; a few bites and you'll feel much better. A lady in your condition cannot go without eating."

"Let us at least wait for Raquel to come down," Sabrina begged. "I cannot believe she would let Percy leave without seeing him off. Perhaps she was overwrought? You don't think she's in love with him?"

Her mother's smile was sad. "No. I think she cares for him, certainly, but I doubt she's capable of loving any man in that manner now. I'm still in shock over how she was treated. As for Lord Falloure, I never would have taken him for the knight-in-shining-armor sort, but he's certainly proven himself so where she is concerned. He's become positively paternal."

Sabrina laughed through her upset. "He's turned into a complete mother hen, you mean." Looking at the clock on the mantelpiece, she frowned. "She ought to have been down by now." She called for a servant, and bade the girl look in on their guest and report back.

When the servant returned, it was with unhappy news. "My lady, I'm afraid I was unable to find Lady Raquel."

"Has her bed been slept in?" she demanded urgently.

"No, my lady. It was still made, and…"

"Yes? What is it?" she asked the nervous maid.

"It's her clothes, my lady. They're here, all of them—the shift she borrowed and the gown she arrived in."

She looked at her mother for a long, terrified moment. "Call everyone together and search the house and grounds," she said softly to the waiting servant. "If she is not found within one quarter of an hour, we shall send for the constable."

Chapter Thirty-Four

THE MORNING WAS CLEAR AND THE SUN BRIGHT AS Henry prepared himself while Percy and Lord Fenton, Fairford's second, readied the pistols.

Just as Fenton was about to call paces, however, a carriage rounded the bend. It was an unmarked, hired affair of poor quality. The vehicle rolled to a stop, and a passenger disembarked.

"Who is that?" demanded Fairford.

Henry squinted. It was a footman, one from Pembroke, by the look of his livery. A piece of parchment fluttered in his hand as he walked across the field.

"Well, get on with it, sluggard," Fairford shouted. "Your master awaits your leisure."

The young man ducked his head submissively and quickened his pace.

Beyond him, the carriage began to roll away, momentarily capturing Henry's attention. Why was it leaving? The lad passed him by, and he turned in confusion just in time to see him walk up to Fairford with the message held out. What was he doing? Why was he giving *him* the message?

Before Fairford could take it, the servant's other hand rose from beneath the folds of his coat, the grip of a pistol held in it.

Henry could do no more than open his mouth before the weapon fired with a loud *crack* and a cloud of smoke. He watched in stunned amazement as Fairford staggered to his knees, clutching his midsection.

Reaching up with his other hand, the footman drew off his hat and wig, transforming into a woman, and Henry recognized Raquel. He ran to where she stood, her attention riveted on the body lying in the grass. His surprise was such that he could not even speak as Percy and Fenton came up beside him.

The girl knelt by Fairford and addressed the dying man. "Your death will not bring back the babe you took from me, or the lives of those that might have followed," she said coldly. "But it will ensure the life of Lady Montgomery and her child."

Fairford opened his mouth to reply, but all that issued forth was a strangled, gurgling noise.

Henry watched as his gaze became fixed and unseeing.

"It is over," whispered Raquel, standing.

Then, and only then, did Henry notice the tears streaming down her cheeks. After a stunned moment, he spun her about. "You should have let *me* kill him! As the challenged, I would've been protected. They'll hang you! Why did you not wait for word at the house with the others?"

"He murdered my child," she said hollowly, continuing to stare at the body. "He took the life of my babe as if it were less than nothing. Had he killed you, he would have gone after yours, too. I could not allow it. Not when I could stop him. I do not regret my action. I accept my fate with peace in my heart."

Henry turned to Percy, already having decided her fate—and it *wasn't* the gallows. "Take her home. And speak of this to no one. Fenton and I will see to the body." Bending, he took up the girl's discarded weapon. He peered at it for a moment in growing confusion.

"I am sorry to have abused your kindness and trust, my lord, but I had no choice," said Raquel, pausing. "He has taken so much from so many. He took our children. And he took their lives, the others before me. I heard him talking to his man. They murdered them. Murdered them all. I could not let him do the same to Lady Sabrina. She and her lady mother were so kind to me, though they had no reason to be."

Tucking his father's purloined pistol away in his pocket, Henry regarded Fairford's body with distaste. "He would have died today by my hand, had you not interfered, though I suppose you had more right than anyone to end his life. Still, that will not protect you if word of this gets out."

"Who *is* this woman?" interrupted Fenton. "And what's all this about Fairford murdering people?"

"She is no one you need be concerned with," Henry replied, piercing him with a cold stare. "A terrible wrong has been righted. That is all you need know. If anyone asks, it was my hand that killed him, and you've never seen this woman. Do we have an understanding?"

Paling, Fenton nodded.

"You do not have to protect me, my lord," said Raquel. "I knew what I was about when I stole the weapon and your servant's livery. As I said, I am ready to accept my fate."

He peered at her for a moment. "If I do not do this, you will most certainly be bound for Tyburn, dear lady. And I would not have that be your end. There is also still the matter of his man."

"Fairford would have had him hiding nearby to ensure your death in the event he missed," she said calmly.

Henry looked about the meadow with apprehension.

"He will not trouble us," continued Raquel. "If he was indeed here, then I am certain he has already fled and is halfway to the docks by now. If not, then he will vanish the instant he learns of his master's death, for he knows he will hang if he is caught, and his loyalty is to himself above all."

"You are willing to let him escape justice? It was he that executed the other women. I know this to be a fact."

"Let God be his judge, for he never laid a hand on me," she replied. "It was Fairford who ordered my child's death. It was his hands that—"

"I know," Henry said gently. "We will see if we can find him, just the same."

She nodded, and he saw that she was trembling from head to toe.

"Percy, get her out of here," he commanded. "And for God's sake, find something more appropriate for her to wear before she is seen and there are questions."

After one last look at the dead man on the ground, Raquel allowed Percy to lead her away.

Henry took off his jacket and laid it on the ground beside Fairford's body. He addressed Fenton. "Help me move the body. We will take Fairford to his family and explain how he died at my hand on the field of honor, in proper fashion, according to the rules of the challenge. His grievance with me is well known. There should be no questions."

The other man did not argue.

When all was done and he finally arrived at Aylesford, he was greeted by the sight of Sabrina rushing into the entry hall, skirts hiked up, heels clattering on the marble tile. He caught her in his arms and held her as she wept into his chest unashamedly.

"Thank the Lord!" she sobbed. "When no one came back with news for so long, I thought I'd never see you again!"

Clutching her tightly, he stroked her back and kissed her hair. If there was ever a doubt in his mind regarding her feelings, there was no more. His father, Sheffield, and Lady Aylesford arrived at an only slightly more dignified pace.

"Henry! What in heaven's name happened?" said his mother-in-law. "No, before that, I must tell you that we have been unable to find Raquel. We've searched the house and grounds thoroughly, but there is no trace of her. The constable has been sent for, and—"

"She is with Percy and perfectly safe," Henry assured her. "I've a tale to tell, but not just now," he said quietly, flicking a glance at the gathering crowd of servants. "Suffice it to say that Fairford has received due justice," he announced a bit louder. "He will trouble us no more."

Shifting to a more comfortable position, Sabrina absently rubbed the gentle swell of her midsection as she read. At last, the uproar over the scandal of her wedding and the duel that followed had died down, and the papers had moved on to other news. *The duel that never happened*, she thought with a smile.

Mrs. Geraldine Childers had disappeared from London, as had Mr. Everett Grimsby, who was now wanted for the Thames murders.

Sabrina grimaced. Upon scanning farther down the page, her eyes widened. "Henry! Look at this," she exclaimed, showing him the paper:

Lady Bidewell announces her daughter's engagement to Lord Thomas Fairford, cousin to the recently deceased Lord Francis Fairford, now heir to the Fairford baronetcy.

She snorted. "Well, that was rather hasty, if I do say so. Her former suitor is barely cold in his grave and already she is engaged to his successor."

Bending to nuzzle her neck before taking a seat beside her, her husband chuckled. "She certainly didn't waste time. Fortunately for her, Thomas is nothing like his predecessor. I knew him at university. He's a very decent fellow."

"I'm glad of it, for her sake. I admit her animosity toward me was largely my fault. I hope she's very happy." Sighing, she tossed the papers aside. "Chadwick is to be married, Miss Bidewell is soon to be settled, and my mother will be Lady Sheffield before Christmas. Only Percy remains unshackled—and don't give me that look," she groused. "You and I both know he needs a wife."

"Yes, well, I doubt you'll convince him of it anytime soon. He was set on having you, remember?"

"Has there been any word yet?" she asked, deliberately changing the subject.

"Give it time." He laughed. "They'll have only just arrived in Paris by now. It'll take a good month to see her properly settled, at the least."

"It's a shame she's decided not to contact her family," she replied, frowning slightly. "But perhaps it's for the best. There would be questions, questions I'm sure she'd rather not answer."

"I only hope he knows what he's doing," said Henry. "It's dangerous business, pouring money into a charity. He has no shortage of funds, but still…"

"Don't you dare impugn his generosity! Let him play the hero for a while, if he's so inclined. He's only just learned what it means to care for someone more than himself."

He shook his head in denial. "Not so, my dear. I'm afraid you were the one who taught him the art of self-sacrifice. For the first time in his life, he did what was right instead of what he wanted." Reaching out, he brushed a wisp of hair back from her forehead. "You've a way of changing people."

"You haven't changed at all," she accused.

"I've changed more than you can possibly imagine."

"Nonsense," she whispered, nestling into his shoulder. "You're still the same man I met all those years ago. I think I might have loved you even then—I must have, or it wouldn't have hurt so much when you made fun of me."

"If that is so, then I certainly hope you've changed the way you show affection. I don't relish the idea of finding snakes in my pockets or—"

"You promised you'd never bring that up again!" she said, throwing a cushion at him.

Wrapping his arms around her, he laughed and held her close. "I promise I'll always love you, my adorable, wonderful Pest."

Sneak Peek: *To Make a Match*

by
Liana LeFey

THE MOMENT THEIR GUESTS DEPARTED, VICTORIA WENT to her room and shut the door, throwing the bolt.

Could things get any worse? Thanks to Withington, she now appeared a complete wanton, and her sister had just insinuated that she was unhinged. Would Cavendish ever come back?

The air in the room was stuffy, and she felt as though everything was closing in on her. She had to get out. Right now. Besides, she needed to have a chat with Primero after his naughty behavior.

Extricating herself from her gown, she changed into her riding clothes. Her shirt was getting rather tatty. She'd need a new one, soon. The breeches still had a lot of wear in them, though, and her boots were decent, at least.

One day, she would order a set of beautiful new riding clothes tailored to her specifications—including breeches—and be damned anyone who disapproved. Plucking out her hairpins, she plaited her inky tresses into a long, loose braid down her back, her nimble fingers working quickly.

Without so much as a glance in the mirror, she took herself to the window. Checking first to be certain no one was about, she climbed over the sill and stepped out across the divide and onto a sturdy branch. Shimmying down the hand and footholds she'd carved into the giant oak's trunk as a child, she dropped to the ground and made for the stables.

Slipping into Primero's stall, Victoria hugged his great neck, taking comfort in his gentle strength. Hot tears spilled down her cheeks. He butted her to show his concern, and she ran her palm down his mane in calming strokes to reassure him that all was well.

But all was not well. Not at all.

Primero nuzzled her shoulder until she rested her forehead against his brow. She gazed into his gentle brown eye. "You *must* stop nipping people, sweetheart," she softly scolded.

He replied with an obstinate chuff that brought a smile to her lips. She stroked his cheek with her thumb in a circular motion and blew gently into his nostrils. "I know you don't much care for gentlemen after the way you were treated, but I'm afraid you must learn to put up with them. I'll be married one day and have a husband, and little Charlie will one day grow up, too. You like him. He's good to you, isn't he? There, now," she soothed. "You don't want to run him off, do you?"

He nickered, and she patted him, accepting the apology with a laugh. "Why don't we go for that ride?"

The huge horse rocked his head up and down as if he'd understood her perfectly. In spite of her sister's disparaging comments this afternoon, Victoria was convinced that he had. What did Amelia know, anyway? She hated horses and made fun of the Romani who'd taught her so much. Far more than anyone knew.

Taking down her light saddle, she fitted it to Primero's back. It was no more than a slip of padded leather compared to a proper one, but she was more comfortable with it, and she knew he liked it better as well.

Without bothering to lead him out first, she hooked a boot in the stirrup and expertly swung herself up. "Hah!" she cried, leaning against his neck.

The horse shot out of the stables with Victoria clinging to his back, and Julius swore as the great beast tore down the path, scattering great clods of earth behind him.

She'd ridden right past without even seeing him.

He had left his carriage and circled back on foot, hoping to find a way to speak with her in private. He'd witnessed her climb down the oak from afar and had followed her to the stables only to miss her, thanks to a gardener he'd had to hide from at the last moment.

The last thing he needed was to be discovered chasing after the wrong Lennox sister.

Still cursing under his breath, he made to borrow a horse. If he hurried, he might catch up.

Once mounted, he followed the well-worn track towards the wood. He slowed on passing beneath its eaves, lest his horse misstep in the gloom. When he at last ascended up out of the valley, he was greeted by a sweeping vista of low, grass-covered hills.

Victoria was nowhere in sight.

He rode on for a while, hoping. At last, a ripple of familiar laughter was carried back to him on the wind. Cresting the next rise, he looked down and caught his breath.

Primero streaked across the valley at what seemed an impossible speed for so large an animal, his powerful haunches bunching and lengthening as he ate up the terrain. Victoria rode astride on his great back, her hair whipping behind her like a long, black banner. She'd let him have his head, and he ran free of all restraint.

Julius watched them approach one of the low stone walls that riddled the hills, and his heart stopped beating. Just as he was about to shout a warning, Primero sailed gracefully over the obstacle, clearing it by at least a foot and thundering down on the other side. A triumphant whoop of joy erupted from his rider as he slowed to a trot.

The wind gusted, and Primero snorted, lifting his proud head and turning towards the hilltop where Julius stood in awe. Even as Victoria spied him, her mount pawed the earth and neighed a challenge. She leaned down, taking a moment to calm him before urging him forward.

As they climbed the slope towards him, Julius marked how she guided her mount purely by the pressure of her knees, flowing with the giant beast's movements as if they were one creature. She held no reins, and her saddle was hardly more than a piece of leather.

Like the Romani, she required neither bit nor bridle to control him.

When she stopped alongside him, he saw that her face was wet with tears. He dismounted, waiting as she swung her leg over and slid to the ground.

"Victoria, I—" He took a deep breath and tried not to sound furious. He was unsuccessful. "Did you completely lose all sense today? I was practically on the verge of challenging my best friend to pistols at dawn over that bit with the rose. I knew to expect some sort of theatrical declaration, but not *that*."

Her smoky eyes chilled to winter rain, and her voice whipped out like a blade. "That was not *my* idea. After the disaster in the stables, I pressured him to act quickly to repair the damage. We did not have time to plan, and I had no way of predicting his actions. I guess when he saw the roses, he thought it the best way for him to truly convince Amelia of his intent without actually laying hands on me. I had no choice but to accept it. Had I refused, she would have known we were lying. He didn't really mean anything by it. You should have seen him afterward. He was—"

"Yes, I know," he said. "He told me. I stopped him after we left the grounds. I rather lost my temper, I'm afraid."

Her eyes widened. "You didn't…"

"No. But it was a near thing. You should have heard him trying to explain himself." He smiled sheepishly. "I'm honest enough to admit I've made a right muck of things. I should have just gone to your father and asked for you from the start."

"That would have been *far* a worse disaster." Her eyes lit with mischief. "On the bright side, Amelia was completely livid."

Her grin was infectious, and he found himself laughing. "She was beside herself. You really enjoy tweaking her nose, don't you?"

She attempted to look contrite, to no effect. He knew better. "I can't help it," she said. "She really is a terrible busybody and meddles in everything I do. The only real freedom I have is here, riding my horses—and now she's trying to take that away. Everyone already thinks me an eccentric, and now she's telling people that I'm mad and that I talk to horses."

It was hard for him not to smile. "But you *do* talk to horses."

She glared.

"And I don't think you mad for it," he added, moving closer. "Even if I did, well…perhaps I'm the sort of fellow who finds a little madness intriguing."

"I'm sure you'll feel quite differently once the gossips pick up the story," she replied sourly. "It's bad enough having your own family making fun of you, but that's nothing compared to public ridicule."

He grasped her by the shoulders so that he could stare right into her wide, grey eyes. "I'm not so easily frightened off."

Taking her in his arms, he determined to prove it to her. Her lips were like berries at the peak of ripeness. He ran his tongue across their crease, teasing until she opened on a sigh. Slowly he plundered the sweet darkness of her mouth, tasting her, learning her.

She was dressed like a boy, but the curves he felt beneath his hands were lush and womanly, unhindered by stays. By Jove, her natural form was crafted to drive a man to madness. With reverence, he confirmed her shape, pulling her into him, pressing her against the sudden ache in his breeches.

To his surprise, she yielded and leaned into him rather than going stiff. Her softness against him was a revelation of pleasure so acute it made his whole body tighten with need. He burned with the desire to touch her.

Pulling her shirt out of her breeches, he reached beneath it to cup a warm, full breast. The goddess in his arms moaned aloud and stilled as he gently massaged the sensitive flesh, lightly rubbing her rigid nipple against his palm. Lifting her shirt, he bent and closed his lips over it, teasing with his tongue.

She moaned and her knees gave. Gently, he laid her down on the grass. When he treated her other breast to the same attention, she tightened her grip on his shoulders in a silent plea for more.

But even as his hand slid downward, Julius stopped. The fact that she was wearing breeches gave him pause, if only because it felt exceedingly odd to encounter a man's button flap that was not his own. Her hips rose invitingly. Looking down at her all flushed and lovely, he knew he could quite happily take her here and now. But she deserved better than to be ravished in an open field.

With a pang of regret and no small amount of physical discomfort in his nether regions, he rolled away.

Her eyes popped open, the question in them clear.

"I'll not take you here in the field like a peasant wench," he rasped, struggling to control himself.

"The hell you won't," she muttered, hooking a leg over his midsection and rolling to sit astride him.

The sudden pressure of her lithe body atop him was a pleasant shock. A shock that instantly galvanized his lust. His arms snapped up, dragging her down across his chest.

It was a kiss that was reckless and uninhibited, a kiss that stole his breath away completely.

About the Author

AN EXCITING NEW VOICE IN HISTORI-cal romance, Liana LeFey loves to tell stories that capture the imagination and bring to life the splendor of the Georgian era. Liana lives in Texas with her husband/hero, two spoiled-rotten "feline masters," and several tanks of fish. She has been devouring historical romances since she was fourteen and is now delighted to be writing them for fellow enthusiasts. To learn more or drop Liana a line, visit www.facebook.com/writerliana.

3551842R00157

Printed in Great Britain
by Amazon.co.uk, Ltd.,
Marston Gate.